Laura

The Adventures of Frank and Joe's Mother

a novel by

Jeffrey Pike

ISBN: 1530438780
ISBN-13: 978-1530438785

DEDICATION

To Mom

With thanks to her, Mr. Gettel, and Phyllis Swank for teaching me how to use the language,

to Georgess McHargue for her old school editing,

and with gratitude to Arthur Gingrande, Esq., my advocate.

CONTENTS

CHAPTER 1
PRESS CONFERENCE DISASTER

The precinct house meeting room stood quiet and empty of people. Early-evening sunlight filtered through the half-open slats of the Venetian blinds at its windows, falling across a showcase filled with tarnished plaques and the curling photographs of long-retired police captains. Next to it on the wall, last year's calendar, 1936, courtesy of the local Chinese restaurant, hung askew by a tasseled red cord. Bits of dust drifted around the room, in and out of the shafts of light.

A young woman, Laura van Duyn, opened the door at the back of the room, and reached to the wall switch to turn on the lights. She stood a moment, taking in the wooden chairs scattered pell-mell across the scratched and dented floorboards, and the podium at the head of the room. She closed the door behind her, stepped to a chair close by the podium, dropped her hat, pocketbook, and gloves on the floor next to it, and sat. So straight did she sit, and so squared were her shoulders, that her back did not rest against the chair.

Laura was a slim, attractive woman, not quite short, dressed in a black, calf-length skirt and, over a white blouse, a belted navy blazer with wide lapels, smartly tailored and crisply new. Against the fashion of the day, short cuts sculpted into elaborate finger waves, she kept her strawberry blond hair long and straight, gathered now in a tidy chignon at the base of her neck. She reached into her jacket pocket, pulled forth a pad and pencil, and held them in her lap.

The door opened again and a loosening congregation of loud men entered, dressed in rumpled jackets and ties and hats with press cards stuck in their hatbands, guffawing and jabbing each other in the ribs. Laura's presence silenced them and then prompted a whispered consultation. One of them stepped forward, grinning and chewing fiercely on a wad of gum.

"Miss van Duyn, you're a ways south of the Waldorf ballroom." Chew, chew. His companions snickered as they pulled up chairs and sat. Laura did not bother to turn as she said, "At least, Mr. Garrity, I know better than to come out in August in a brown pair of shoes." More snickers. Garrity's face reddened. "I'll tell your editor you're down here. He'd never let a society page dame cover the police beat."

"I'm here on my own time, Mr. Garrity. My editor has no jurisdiction."

Garrity snorted. "Pretty big word for a dame."

"Aw, Garrity," another reporter chided, "let her alone. She's not doing any harm."

Garrity sat down grumbling. A third reporter spoke up. "I heard a rumor Hardy's going to break a big case. Anybody heard anything reliable?"

"No!" Garrity complained, "I wish I had. I got a deadline."

"Good afternoon, gentlemen. Thank you for coming." At the back of the room, a smiling Detective Fenton Hardy filled the doorway. He wore a brown suit, a sharp crease in the trousers, a white shirt, a cream and maroon-striped tie, and spotless, shining brown shoes.

"About time you showed up, Hardy," Garrity joshed. Laughter followed the detective as he strode to the podium. He paused for absolute silence, then, nodding towards Laura, he said, "It's nice to see a member of the fairer sex here. I don't believe we've met."

"My name is Laura van Duyn," she replied, "I write for the Herald Tribune."

"Parties and gossip," Garrity muttered.

Fenton cocked an ear. "What was that, Mr. Garrity?"

"Nothing! Can we get on with it? I got a deadline."

"OK, Mr. Garrity, as you wish. I want this information in the late editions anyway. I'm here to inform you that I've been investigating a gang that's got its fingers in every piece of illegal business in this city. I am taking personal responsibility for apprehending all of its members and putting them away for a long time."

A grizzled old man stood, took a drag off his cigarette, and blew smoke in the detective's direction. "Smith here from the Daily Mail," he rasped, "Detective, I checked around. Nobody else has heard of this gang. You say you got a line on it. Where from?"

"Yeah," another one piped up, "I heard it was your sister." The reporters snickered again.

A line of red started up from Fenton's collar, but he forced a smile. "I'm sorry, I can't reveal any details without compromising the investigation."

"Then why'd you bother to call us down here?" Smith jeered, "You going to start bragging on your college degree again? Two years on the force and all it's got you is a great big salary. Three beat cops could work on what you make, and arrest three times the crooks. The real story is, you've come up empty again. How much longer should this department carry you? Can you answer that question?"

Fenton replied through gritted teeth, his balled fist banging the podium. "This is about my case, Mr. Smith, not about my conduct. If you have a question about the case, I'll answer it."

"No, Hardy, no more questions. I got my story." He stalked out.

Garrity poked his pencil at Fenton and squinted. "Say, Hardy," he sang out, "can you give us that sister angle?"

The other reporters yelled for confirmation.

"You leave my sister out of this! It's one thing, roughing up a man in the papers, but a woman? You'll ruin her reputation!" He paused, catching sight of Laura. "No offense intended, Miss van Duyn."

"None taken, Detective, although I don't believe our reputations are nearly that fragile. But I am interested in your investigation. What more can you tell us? Will there be arrests soon?"

Fenton cleared his throat and fidgeted with his tie. "Well, it would be premature to release any more details at this time."

The room fell silent. The reporters shifted their chairs and glanced through their notes. Finally, one fellow pushed his hat back and scratched his forehead. "Guess that'll do for me. I got to get this story to my editor. What there is of it."

The other reporters all nodded or said it was about time they got to work, too. They stood, stretched, and left, one after the other. Only Laura remained. She rose, absorbed in her notes, silently mouthing the words, and drifted towards the door.

"Miss van Duyn?" Fenton held out her pocketbook, gloves, and hat.

"Thank-you, Detective." She took her things, and, catching the dejection in his face, said, "Why, you look as if all the wind's gone out of your sails."

He shrugged his slumped shoulders. "Miss van Duyn, you don't know the half of it. You heard Smith. Tonight, this case, well I thought maybe I could finally prove something to them, but I couldn't tell them anything they wanted to hear."

Laura sought some words of encouragement. "I think you just called your press conference a little too soon, but I'm sure you'll conduct the investigation just fine. I admired the way you defended your sister."

Fenton gave a short, bitter laugh. "That's the worst part, Miss van Duyn. My sister's dating the prime suspect."

CHAPTER 2
THE REAL STORY

"But Detective, she might be in danger!"

"Well, I don't know. He is still only a suspect."

"Why do you suspect him?"

"I'll tell you the whole story. Off the record?" She nodded.

"Well, okay, there was this guy started coming to her church a few weeks ago. The very first day he talked her up, said he'd seen her at the restaurant where she had lunch and wanted to get to know her better. The next week he asked her out. Gertrude had some reservations because they'd just met, but…well…she was in kind of a dry spell, if you know what I mean, so she said yes. Gertrude told me she was seeing him. Said he wasn't polished, but he didn't smoke or play the horses. Came to church nearly every Sunday. Set with money, but didn't flash it around. Treated her to movies and sensible meals. Pretty soon, she started to fall for him, not in a big way, mind you, but she said she was comfortable around him, liked his company. I was happy for her. I started to think maybe she'd found a fellow to settle down with."

"We share an apartment to save expenses. One day she came home and said that he knew who I was and had started asking her questions about police work, like what cases we were working on, did we have any leads or suspects. Just general questions I thought any curious person might ask. I didn't figure I ought to take any chances, though, so I asked Gertrude if she would mind if I checked him out. She didn't like the idea much, but when I explained that she was the sister of a policeman, after all, and although it was probably nothing, it would make sense to see if he was trying to keep tabs on us, she said okay. I looked him up. Police records didn't have anything. I got Albany to send down copies of his driver's license and car registration. Here, I've still got them." He reached into his pocket, pulled out two folded sheets of paper, and handed them to Laura who began to read them.

"We went around to his address, a residential hotel out in Brooklyn. His landlady said he was quiet, paid his rent every week. That was good enough for me, so I let it go."

"Then yesterday evening Gertrude came home and said he'd asked her was I snooping around? She told him it was just routine. Asked him was that a problem? He started yelling at her, said I should mind my own business, he was just an interested citizen, and she'd better watch her step if she still wanted to see him."

"Well, my sister doesn't take trouble from anyone. I was just doing my job she said and maybe she wasn't sure she did want to see him anymore. When he realized the tables were turned, he calmed down and apologized for yelling at her, and asked her please not to split up. Gertrude said she'd think about it. They had a date tonight, and she would tell him what she had decided to do then."

Laura frowned. "He doesn't sound at all nice. You must convince her to break it off."

"It's complicated Miss van Duyn. Even though he has no record, his actions are suspicious and criminals rarely act alone. If there is a gang, Gertrude's seeing him makes it easier for me to investigate."

"Isn't that dangerous?"

Fenton smiled. "You don't know Gertrude. He's the one ought to be worried. But you're right, and there are other ways I can keep tabs on him. I'll suggest she stop seeing him when she gets home tonight, if she hasn't already told him herself."

"Thank you, Detective. That makes me feel better." She held out her hand. "I don't want to take any more of your time. It was nice to meet you." They shook and left the room, started down the hallway together.

"Going back to write your story?"

She smiled, showing fine white teeth. "Yes, in a manner of speaking."

He raised his eyebrows, questioning.

"You see, as Mr. Garrity hinted, I write for the society pages, but I'd prefer something more…substantial. So I've been coming to functions like this and going home to practice."

"Good for you. I admire someone with initiative."

He stopped outside an office and gestured toward the door. "I have to get my things."

"May I use your telephone? I need to call a cab."

"Why don't I give you a lift?"

"I wouldn't want to put you out…"

"No, not at all. It'll be payback for bending your ear."

"All right."

As they entered the office, the telephone rang. He snatched up the receiver.

"Fenton?" a woman's voice whispered, "It's Gertrude. Can you come get me? I told him I don't want to see him anymore, he didn't let me go, he drove me to his place, what a dump, and has me locked in somehow. I tried jimmying the lock with a butter knife. No go. He seems very angry, he's left. Says he's bringing some people back."

"OK, Gertrude, you just hang on. I'll be right there."

"I'm in room 302. I do have my little pistol if he gets ugly. Wait, here he comes." She hung up.

"Miss van Duyn?" Fenton called, "That was my sister. She's broken up with that fellow, and he isn't taking it well. She needs me to come for her. I guess I can't give you a ride after all."

Laura paused, considering. "May I come with you, Detective? You could drop me home afterwards."

Fenton shrugged. "Sure, no harm, I guess." He swung to the coat rack behind him, slung his service revolver over his shoulder, and pulled on a trench coat. Back in the hall, Laura had her hat and gloves on. "I'm ready," she said, and smiled. "Thank you."

"Don't mention it," he answered, and strode down the hall so fast, Laura had to scamper to keep up.

CHAPTER 3
DESPERATE RESCUE

Fifteen minutes later, Fenton pulled up to a square brick building set behind a well-kept lawn. On the roof, "Royal Arms Hotel" blazed in red neon. "Wait here. I'll only be a minute," he told Laura.

He got out, left the engine running, and crossed behind the car, watching the only room on the third floor with lights on. The shadows of more than two people moved behind the blinds. He bent to Laura's window, open for the breeze.

"Miss van Duyn, can you drive this car?"

"Yes," she replied, her gaze steady.

"Look, I don't think there will be any trouble, but maybe you'd better get over into the driver's seat in case we need a fast getaway. Just in case."

"I can manage, Detective." She slid across and took the wheel. "You just get your sister down here safely."

"Thank you, Miss van Duyn." He proceeded to and entered the hotel, after pausing to give her a thumbs up.

Laura put her hands on the steering wheel. Her heart thumped. She took in her surroundings. Four and five story apartment buildings lined the street for several blocks. Street lamps pooled light at the corners. She noted the next cross street on the left, two blocks down, and three blocks farther on, a major intersection marked by a traffic light. She tested the clutch for throw and stiffness.

A commotion over by the apartment door drew Laura's attention. Fenton had emerged with a small, angry woman hoisted against his hip. She struggled to free herself, shouting in undignified rage and waving a pistol. Fenton strode to the car, big enough to endure her wrath, thrust her into the back seat and jumped in after her. "Miss van Duyn, meet Gertrude, my hot-headed sister. And get us out of here, please."

Laura released the clutch and pushed down hard on the gas. The car leaped from the curb. A man lunged from the Royal Arms brandishing a revolver. A black Packard roared out from behind the building, screeched to a halt long enough to pick up the man and then came hell-for-leather after them. Gertrude cranked down her window, leaned out, and aimed her pistol at their pursuers. Fenton hauled her in. "Now cut it out! You're going to hit someone."

"That was my intention."

"I meant someone who didn't deserve it."

"I never miss. You know it." But she subsided, the adrenaline, apparently, having run its course. Instead, she sat, and muttered. "I will never look at another man as long as I live! They're mean, lying, treacherous trouble!"

Fenton patted her shoulder. "You can't write us all off because of one bad apple."

"Detective," Laura said quietly, "that car is gaining on us."

She shifted up through second to third gear, accelerating towards the traffic light, but the black sedan drew ever closer. A bullet crashed through the back window. Laura gasped and tears filled her eyes, but she held steady. Gertrude, roused again, aimed her pistol through the gaping rear window. Fenton pulled her arm down and reluctantly took out his own revolver. "I'll do the shooting, Gert, just keep your head down. Are you all right, Miss van Duyn?""

"Yes, the bullet just grazed my arm." Her voice was shaky, but her jaw firm. Fenton nodded. "Well keep it up, you're doing fine." He aimed carefully and squeezed the trigger, blasting a headlight, but the sedan sped on.

"I'm going to turn left at the light. Hang on please."

Laura cranked the steering wheel over and ran through the intersection just as the light changed from yellow to red. For a moment, it looked as if their pursuers would not make the turn, but they skidded around at the last instant, up onto the sidewalk, and back onto the street. Laura made a quick right onto a nearly deserted thoroughfare. Fenton glanced back.

"I think you lost them, Miss van Duyn. No…. Wait, they're still coming." Fenton let off another shot. Steam billowed from the Packard's radiator.

"Detective, I am going to slow up. When they get close, you can shoot out a tire."

"It's risky, Miss van Duyn, but I think it's our only chance."

Laura lifted her foot from the gas pedal and her gaze to the rear-view mirror. "Don't shoot until you see the whites of their eyes, Detective." She smiled at him, and he returned her smile.

"Thank–you, Miss van Duyn. I shall fire when ready."

"Here they come, Fenton," Gertrude yelled, glaring again out the rear window.

"Miss van Duyn, turn at the next street. That will give me a clearer aim."

As she gained the intersection, Laura turned. In the instant the pursuing automobile stood broadside to their car, Fenton squeezed off a shot. A bang signaled a direct hit. The car skidded across the intersection, pivoted around a fire hydrant, and slammed up against a building. Laura pressed the brake, bringing the car quickly to a stop. Fenton leaped out, pistol brandished and pursued the men on foot, but they vanished into the crowd and were gone. Fenton hastened to the police car and reached past Laura for the radio handset.

"Drat!" he exclaimed, "that bullet took out the radio." He tossed aside the ruined instrument. "I need to get down to headquarters. Miss van Duyn, can I drop you both at your place? They know where she lives."

Gertrude snorted. "Nonsense, Fenton, I've got my gun. I'm not about to impose on Miss van Duyn."

"Please, it's not an imposition," Laura said, "I would welcome your company."

CHAPTER 4
COMPARING NOTES

She paced alone through the dark apartment lit only by the glow from her cigarette, the distant streetlamps, and the neon sign that read "Royal Arms Hotel" on the building's rooftop. Heavy men shuffled outside the door, and then came a knock. She flung the door open.

"Come in, quickly." She thrust the door closed behind them. "Where is Tony?"

"Don't know."

"He wasn't with you?"

"No, he must've lit out after the action. Down the fire escape, maybe. I know where he'll hole up, though. I'll take care of him in the morning."

She took a final drag on the cigarette, dropped it and stubbed it out, then blew the smoke in his face. "If there's any killing to do, Bruno, I'll do it."

Bruno shrugged. "Not if I find him first."

She glared at him, then put the issue away. She had more urgent considerations.

"Where are the Hardys?"

He shrugged again then gave her a brief rundown of the evening's events.

"I can't imagine what you were thinking, chasing through the streets, shooting." Sirens whined in the distance. "There's the detective come to arrest us. You've found another car?"

Bruno nodded.

"Let's go, then."

***

Fenton dropped them at Laura's building, promising to return as soon as he had finished downtown. The building was fifty years old, originally a Gilded Age mansion remade into ever-smaller apartments. Laura's was the done-over maid's quarters. Its dark and ornate wainscots had been demolished and the rooms finished in gentle Art Deco shades -- the walls dove grey, the carpet thick and green as grass. On one wall hung a painting, an incandescent pre-Raphaelite of a blonde lady sitting sidesaddle upon a pale horse, led by a woman with flowing black hair astir in the wind. Beneath it, a plush club chair in royal blue leather stood beside a reading lamp and a bookcase crammed with classics, college textbooks, and the latest popular novels. Framed and set on top of the case was a signed photograph of a woman in slacks and a pith helmet astride a camel. On the chair, a leather-bound volume of Gertrude Bell's *Arabian Diaries* lay face down, a pair of wire-framed eyeglasses sprawled across its spine. Hard against the bookcase was a small desk. On it sat a black Royal typewriter with a half-filled sheet of paper and beside it a stack of tabloid newspapers. Opposite this suite stood a black-lacquered coffee table and, the chair's companion, a sofa beneath the windows. There Gertrude sat winding a band of gauze around Laura's biceps, where the bullet had, by good fortune, just grazed her skin.

"All fixed up," she said, patting Laura's arm, "How do you feel, a little shaky?"

"Oh no, I feel as if I could go on all night."

Gertrude smiled. "Excitement can do that to a person." She stood and went to examine the painting. After a moment, she exclaimed, astonished, "This is real! I can see the brushstrokes."

Laura blushed. "Well, yes, I've had some good fortune in my life."

"More like you're worth a fortune." She turned to Laura, questioning, but Laura remained inscrutable. She caught Gertrude's eye. "How are you?" she asked.

Gertrude straightened herself. "Disappointed," she said, matter-of-factly. "I know it looks as if Nathen was just using me to keep tabs on Fenton. I could tell, though, he felt something for me, a man can't hide that."

"But he behaved miserably toward you."

"Yes, and I understand I have to let him go. I can't abide a man with a temper. Still, I'm not angry with him anymore, I'm worried about him, and I have no way to find him. I hope he will be all right."

"Why worry?"

"I'm just afraid those people will blame him for what happened. They didn't seem nice, well the men, anyway."

"There was a woman?" Laura leaned in.

"Yes, she…I'll tell you the whole story. After I called Fenton, Nathen came back with two men and a woman. The men were just thugs, but the woman was different. Cool and self-assured, sophisticated almost. She had Nathen by the arm. I couldn't tell if he minded, although he didn't shake her off. But the men worried him, I could see, especially one of them, a great big bruiser. Even I was a little scared of him, he was huge and not happy. The woman turned to me and actually told me not to see Nathen anymore, to go home and just forget him. Well, that upset the big fellow, he started carrying on about how they couldn't just let me go, I knew too much. She stared him right down and asked him what it was he thought I knew. That nearly shut him up, all he could say was he wasn't going to take a chance on some dame interfering with his paycheck. She turned back to me, said I could leave, and asked if I needed a cab. I said no, Fenton was coming to get me. That set the big guy off again, he started yelling at Nathen, said he'd brought the cops down on them. He looked like he was going to hit Nathen, and that's when Fenton knocked on the door. The galoot threw it open, grabbed Fenton by the shirtfront, and dragged him into the room. Well, I'd had enough by then, so I drew my little pistol and shoved it into his back. He let go of Fenton real quick. Fenton took a swing at him, a roundhouse right to the jaw, but the guy didn't even flinch, left Fenton standing there shaking his poor knuckles. Then that woman stepped over to the wall and shut out the lights. She pushed us both out the door and we started to make a getaway, but that big man came after us. I was ready to drop him, but, as you know, Fenton thought better of that. He was right, I guess, after all. And you know the rest."

"If the woman is in charge and she was protecting Nathen, maybe you have nothing to worry about."

"I hope so." Gertrude sighed. "And it's out of my hands, I guess." She patted her belly. "Best thing for me at a time like this is to keep my strength up. Where's the kitchen? I'll make us a sandwich."

Laura stood. "Why, the kitchen is full of food. Follow me." She pushed through a swinging door into the kitchen, a cozy room papered in gold, cream, and red. A small table and two chairs sat along one wall. Opposite them stood a white Westinghouse range and refrigerator. A counter and a double sink separated them beneath a window that looked out onto the street two floors below. Laura opened the refrigerator and spread across the counter a pitcher of lemonade and several plates covered in tin foil. She unwrapped them to reveal dilled salmon filets, roast chicken, a Linzer torte, chilled white asparagus with vinaigrette, and soft, white dinner rolls. She placed them on the table in front of Gertrude and added a butter dish and jam, two plates and two glasses from a cupboard and knives, forks, and spoons from a drawer.

"Surely you didn't make all this just for yourself," Gertrude exclaimed.

Laura blushed. "No, it was…brought in."

Gertrude gave Laura another shrewd glance, but decided again to let her keep her secret. She took the empty plate Laura offered and filled it. She poured herself a glass of lemonade, closed her eyes and murmured a short blessing, then set to with gusto. Laura apologized for not offering sustenance sooner to her apparently famished guest, but Gertrude waved her off. "I always eat like this. It shows God my appreciation for what He's set before me."

"And I see He thanks you by preserving your figure." Laura nodded at Gertrude's petite frame.

"Just my metabolism," Gertrude replied, "I'm a little high strung."

"You seem perfectly calm now."

"Yes, but I'm easily excited."

"Maybe you should eat more."

Gertrude laughed as she speared another slice of salmon. Laura took her own plate and dished up a dab of salmon, a slice of chicken breast, and two spears of asparagus. She pulled two sheets of paper from her skirt pocket. "You know, there's a clue here. It should have tipped your brother off. I don't know why he didn't see it." She pointed to the name on the automobile registration that Fenton had given her earlier. "'Nathen Stoico'. Nathen is misspelled, it should be N-A-T-H-A-N, and there's more. If you take off the first "N" and add the "S" from Stoico, you get Athens, where the Stoics had their school in ancient Greece. The name is obviously made up."

Gertrude whistled in appreciation. "You're one smart cookie, Laura."

"And so is she." Laura fell silent, lost in thought, and Gertrude offered her a penny.

"I don't know, wondering who she is, I guess. What's she up to and why. She must lead an exciting life."

"On the wrong side of the law!"

"Yes, I suppose." She glanced at Gertrude's empty plate. "Are you finished?"

"Yes, and you?" Laura nodded. "Then I'll do the dishes." Gertrude gathered the plates, silver, and her glass, took them to the counter beside the sink, and ran hot water. Laura retrieved the leaves of foil and began to cover the food.

With the kitchen tidied and themselves replenished, Laura and Gertrude returned to the living room. Gertrude put on the table radio that stood next to the bookcase and sat in the club chair. Laura reclined upon the sofa. A steady stream of tunes lulled them. A moment later, it seemed to Laura, a knock at the door awakened her. Fenton had returned.

"We went back out to the Royal Arms, but they'd already cleared out. I thought they might have. I'll go back tomorrow and give the place a thorough going over. Say, I'm starved. Is there any food in this place?"

"Mind your manners, Fen," Gertrude scolded, and he dutifully apologized.

Laura showed him into the kitchen and handed him a plate, invited him back to the living room to eat, and returned to keep Gertrude company. Fenton emerged from the kitchen, his piled high plate and a beer he'd bought balanced in one hand and a cigarette waving from the other one.

"Do you have an ashtray?"

"Well, no, Detective, I don't. I can't abide that habit. I would urge you to give it up."

"Why, here's just the girl for you, Fen," Gertrude declared. "You oughtn't to let her go."

"Since you've sworn off men, Gert, I wouldn't think you'd be encouraging relations between the sexes."

"Pish-tosh, Fenton. The way you go through girlfriends, I don't think I have anything to worry about."

Fenton bridled. "Gert, you know I just haven't found the right girl yet. I can look, can't I?"

"I wonder if you're not looking at the right girl sitting just across the room from you."

"I'll save you both the trouble." Laura smiled. "I'm not looking for a boyfriend just yet. Detective, eat your supper."

He shrugged, slouched in the club chair, and set the plate and beer onto its wide arm. He pulled a silver cigarette case from his coat pocket, slid the cigarette into it, set the case beside the plate, and dug in. "Say, this is good," he said, his mouth full, "You can cook, too?"

"Well, no, somebody else made it."

He continued to chew and began to mash all the individual dishes into one big pile. "Yeah? Who?"

"Fenton, that's not important," Gertrude interjected.

"No, that's OK, Gertrude. It's from my mother," Laura said. "She thinks I'll starve if I'm left on my own. It may be true, I haven't learned to cook yet."

Fenton scraped up the last of the pile from his plate and shoveled it into his mouth. He set the plate back on the chair's arm and took a long pull at his beer. "You know, it's a good thing you decided to come to my press conference. You surely got me out of a jam. Where'd you learn to drive like that?"

"I never did, Mr. Hardy. I guess necessity brought out the best in me."

"Well, necessity or whatever it was, we'd have been in a real pickle if it weren't for you. Why, you ought to be in the papers."

"I am in the papers, Detective."

"Well, of course, but I didn't mean it like that."

"You meant in the sense that my reputation would be ruined?" Laura smiled.

"No, not like that, either, I meant in the good sense. Gosh, now you've got me all confused." He threw his hands in the air.

Laura's eyes sparkled. "That was not my intention, Detective, and I apologize." She continued, "I think you were right to suspect that man. I'm sure he's not the person he presented himself to be. I noticed something odd about his name." She pulled the registration from her pocket and ran through what she'd found.

"I know where Athens is," he responded, "but what's a Stoic?"

"Stoics were Greeks. They shared a particular philosophy. I know you went to college, Detective."

"But I didn't study that old-fashioned stuff. My education was up to date."

"The 'old-fashioned stuff' is the foundation of our civilization."

"Sorry, but if it doesn't help me solve crimes, it isn't any good to me."

"If you'd known about the Stoics, perhaps you would have noticed that clue."

Rueful, he could only shrug his shoulders. "If she made up the name like that, I guess she's pretty smart."

"Yes," Laura mused, "and clever, too. If you'd guessed it, she would have known you'd found her out."

"How do you mean?"

"One of you…" she nodded at Gertrude, "would have confronted him with it."

"Ah, a tripwire. We're not dealing with a common criminal."

"What could she be planning?"

"Bank robbery. Maybe smuggling."

"Have you considered, she needn't be a criminal at all?"

"Well of course she's a criminal. Shooting people is against the law!"

"She wasn't shooting. She wasn't even there."

"Now you're splitting hairs. She's smart enough to let her goons do the dirty work, that's all."

"They might have gone off on their own to shoot at us. You don't have a single bit of evidence she's done anything wrong. What could you charge her with?"

"Accessory! Say, why are you taking her side, anyway?"

"I like to give people the benefit of the doubt."

"Why go to all the trouble to keep tabs on me?"

"Because whatever she's doing, even if it's legal, would appear suspicious if the police found her out. They would interfere with what she's trying to do."

"Well you're so smart, you tell me what she's doing?"

"I don't know Detective. My intuition can take me only so far."

"Intuition!" he scoffed. "You can't prove a case on intuition. You need facts. Demonstrable proof. What'll stand up in court."

"And how many times have I heard about the police proceeding on hunches?"

"The only ones you heard about were the ones that worked out. And you read about them in the papers, right? Reporters never report the ones that didn't. No ma'am, real police work means building a case from observation and verifiable clues."

Laura sighed. "Is there no way I can convince you, Detective?"

"You're a reporter. Think about it, that's not so different from being a detective. We're both trying to find things out, right? So prove your case, Miss van Duyn. If you think she's innocent, then get me the proof. If I can't deny it, I'll believe you."

A loud yawn came from behind the club chair. "Fenton, can we go home? I'm beat, and we're safe now, aren't we?"

Fenton grinned. "Yeah, I think we'll be all right. Time to go." Gertrude went to take Fenton's plate into the kitchen, but Laura insisted that she not. And so brother and sister gathered up their coats and hats, cigarette case, and car keys, plied Laura with their eternal thanks and gratitude, and left.

CHAPTER 5
THE NEXT MORNING

Laura awoke early and restless. She fetched last night's dishes from the living room and piled them in the sink. While her cup of tea brewed, she fetched the newspaper. The lead article, all about the car chase and shootout the previous evening, did nothing to improve her mood. Though her name was not mentioned, still she felt hemmed in, watched. She ate some leftover salmon and a spear of asparagus, bathed, dressed, and went out. She wandered for a while, finally descending into a subway station to escape, she would have said, the muggy air; afterwards, she could not have told anyone which station. Her riding seemed random to her as she thought, but eventually she realized she was in Brooklyn, near to the Royal Arms Hotel. After explaining herself to the landlady, who she was and why she was there, the landlady handed her two keys, each stamped with an apartment number. Laura mounted first to the third floor and went along the hallway to number 302. The key let her in. A potent scent assaulted her, sweat and cheap cigars, cheaper booze, burnt toast and fried onions, and not a hint of cheap perfume, Laura noted. A few old police gazettes, some empty bottles, and a stale ashtray stood on a flimsy coffee table in front of a sagging sea-green couch. Laura paced the rooms a while, crouching to look under beds and tables and peering into closets, finding nothing but balls of dust and tattered cobwebs. To her eyes, the flat yielded no clues. Nathen had lived lightly in this place. Or not at all.

Laura abandoned 302 and its reek and climbed to the fourth floor.

Her spirit lightened when she entered the second apartment. The little room and the few objects it held -- a broom and a dustpan, a rude iron bed with a nearly-sprung mattress, a cupboard, a sink, and, on the counter next to it, a hotplate -- conveyed an aura of nearly obsessive neatness. Laura was reminded of a nun's quarters she'd once visited. The floor was swept clean. The window glass shone. A light and airy essence hovered just beyond her nostrils' ken.

She spied a closet door across the room and start towards it. Along the way, her foot caught on a loose floorboard and her heart leaped, but when she stooped and lifted it she found merely an empty cavity.

Some men's dungarees and a work shirt hung in the closet. The scent lingered stronger here, anise, something almost like pine, tobacco, jasmine. "What an odd smell for the city," she thought. She rummaged in the dungarees' pockets, but her search yielded not even a shred of lint. She shut the closet and turned, her eyes running towards the bed. A book lay on the floor beside it. She knelt to pick it up and opened it. The title page read "Philosophies of the Greeks." Beneath the title was stamped the name of an English public school. As a bookmark, she found a receipt from a Fourth Avenue book dealer, one Laura had herself visited many times. "I could have seen her there," she thought. She closed the book and laid it on the bed. A beam of sunlight struck the wall above her and a flash of color caught her eye. Tacked to the wall was a blade of grass, emerald against the dun-colored paint, its edges just beginning to curl. It held her gaze, so out of place. A tremor disturbed her heart, of wildness and the unknown. She stood and stroked the blade with the tip of an index finger, smooth going up, rough coming down, and wondered at its purpose, a symbol? Or a sign?

"Hey, you're not ruining my crime scene are you?"

Laura, startled, snatched her finger back. Detective Hardy stood in the doorway grinning. "Did you prove your case yet? Got anything for me?"

She shook her head.

"Yeah, they cleared this place out pretty well." He strode into the room carrying a satchel held closed with a clasp. "I'll give it the works anyway." He looked around. "Something might turn up."

"Would you mind if I watched?"

"No, help yourself. Although I can't promise it'll be stimulating, police work's mostly not about car chases and gunplay."

He opened the satchel, removed equipment, and spent a half an hour dusting for fingerprints, pulling open drawers, inspecting with a magnifying glass. Finally finished, he ran a hand through his hair. "Nothing, just some prints on the closet doorknob, but those are yours."

Laura nodded. "How did you know?"

"Seems pretty clear nobody's been in here but you since she left, it's so clean. She's very careful, a pro I'd say, at hiding herself." He nodded at the blade of grass. "What do you make of that?"

"I couldn't say."

"Yeah, weird. Could be some kind of secret message." He reached out to take it, but she caught his wrist.

"No. Leave it. Please."

He lowered his arm and grinned. "Well, all right."

Laura blushed. "It's just that, it's just a blade of grass. It couldn't prove anything."

"As a matter of fact, it could, but I get the feeling though that's not your real reason."

"What other reason could I have?"

"I don't know, it just seems like you've taken an interest in this woman."

"She could be a good story."

"Ah, the reporter. I forgot. Well, I guess there's no harm in leaving it. It's not likely it'll tell me anything." He picked the book off the bed. "I'll take this, though." He opened it and chuckled. "You sure pegged that one. Good for you!" He also took the clothes from the closet, and stood there with them and the book in his arms. "That's all I can do here for now. You need a lift over to Manhattan?"

"Yes, thank you," she nodded, "that would be nice."

***

The detective had requisitioned a standard-issue and well-used squad car. Laura got in through the passenger door before he could open it for her. The leather upholstery shone, smoothed by years of sitters, but the rest of the car's interior was dusty and smelled of sweat and old cigarettes. Fenton climbed in behind the wheel. When he turned on the ignition, the radio squawked and he shut it off.

On the drive back, he asked her, "Why aren't you married, Miss van Duyn?"

"I don't want to be, Mr. Hardy!"

He glanced at her calves. "Just seems a gal like you'd at least have a beau. Or two."

"If I had a beau, he'd be more interested in what's up here…" She tapped her temple with her fingertip. "…than what's down there."

He whistled. "No offense meant. Say, you're a little saucy."

"And you're a little cocky."

He laughed. "All right, all right, I'll lay off." He drove on.

She stared out the window. After a moment, she said, calmer, "I don't need anyone. I'm doing fine on my own."

"You can do fine and be with someone. It's not either or, and there's nothing wrong with companionship, helps ease out the bumps."

She smiled. "Bumps?"

"You know, the bumps in the road of life."

"Why, Detective, you're quite the philosopher."

"Now, see, you're just making fun of me, like last night with those Stoics. I'll bet I learned things you never did. Besides…" he reached into the back seat and brought up a book. "…here, got it this morning."

She read the title, embossed in gold: Stoicism. "By St. George Stock, isn't it?" She ruffled its pages. "I've read it myself, it's quite good. I hope you enjoy it." She set the book on the seat between them. "And why aren't you married, Detective?"

"Me? Are you kidding? I got a lot of living to do before I saddle myself with a wife and kids and a dog and a mortgage. Nothing but tie you down."

"And what about companionship, Detective, easing the bumps? Seems to me you set a double standard."

"Why, how do you mean?"

"A woman ought to be married, but a man can sow his oats?"

"A woman needs taking care of."

"Except for Gertrude."

"But Gertrude's not…"

"A woman?"

"Now don't go putting words into my mouth, Miss van Duyn, I

mean she was raised different, not like most women. Say, I'm not surprised you haven't got a boyfriend, you take them apart like that. A lot of fellows don't like a smart girl, makes them feel threatened."

"I don't intend to threaten you, Detective."

"No, I'm not threatened, I like a gal knows what she's talking about, they're more interesting that way."

"You like interesting women, then?"

"Well sure, I mean they've got to have nice legs, but who wants to be bored on a date?"

***

Back across the East River, Fenton stopped in front of her building. "I've been thinking, Miss van Duyn, we ought to cooperate. I'll be the detective, work the case, and you'll be the reporter who tells the story. Scratch each other's backs."

She considered his proposal. "Yes," she said, "I might be interested. I'll let you know."

"You'll let me know? This could make your career! Isn't that what you're looking for?"

"I'm looking for something, Detective. Maybe this is it, I'll have to think about it."

He tipped back his hat and scratched his forehead. "I sure can't figure you out."

"You don't have to, Detective. It is, fortunately, not your job."

"Well, yeah, that's true. Oh, say, do you have any plans for tomorrow morning?"

"No. Why?"

"Gertrude wondered if you'd like to go to church with her."

"Yes, I'd love to. Which church?"

"First Presbyterian. Do you know it?"

"Yes, I do. I'll meet her there. And will you accompany us?"

"Naw, I got better things to do."

"Are you not concerned about where you'll spend eternity, Detective?"

He snorted. "No! If God's anything like they say he is, he already knows where I'll end up. Nothing I can do about it."

"That's very sensible."

"Yeah, I thought so, too. Hey listen, you'll let me know about that reporter thing won't you? I've got to talk to the press at some point, if it's not going to be you."

"You can talk to the press whenever you'd like. You don't need my permission. I would appreciate your not mentioning my name though. Is that all right?"

"Deal."

"I'll be going, then. Thank you for the ride."

"Don't mention it."

She lunched on the rest of last night's dinner and set out for the library, where she spent the afternoon and evening. While the librarians were tenacious in their research, no source they consulted hinted at any explanation for the blade of grass. She left discouraged. As she approached her apartment, she noticed several men loitering outside. The light over the door fell on their faces, and she recognized Garrity, his jaw working hard on that gum. He assailed her.

"Hey van Duyn, there's a rumor you were driving that police car last night. Got anything to say about that?"

She put her head down and tried to bowl right through them, but Garrity caught at her elbow to restrain her. She shook him off and started at him, fierce, so he backed away and then caught himself. "Listen, you can't sit on this story. You got to talk to us."

"No I don't Mr. Garrity. I'm a reporter, too, and I will tell my own story. I'll thank you to stay off my doorstep."

As she ascended to her floor in the elevator, she asked of nobody in particular that she be granted patience and grace.

CHAPTER 6
"...ALL MY FRIENDS DO."

On Sunday morning, sunny and warm, Laura and Gertrude approached an imposing Gothic church. Laura asked Gertrude, "Have you heard from Nathen?"

Gertrude shook her head. "No, not a word. It's hardest not knowing if that's good or bad."

"If he'd needed your help, surely he would have found you."

The two women had passed into the church and stood now in the foyer waiting for their eyes to adjust to the dim light. A man hissed Gertrude's name. She looked around, bewildered.

"Where's that coming from?"

"Over there." Laura pointed to a corner between the church wall and an unopened door where the sunlight did not penetrate. Gertrude started towards it, but Laura grabbed her arm. "That might not be safe."

The man called a little louder, "Gertrude, it's all right, it's Nathen." He came part way into the light. He hadn't shaved, and his rumpled clothes were dusty. His bloodshot eyes, shadowed by dark crescents, shifted from Gertrude to Laura and back.

With a concerned cry, Gertrude broke Laura's grip, strode to his side and took his arm. "Nathen, you're a mess. Let me take you home. You'll be safe there."

"Naw, I'm all right. I just need to hide out a couple days until everyone cools off. Me and my brother got a house in Jersey, I'll go over there. Listen, Miss Hardy, I know it looks bad for me, like I was just using you to keep tabs on the police. It might have started out that way, but after a while, honest, it got to where I enjoyed your company. I know I hurt your feelings, and I feel awful, I been walking all night thinking about it. I come to apologize and to find out if you could possibly forgive me."

Gertrude, blinking back tears, took his hand. "Why, Nathen, of course, I already have."

"Mr. Stoico?" Laura asked, "Can you tell us why you were asked to watch the police? Was it the woman who asked you?"

"Yeah, Halliday, that's her name. A couple of months ago she caught up with me playing pool over in Jersey. Told me I needed some help." He grinned. "I'd beaned a cop in a bar fight, they had a warrant out on me, somehow she knew about that. Anyway, she asked would I be willing to follow this woman -- that would be you, Miss Hardy. Her brother was a detective with the NYPD and she needed to keep tabs on the cops. She was offering money and protection from the cops, I don't know how, but it made sense so I said, sure, what the heck. She put me up in that room in Brooklyn, got me a nice suit. All I needed to do was report back to her anything you said about what the police was up to. After a while, there wasn't much to say, I got to feeling kind of bad about her spending that money on me and no results, so that's when I pushed you a little, Miss Hardy, I wanted her to get her money's worth, but, well, that blew the whole thing."

"And this Halliday," Laura continued, "why did she need information about the police? What are her plans?"

He shrugged. "No idea, Miss. She's big on only letting on to what a person needs to know. She never said, and I wasn't in no position to ask."

"Nathen, are you in any danger?"

"From Halliday? No, Miss Hardy, she always treated me good."

"What about that large man from last night?"

"Bruno? Heh. I can handle Bruno. Don't worry about me, I'll be fine."

"But what will you do now?"

"I don't know, I always find something."

"Mr. Stoico," Laura chided, "you really ought to go to the police."

Stoico faced her. "Lady, I got that warrant out on me. They'd just throw me in the can. I got a brother to support and taxes to pay."

Gertrude sighed and opened her purse. "Laura, let him go. I believe him." She pulled out a business card and handed it to him. "You are a decent man after all, Nathen. Please, come see me. I have some pull with the police, and I know I can help you find something honest to do."

Nathen took the card and shook Gertrude's hand.

"Thank you, Miss Hardy." He bowed his head, then looked her in the eye. "You know my real name ain't Nathen. She give it to me. My real name is Anthony, Anthony Difaro. You can call me Tony, all my friends do."

He stepped towards the door, gave Gertrude and Laura a thumbs-up and a smile and vanished. Gertrude took Laura's arm and guided her into the sanctuary. "Now, I like that pew over there because the preacher can't see you when you fall asleep."

CHAPTER 7
A FATAL TURN

Tony stepped from a cab in front of his big brother's house in Jersey City. The once-sunny day had gone cloudy and cold. He hunched his shoulders, shivering under his thin coat. Triple-deckers lined both sides of the street, clad in asphalt shingles or clapboards, all painted some shade of gray. The sidewalks were empty. People, finished with church, were either home with the family or off visiting.

It was not strictly Carlo's place. Since his wife kicked him out, his brother had lived in their folks' old place, but the folks had left it to the both of them when they passed on a year ago. Neither of them kept it up. Carlo had no job and no money. Tony just didn't care. A shabby edifice greeted him of cracked glass and peeling paint. The door swung loose. Fresh wood showed at the latch where someone had forced it. Tony peered cautiously inside, but the place was dim, and he could not see.

"Carlo?" he called, "You in there?"

Nobody answered. He pushed through the wrecked door and swung right into a long, narrow living room. Gray light came through the bay window behind his back. At the end of the room, two wing chairs stood in front of a fireplace. Bruno sat in the chair to the left and cracked his knuckles while he warmed his hands over the fire. He spat, and the fire hissed. He stood to face Tony; he was huge, six-two with shoulders wide as the fireplace, in a sharp suit, dark and double-breasted. He glared from tiny, black eyes and rubbed his meaty, dimpled nose.

"That your brother I run out of here?" he asked, "He's yellow, wet his pants going out the back door."

He put his hand into his jacket and pulled out a snub-nosed revolver and a silencer, which he commenced to screw onto the end of the gun's barrel.

"You a prayin' man, Difaro? 'Cause if you are, you better start prayin." He looked around the room. "You might end up someplace nicer than this."

Tony pulled himself up, the smaller man but bold. "I didn't sell you out, Bruno. You got no right to kill me."

"You're a loose end, Difaro. You panicked and now you might do anything. You might go to that cop, sell me out after all. I end it here, and I don't have to worry about you." He aimed the pistol and set his finger on the trigger. "Besides, my car's wrecked. Somebody gotta pay." Tony squinted his eyes shut and steeled himself, wondered if it would hurt, then felt a cool hand on his wrist. The air moved in front of him, sweet, and a voice murmured, "Put it away, Bruno." Tony opened his eyes and saw a vision in the gloomy light. Halliday!

She faced him over her shoulder, tall, five-ten, in a loose white linen shirt and dungarees. Black hair tumbled in lavish waves down her back. In that pale light, her face shone, set with indigo eyes and full lips, and a scatter of freckles across the bridge of her nose. Around town, there was a new word for what she was: A knockout. She smiled, squeezed Tony's arm, and turned back to Bruno, who still held the pistol, pointed now at her.

"I asked you to put it away, Bruno."

Bruno snorted and jerked the gun. "I'm doing the asking now."

She spun to face Tony, and began to fuss with the lapels on his jacket. "Is it so bad Bruno? Could you not just let him go?" Still quiet and calm, and in some foreign accent Tony could not place. "A different one every day," he thought, "like it's part of her disguise."

"I told you it was a dumb idea, sending him to keep tabs on the cops. Turns out I was right, now I gotta fix the mess."

"And the only way it can be fixed is that Tony must be dead?"

"The way I see it."

She looked into Tony's eyes and smiled again, and stroked his cheek. "Bruno, did I ever tell you I was a conjurer?"

"No. What's that mean?"

"I can pick a needle out of thin air." Her fingers, with painted red nails, moved from Tony's cheek and, briefly, a needle stood upright between thumb and forefinger. Then, just as briefly, she pricked Tony's neck and he fell, disheveled, to the floor and lay still with wide eyes staring at the ceiling.

"I said I would do the killing, so it is fixed. Now you will put your gun away and we will go back to work."

CHAPTER 8
SHADOWED

"Brrr," said Gertrude, "what happened to the sun?" She stood with Laura in front of the church.

"I don't know," Laura answered, shivering. "Let's go someplace warm for lunch."

"There's the Automat across the street," Gertrude said, "I love their lemon pie."

Inside the restaurant, they collected their nickel tokens and found the food they wanted behind tiny, windowed doors -- meatloaf and pie for Gertrude, and for Laura, a lettuce salad. They sat at a table by the window.

"What do you do for work?" Laura asked.

"I'm a social worker," Gertrude replied, "for a relief agency downtown."

"I don't wonder that you carry a gun."

Gertrude waved a dismissive hand. "Never needed it. Poor people aren't any more dangerous than other people. Surely you must know that from your mother's work."

"You know who my mother is?"

"Of course, dear. Van Duyn's not such a common name and her foundation underwrites a good part of my agency's budget. I read the society pages, too. I've seen your by-line and your mother's name all over them. Wasn't hard to make the connection."

Laura blushed and hung her head a little. "I'm ashamed to say I have stayed as far from my mother's work as I could. I assumed poor people were dirty and dangerous."

Gertrude smiled and reached across the table to pat Laura on the shoulder. "Come with me sometime on my rounds. You won't be afraid. 'Blessed is he that considers the poor. The Lord will deliver him in time of trouble'."

Laura returned her smile. "I will accept your invitation. You can make me a better woman." She gave Gertrude a puzzled look. "Why do you carry a gun, then?"

"Force of habit," laughed Gertrude. "My father had me shooting by the time I was four years old, and gave me a pistol to carry when I went off to college. 'It's what every girl needs to protect herself' he'd say. I guess he didn't trust college boys too much, with good reason I found out. I only ever had to use it that once, though."

"Gertrude!" exclaimed Laura, scandalized, "Did you hurt him badly?"

"Not any worse than that little scratch you got."

"Didn't he call the police?"

"And ruin his reputation as a lady's man? Heaven's, no! He even helped me pass Physics when I threatened to tell, he was that anxious that it not get out. I guess it did, though, because no boy was ever fresh with me again."

A fit of giggles overcame Laura, and she leaned back taking in the street scene outside the window. The giggles stopped. "Gertrude, that man across the street reading a paper…I think he was sitting behind us in church. Do you think he might be following us?"

Gertrude opened her purse, pulled out a compact, and glanced into its mirror. "He's one of the men from last night." Her face brightened. "He must be following us! Let's wait until he leaves and follow him."

Laura's mouth gaped. "Gertrude, don't be silly."

"Silly! Laura, he might lead us straight back to the gang. Talk about a scoop for you!"

Laura reconsidered. "But he's following us. I mean, if we leave, he'll follow us, and he won't leave as long as we're here."

Gertrude frowned. "Good point."

"He has to think he's lost us."

"How do you mean?"

"We have to get out of here without him seeing us. He'll think he's lost us, and he'll leave. Then we can follow him."

Laura made sure their tag wasn't looking, then stood, took Gertrude's hand and led her to the back of the restaurant and out through a door into the alley. She strode left to pull open a door leading into the neighboring shop. With Gertrude at her heels, she moved quickly down a short hallway into the shop proper and to the storefront window.

"Gertrude, he's not there," she said, dismayed.

"Ahem." The shopkeeper announced her presence. "Can I help you?"

Gertrude spoke over her shoulder. "There's a man following us. We're going to turn the tables on him."

Her interest piqued, the proprietress joined them at the window, craning to see. "Where is he?"

"We don't know."

Laura grabbed Gertrude's arm. "There he is, down the street. He's already left." She started for the door.

"Ladies, wait." The shopkeeper took two silk headscarves from a shelf. "Take these. They're not much of a disguise, but men are easy to fool." She smiled.

Laura and Gertrude thanked her, and Laura promised to return for a proper purchase. Outside, they spotted their man quickly but hung back, keeping a half block behind him and pretending to window shop. He did not hurry, so they easily kept him in sight.

"He's probably not too anxious to tell the boss he lost us," snickered Gertrude. They followed him for several blocks until he came to his apparent destination, a bus stop. Another man came up and began speaking with him. Gertrude slowly leaned her head towards Laura's as they gazed into a window.

"We have to find out what they're saying."

"How?" Laura asked, glancing sideways.

"They haven't noticed us yet. Let's just walk up to them."

The women approached the men, who remained deep in conversation, oblivious to anyone around them. The sidewalk was, fortunately, bustling.

"Yeah, I caught Stoico talking to that Hardy dame. I called Halliday after he lit out, told her I figured he was going over to Jersey. Between you and me, with her and Bruno on his tail, I guess his time's getting short."

"They're going to do him in, you think?"

"You heard them last night, they both pretty much said so. I'll bet the deed's already done, she don't have much time to tie up her loose ends before that ship comes in. Hey, here comes the bus."

It pulled to the curb, and the doors opened. The waiting crowd pushed forward, carrying along Gertrude and Laura who jostled the two men. Their eyes widened as they recognized Gertrude. One of them made a grab for her arm, but the surging crowd separated them. Laura and Gertrude were between the men and the bus. Laura tried to turn out of the way, but it was too late, the crowd had them trapped. It swept them onto the bus with the two men after them.

CHAPTER 9
TABLES TURNED

Laura took some coins from her purse and dropped them clattering into the fare box. The impatient queue pushed her and Gertrude toward the back of the bus. Men offered to let the ladies sit, but Laura and Gertrude thought they could keep better tabs on their adversaries if they remained standing. The two toughs came up the steps, deposited their coins, grabbed poles and whispered, darting occasional glances at the women. The clogged aisle prevented their approach. Laura thought they weren't likely to be harmed with so many people around. She turned to Gertrude and saw her eyes filling.

"Gertrude, what's wrong?"

"You heard what they said. Tony's dead!"

"You don't know that. It's only hearsay."

Gertrude glared. "Laura, you have to face it now, that woman is evil."

Laura tried hard not to be exasperated. "I admit it doesn't look good for her, but there is no evidence to prove she's done anything wrong. We need more information." She glanced back at the men, now casting leers their way. "We need to have them arrested."

Gertrude wiped her cheeks. "How can we do that?"

"They know we overheard them, so they will try to come after us, don't you think?"

Gertrude nodded.

"Are you armed?"

"Of course."

"If we get off the bus, they'll follow us. There are too many people around for them to attack us. We can bide our time and look for a place to set a trap. While we're walking, we should pretend that we're scared of them. That will make them less cautious. And when we've sprung the trap, you hold them with your gun while I get the police."

At the next stop, Laura and Gertrude made a great show of clutching their purses and hurrying off the bus through its rear doors. Just as Laura thought, their pursuers struggled through the crowd and jumped onto the street at the last moment. Laura, half a block ahead, made sure they saw her fearful glance. The two men turned to each other, grinned, and set off in pursuit.

Gertrude and Laura lured the men on, looking over their shoulders as if nervous. Horace and Gus paced them half a block back. As Laura expected, they weren't going to try anything on the busy street. When they passed in front of a narrow, dark alley, Gertrude grabbed Laura's arm and pulled her in. They hurried halfway down and crouched behind some wooden crates. A moment later, Horace and Gus came sprinting into the alley's mouth and dashed right past the women, coming up hard against a dead end a few feet beyond. Gertrude snatched her pistol from her handbag.

"Freeze, or I'll shoot you!"

They spun back to face Gertrude with astounded faces. One of them made a grab for his jacket and Gertrude squeezed off a shot that chipped a brick not three inches from the side of his face. The ricochet nicked his cheek as it whined off. That stung, and the man put a hand up with tears actually starting in his eyes. His partner stood very still.

Gertrude kept her gun on them. Out of the side of her mouth, she said, "Go find the police."

Laura sprinted to the street and, turning with shaded eyes, searched the throng for a policeman. A burly man looked up from the edge of the sidewalk.

"Looking for someone, lady?" he shouted. He stepped away from the moving van he was unloading. His equally burly partner jumped out the back.

"What's up, Joe?" he yelled.

"I dunno, Pete, looks like some lady needs a hand."

Joe waded through the crowd to Laura. "Can I help you ma'am?"

The words spilled out of Laura almost faster than she could say them. "Oh, thank you, yes, my friend is holding two criminals at gunpoint down that alley. They know about my friend's boyfriend's murder and he was following us, but we turned the tables and followed him and he met a friend, and then we got shoved onto a bus, and we got off and trapped them in the alley. My friend's holding them, but I don't think she can hold them much longer, she has a very tiny gun, so if you could please just help her watch them until I find a policeman, I'd be obliged. Thank you."

Joe frowned. "Murder...gunpoint...she?" He turned to his partner. "Come on, Pete." They lumbered down the alley.

Laura spotted a policeman sauntering her way and waved her arms overhead to catch his attention. She pointed down the alley, and then ran back to Gertrude's side. The sight that greeted her nearly made her giggle. Gus and his friend squirmed on the dirty alley pavement with a large mover perched on each one.

CHAPTER 10
GERTRUDE'S TRIUMPH

Ten minutes later, with the help of the movers, Joe and Pete, Officer Flanagan had Gus and the other fellow, Horace, handcuffed and standing sullen and subdued on the sidewalk, waiting for the paddy wagon. Officer Flanagan had affixed an adhesive bandage to Gus's cheek.

Laura watched Gertrude strike up a conversation with Joe. She was explaining about her pistol and how she knew how to shoot it so well. As she held the pistol in her right hand, she took hold of Joe's large biceps with her left and sidled up close to him. She spoke softly so Joe had to bend down close to her to listen. She abruptly stuffed the gun into her purse and whispered into his ear while she squeezed his arm. Joe nodded slowly. Gertrude whispered again, and then let go Joe's arm and scooted across the sidewalk to Laura. She turned and gave Joe a little wave. He waved back and then got into his truck and drove off.

Gertrude said, "My, what a handsome, strong man he is. I just love brown eyes."

"You asked him out! Gertrude, I thought you'd sworn off men."

Gertrude laughed and waved her hand. "Passed like a summer storm," she said, "and he never would have asked me out. How else could I see him again?"

Officer Flanagan stepped over to them. "It's lucky those two movers came along. You girls had your hands full. You shouldn't ought to get involved in dangerous stunts like that on your own."

Gertrude rounded on Flanagan, getting up full in his face. "Officer, you shouldn't lecture grown women on what they should and shouldn't do. For your information, Miss van Duyn, who happens to be a reporter for the Herald Tribune, and I planned and executed our dangerous stunt with perfect precision. There was no danger. Those two are like most bullies, once you get the advantage of them, they back down pretty quickly."

Flanagan's face reddened under Gertrude's onslaught. Nudging Gertrude aside, Laura said quickly, "Of course Officer, we appreciate your concern for us. We are entirely grateful you happened along and brought these dangerous criminals into custody. Thank you very much, and I will be sure to mention to Gertrude's brother, Detective Hardy, and to my editor, the honor you have done your badge and your department this afternoon."

Flanagan relaxed, but his voice was still stiff. "You're welcome Miss van Duyn. Thank you for your consideration." He pulled a small notepad and a pencil stub from his shirt pocket. "Now, I'll need to take your statements. Miss van Duyn, you first." He nodded towards Gertrude. "Since you have the cooler head."

Gertrude fumed, but Laura gripped her forearm to keep her at bay, and quickly summarized the day's events. When she finished, Flanagan glanced over his notes. "I haven't heard anything about a murder, but you say this fellow lived in New Jersey, so if it did happen maybe it was over there. We'll start contacting police departments and see if they have any information."

"Thank you Officer," said Laura. "Can you tell me what will happen to those two?" She nodded towards Horace and Gus.

"Yes, Miss van Duyn. We'll take them down to the precinct house and book them on suspicion based on your statements that they are accessories. Since Detective Hardy's on this case, we'll let him know we're holding them, and he can have first crack at interrogating them. We'll hold them overnight, helps if these tough guys have the chance to stew a little."

A paddy wagon pulled out of the traffic and stopped at the curb. Two officers got out and approached Flanagan. "These the two Matty?" one of them asked, jerking his thumb at Horace and Gus.

Flanagan turned to him. "Yeah, Robby. That fellow on the left got nicked by a .22."

Robby turned to Flanagan. "You don't carry a .22, Matty."

"No, it wasn't me, was this...er...woman here."

Robby turned to her. "That's some shooting, lady. Maybe you ought to try out for the force."

Gertrude smiled in triumph. "Thank you, Officer. It's so nice to talk to an enlightened man."

Laura kicked Gertrude's foot. Flanagan glared. Robby and his partner herded Horace and Gus into the back of the paddy wagon and left.

Flanagan said, "Well, I've got to get back to my beat. You ladies are free to go." He set off down the street. Laura sagged against a mailbox. "Gertrude, I'm exhausted."

"Me too, Laura. Let's get a cab. I can't walk another step."

CHAPTER 11
BACK TO BROOKLYN

Laura was up at 6:00 the next morning and gone by 6:30. She stopped at the corner for a doughnut and coffee. Back outside, she hailed a cab and around 7:15 pulled up at the precinct house where the police held Horace and Gus. Outside the station, a paddy wagon waited with its engine running. A man in a trench coat and a gray fedora leaned on its fender, smoking. He nodded at Laura as she passed, flicked the butt, and climbed in beside the driver. The truck whined off. Laura stopped, wrinkling her nose. What was that scent, shrouded in cigarette smoke? An instant later, she knew. She spun back; the truck was only half a block away. She sprinted after it, but it accelerated and outpaced her. She stopped in the middle of the street, then strode back towards the station. A flash of white out of the gutter caught her eye, the remains of the cigarette. She folded them into a handkerchief and thrust them into her pocket, then dashed up the steps and through the station's double doors. "Tell me," she demanded of the desk sergeant, "who was in that paddy wagon?"

"Can't, ma'am. Police business."

"Was it two men, brought in yesterday, one nicked in the cheek?"

"Yeah, how'd you know?"

"I helped to bring them in."

"No kidding. You that reporter?"

"Yes. Now tell me where that wagon is going."

"Moving 'em to Riker's. Why?"

"I think you were set up, Sergeant."

"Naw, that detective, Hardy, he had all the paperwork, dotted and signed."

"Fenton Hardy?"

"Yeah, the one in the papers."

"That wasn't Fenton Hardy, Sergeant. May I use your phone?"

"Yeah, sure." He shoved it towards her. She dialed the Hardy's apartment. Fenton answered.

"Detective, it's Laura van Duyn. Those two men have been sprung."

"When?"

"Just now, by that woman. She posed as you, with paperwork to move them to Riker's Island Prison."

"Are you at that precinct?"

"Yes."

"Put the Sergeant on please."

She handed the Sergeant the phone. After a moment, he shuffled some papers and read a number into the mouthpiece. Then, his voice wound up, he said, "I'm sorry, Detective Hardy, for letting 'em go like that." At Fenton's reply, his shoulders relaxed, and he answered, relieved, "Thank you, Sir, I'm very grateful...Yes, here she is." As he handed the phone back to Laura, he pulled up a microphone and started to broadcast an APB.

Laura took the phone. "Yes?"

"I guess you have to admit she's guilty."

"Have you found a body?"

"No," he conceded, "but I was over in Jersey City yesterday at DiFaro's place, and it doesn't look good. The door was busted in and nobody around. I lifted some fingerprints. Big hands, I expect at least that fellow Bruno was there. Crazy thing is, I found another piece of grass stuck to the wall."

Once again, Laura's heart trembled. She caught a whiff of licorice.

"Detective, I hate to cut this short, but I need to go on to work. Just one more thing. Did Gertrude tell you those men mentioned a ship?"

"Yes."

"Will you search for it?"

"No, without more specific information, it would be like picking a needle out of a haystack. I'll put my hopes on these fingerprints and us catching that paddy wagon."

She said goodbye and rang off. She asked the sergeant to call her a cab and thanked him for his help.

***

As the truck pulled away from the curb, Bruno glanced at his side view mirror. "That dame's chasin' us!" He pressed down on the gas. "Why'd she do a thing like that?" Halliday watched Laura out of her own mirror. "I believe, Bruno, she's discovered who we are and would like to question us."

"Yeah? Why's that?"

"Because she's a reporter." She frowned as Laura bent to pick up the cigarette end. In a couple of blocks, they'd switch vehicles, but still she ought not to leave clues lying around. She'd slipped up. She glanced at the paper on the seat beside her, its front page story the capture of Horace and Gus. What, she wondered, had given her away to Miss Laura van Duyn? She watched Laura recede in the mirror until they'd turned the corner.

***

Laura fidgeted in the back of the cab. How, she thought, would the confrontation with her editor go? She considered that she might not have a job. She twisted the handkerchief in her pocket and wondered if that would be so bad? Out the window she saw a sign for a tobacconist's shop. She asked the driver to stop. The store was not yet open, but she could see a person moving around inside, so she rapped on the glass. A man came and waved her off, but she persisted until he opened the door.

"Madame, can you not see we are closed. Please, come back in an hour."

"I'm a reporter. I only need a moment. I'd be very grateful."

The man, still exasperated, opened the door wider and let her in. His shop was all dark wood, with the heavy, sweet scent of cured tobacco, newspapers and men's magazines.

The proprietor was a thin man, tall, with thick black hair, dark eyes, and olive skin. He wore a white shirt with tan slacks and had a dark mole on his left cheek. He went to stand behind the counter. "What is it you want?" Laura took the handkerchief from her pocket and unwrapped it on the counter. "Can you tell me anything about this? What kind of tobacco? Where someone might buy it?" The man lifted the kerchief to his nose and inhaled. His face broke into an improbable grin.

"This is the tobacco of my country. Peasant tobacco, very harsh. The anise is for better flavor." He smelled it again. "It is what my father smoked."

"Do you sell it?"

"No. My customers are a higher class."

"Where could it be bought?"

"On Atlantic Avenue in Brooklyn, where Syrians shop, maybe."

"Can you tell me anything about the woman who smoked it?"

"She is not Syrian and she is not married. Her husband would not let her smoke."

"Nothing else?"

"No." He smiled. "I am not a detective. Maybe you should take it to that detective in the papers, that Mr. Hardy."

"Yes. Maybe I should." She took a business card from her purse and gave it to him. "If you think of anything else, please call me. Thank you for your help."

"You are welcome. It has been my pleasure."

***

At the offices of her paper, Laura entered an elevator and gave the attendant her floor. He looked up from his copy of the morning edition, his face alight with excitement.

"Miss van Duyn, they been looking for you. You made the front page!" He held up the paper and there under a bold headline and file photo was an account of her adventure with Gertrude the day before. "The city editor told us all we was to send you up soon as we saw you."

"Oh. Well, okay, I suppose that's what you should do." She wondered if this were a good or a bad omen.

The boy pulled closed the doors and cranked over the lever that sent the elevator upwards. As they ascended, he read out loud and ever more breathlessly the paper's report of the previous day's events, finishing just at her stop and waving her off with an admiring smile. She stepped into the crowded city room, full of light from the floor-to-ceiling windows off to her left and the cityscape beyond, desks and clacking typewriters, and she stopped, uncertain where to go. The reporter nearest her looked up.

"Van Duyn?"

"Yes."

He pointed to the opposite wall with its row of offices. "Editor. He's waiting." He bent back to his work.

She threaded her way through the desks, jostled by copy boys and reporters speeding off on assignments, jackets over their shoulders and cigarettes dangling. She found the door whose plaque read "Daniel Hirsch, City Editor" and knocked. A gruff voice yelled, "Come in." She opened the door.

A beefy man, Hirsch sat reading copy in shirtsleeves and loosened tie, wielding his blue pencil with flourishes of satisfaction. "Mr. Grant," he yelled, "where'd you learn to write?" He looked up. "Who are you?"

"Laura van Duyn."

He put down his pencil, took off his hat, and straightened his tie. "Sit down, please, and explain," and he held up three or four different papers with nearly the same headline. "How did my competitors get this scoop and why weren't you down here yesterday afternoon filing your story?"

"Sir, I'm just a society reporter..."

"That's bull, van Duyn. A reporter's a reporter's a reporter. If you're on the scene of the story, you get the story. That's what reporters do."

She nodded.

"I checked up on you. Got your degree at Barnard, your dad pulled some strings, got you up there on the society beat, but I know where you went last Friday, on your own time, and I'm willing to bet you're not just a rich girl dabbling. Am I right?"

"Yes sir."

"Well all right, then. I'm glad we understand each other. Now, I pulled a couple of strings myself and got you transferred down here." He caught her eye. "That all right with you?"

She grinned, hugely. "Oh, yes, sir."

"Careful, van Duyn, you still owe me. First thing, you're going to give me a thousand words for the evening edition, your firsthand, eyewitness report. It'll run under your byline. I need it by lunch.

Second thing is I want you dogging that detective every step of the way. This looks like a big case, and because of you, we've got an exclusive. You up to that?"

She hesitated.

"Something you don't like?"

"Sir, I had a different idea. There's a woman, whatever is going on, she seems to be the leader, the planner. I want to find her."

"And you think there's a story in it?"

"Yes."

"You got a plan?"

"Yes."

He ruminated. "I'm out on a limb for you, van Duyn, but get me that feature by lunchtime and we've got a deal."

"Yes, sir. I won't let you down."

He held out his hand. "Good. You write well, and we'll get along. Talk to Janine out there, she'll show you your desk."

She stood and shook his hand. "Thank you, sir."

"You're welcome."

Janine got Laura settled, set a ream of paper beside the big Royal typewriter, and asked if she needed coffee. Laura declined, and Janine retired to her own desk. Laura rolled a sheet of paper into the typewriter and began to type, and it was as if her fingers were siphons to her thoughts; her recounting of the past three days' events streamed freely and without interruption onto the paper, from the Detective's press conference to her encounter that morning at the tobacconist. She reserved for herself only her observation of Halliday's scent. She had just finished and was neatening up the five typewritten sheets when the telephone at her elbow rang, and the switchboard put a call through. It was the tobacconist.

"Miss van Duyn, I have made some inquiries this morning on your behalf. I have located a tobacco merchant on Atlantic Avenue in Brooklyn. He has a female customer and she is buying tobacco there like the kind that you brought me this morning. Would you like the address?"

"Yes, please." She jotted it down. "Thank you very much for your help."

"Miss van Duyn, do not mention it. It was my pleasure to help you." He hung up. Laura took her story to Mr. Hirsch. With his blue pencil he went to work, and so did not immediately notice that Laura tarried in his office. Eventually he looked up. "Yes?"

"Mr. Hirsch, I have been given a lead, an important one, I think. May I leave to follow up?"

"Is this part of your plan?"

"Yes, sir."

"You mind tidying this up first?"

She looked stricken. "No, but is it…is it that bad?" She couldn't know how he hated to see a woman upset. He rushed to assure her.

"No, no. No, it's good. Just needs a little brushing up, I'll do it myself. Please, follow up your lead." He waved her out the door and went back to editing. Five minutes later, she was on the street hailing a cab.

CHAPTER 12
THE FATE OF HORACE AND GUS

A green utility van made its way east, slowly so as not to attract attention, on 56th Street toward the Queensboro Bridge. In the back Horace and Gus, still handcuffed, sat on the bare floor in the dark, fidgeting and speculating on the circumstances of their liberation. They'd been hauled from their cell, handed over to Bruno and some stranger done up in a cheap trench coat and fedora like a dime novel detective and tossed into the back of a paddy wagon. Minutes later, Bruno stuffed them into this second truck. They were both thinking, was their liberation and were they themselves, bound to be short lived?

Horace, fatigued and tense, said in a hoarse whisper, "Bruno ain't smart enough to spring us like that on his own. It must have been Halliday's plan."

Gus just nodded.

"I don't trust either one of them. We ought to get ready, Bruno might be taking us out to shoot us. Think we can take him if we rush him?"

Gus held up his hands and rattled the handcuffs. "I don't see how."

Horace nudged him, shoulder to shoulder. "Listen, buddy, we been in jams before. I always see us through, don't I?" He could only feel Gus's shoulders shrug.

"Yeah, I know it's bad, he opens those doors, we're blinded. I guess we just got to wait and see." He thought for a minute. "Look, he ain't gonna shoot us in here, he's gonna take us out first, so we'll have some time. If I talk fast enough, I can convince him."

"What are you gonna say, Horace, you'll bake him some cookies?"

"Hey, don't get wise on me, huh? We didn't spill the beans to the cops, I'll tell him that."

"Yeah, but they know who we are, you can bet our mug shots will be all over the city. Ain't Bruno gonna see that's a liability?"

"I don't know if Bruno's that smart. And look, Gus, they hired us. If we weren't essential they wouldn't have. They need our backs and our experience. We been around, we know the ins and the outs. Guys like us, we're not easy to come by. And it wasn't even our fault, just those two dames had some dumb luck."

Gus began massaging his wounded cheek. "Geez, Horace, don't remind me about those dames. Dang it, I hate getting shot. This thing's starting to itch like crazy. I'm not gonna get any peace for a week."

"And that's another thing, Gus, you was wounded in the line of duty. They gotta appreciate that. And it's just until tomorrow night, then we get paid and we can tell Bruno we're gonna vanish, we won't be no more trouble. So don't you see he's gonna buy that story, he loses by getting rid of us, and there really ain't no risk if he keeps us around."

"I hope you're right Horace, I hope you're right." Gus leaned back against the van's wall and lapsed into worried silence. Horace picked at his handcuffs, twisting them around to ease his chafed wrists. "At least he could've taken these cuffs off," he muttered. He stretched out on the floor and closed his eyes. The van was warm, and its gentle rocking lulled him to sleep. A minute later, it seemed, Gus shook him awake.

"Horace, get up. We're here."

Horace sat up and yawned. "Where's here?" he asked.

"I don't know," Gus carped. "You see any windows in this thing?"

"Easy, easy, Gus. I tell you, stop worrying."

They heard the passenger door close, and footsteps, the stranger's, scuffed away from the truck. The truck shifted, as if relieved of a massive weight, and the driver's door slammed. The back doors flew back. Horace and Gus squinted, dazzled by the gleaming sun. Bruno climbed in, looming over them, nearly filling the box. He reached out with bulldog arms, hauled Horace and Gus to their feet and shoved them outside. Horace lost his balance and tumbled to the ground. He jumped up and rounded on Bruno as he lumbered out of the van.

"Listen, jackass," he shouted. "Just because you're Halliday's muscle don't mean you got to rough us up."

Gus pulled Horace back. "Easy there, Horace, friendly, remember? He's got a hundred and twenty pounds on you."

"Yeah," snarled Horace, "but he ain't gotta throw it around."

Bruno, ignoring Horace's outburst, shut the van's doors, collared Gus and Horace, and quickstepped them across a rundown dock toward the door of a dilapidated warehouse. He shoved Horace and Gus up against the building and held them both there with one hand as he fumbled the door opened.

"You got a appointment with Halliday. She knocked off Stoico yesterday for bringing the cops down on us. Since you done the same, I feel like I'm saying so long to the both of you, and if she don't do it, I got half a mind to do it myself." He treated them to a wicked, coarse laugh, thrust them through the door, and pulled it closed on screeching hinges. Horace and Gus stood blinking in the dim, dusty light. A sultry voice spoke out of the shadows in front of them, as near as Horace and Gus could tell, from someone resident in the British Isles.

"Mr. Gilbert. Mr. McMahon. How nice to see you again."

Horace, scrawny as a rooster, puffed himself up. "I never knew no limeys, whoever youse are, you might as well show yourself."

Halliday stepped forward into a shaft of light, revealing herself as the keeper of the voice. From beneath the gray fedora, her lustrous hair curled around her face and fell across her shoulders. She still wore the trench coat. The men gasped.

"You sprung us?" Horace sputtered. "But you're just a dame!"

"Geez, Horace!" Gus bawled.

"And why, Mr. Gilbert, out of your infinite wisdom, could a "dame" not "spring" you?"

He tried to backpedal and keep intact some portion of his dignity. "It's not that you're dumb or nothing, don't get me wrong, it's just not something I'd expect a dame could carry off. It's complicated."

"Mr. Gilbert, let's ignore for now the fact that I did, as a dame, successfully spring you, and why don't you explain yesterday's events to me. You were supposed simply to follow Tony Stoico and let me know his movements."

"Which I did."

"And then what did you do?"

"Yeah, I stuck around. It was cold, and that church was warm. And afterwards, I was meeting Gus here, we was gonna go out to the track, I had to read the racing form so's I could place my bets. Why should I wear out my legs when there's a nice bench to sit on?" He worked up the nerve to glare back at her. "My job was done, I didn't owe you nothing more."

"Did you see the two women go into the restaurant?"

"Yeah. So what?"

"And still you sat right where they could see you?"

"I'm still not getting your point. They was two dames, jabberin' away, how could I know they'd even notice me?"

"But they did, and because they did, you've got the police once more breathing down our necks. Tell me now, Mr. Gilbert, who has best accomplished their tasks, you or this "dame"?

Horace, finally realizing the risk in his brashness, made a valiant effort to redeem himself, figuring the grovel as the most practical means. "Guess I was kind of dumb, huh?" he shrugged.

"Yes, very dumb." Halliday frowned. "It's not worth my time dealing with your foolishness. Apparently Bruno expects me to shoot you. I'm not going to do that, but apparently he still may, although I think I can hold him off until your job is done, and what I expect from the both of you is a good day's work tomorrow, and no complaining. You'll get paid, and then I hope never to see you again. You'll have to make your own peace with Bruno. Now stay out of my sight."

CHAPTER 13
GOOSE CHASE

Atlantic Avenue was busy that Monday morning with delivery men and shoppers. The taxicab idled in clotted traffic, and Laura grew impatient with waiting. She handed over the fare and walked the last few blocks to her destination. Blinds were drawn against the morning sun, but a small sign posted on the door said "Open". A bell jingled overhead as she entered. She shut the door behind her, muting the traffic's noise and the shouting crowds. The proprietor looked up from his newspaper, causing the tassel on his white fez to sway. He was a slim man, dark-skinned, with an aquiline nose and a severely and neatly trimmed moustache. "Yes, may I help you?" he asked. He drew from a cigarette in his left hand, which he raised elegantly to his ear and turned, with fingers bent and palm outward, as he inhaled. The diffuse sunlight at Laura's back still burnished the tendrils of smoke as they rose from the cigarette's tip.

"I'm Laura van Duyn. I'm a reporter."

He gently released the smoke. "Ah yes, the telephone call from my associate. You wanted to know about the woman who comes here?"

"Yes I did."

"What is your interest in this woman, Miss van Duyn?"

"I would like to know what she's doing."

"Her activities are no concern of the newspapers. That is what I brought you here to tell you."

Laura started. "You know her?"

"I am honored to supply her tobacco." He returned to his

newspaper and his cigarette. After a minute, without looking up, he said, "You should leave now. I will say no more."

Laura resisted the urge to stamp her foot, but she brought the door smartly to behind her as she left the shop. Traffic still was not moving, so she set off in search of the stalled cab.

***

The bell jingled again. The tobacconist looked up and scowled. "I have told you to keep out of my store. Where is Miss Halliday?"

Bruno loomed over the counter. "She'll be along. She gotta take care of that dame was just in here. What'd you tell her anyway?"

The tobacconist smiled. "That is none of your business."

Bruno hoisted a fist. "I can make it my business."

The tobacconist's blithe laughter filled the shop. He stood, extended his arm and enclosed Bruno's fist in his hand. "I met a Chinaman once in Berlin. He taught me how to deal with brutes like you. Try. You cannot resist me." Bruno pushed back, grimacing, but could not dislodge his opponent. He dropped his fist and came up in the tobacconist's face, lowering his voice to a growl. "You're playing a dangerous game."

"Danger makes life worth living, Bruno."

***

Laura stood on a street corner shading her eyes against the morning sun. Movement half a block ahead caught her eye -- someone waving to her, a woman, Halliday, it must be her! She stepped off the curb and a horn blared. A delivery truck bore down. It passed, and Halliday was gone. The signal turned, and Laura hurried down the block. An alley opened on her left, full of light, and Laura decided that must be where Halliday was. She went down it, picking her way through the trash scattered along the uneven paving. She passed a gap between the backs of the opposing rows of buildings and felt the air stir suddenly behind her, carrying Halliday's scent. Hands pinned her arms at her sides. Laura did not try to resist. She was drawn into the gap, too narrow and high for the sun to have reached. She could not see after the dazzling light.

A voice close to her ear whispered, "Please don't turn around."

"I won't."

"Miss van Duyn, how do you know me?"

"From your…your smell. It was on your clothes at the Royal Arms and in your cigarette."

There was a pause, then, "You should be the detective." There was a smile in her voice. "While I admire your skill, I must, alas, ask that you leave me alone."

"Why?"

"I don't let people get in my way. You might get hurt."

"Can't you tell me anything? The blade of grass, what is the blade of grass?" But her arms were now free and nobody was there to hear her.

***

Halliday entered the shop to find Bruno and the tobacconist confronting each other. "Bruno, outside. You know he doesn't like you in here."

Bruno rounded on Halliday. "You got to respect me, lady. It was you asked me for help, remember? What if I was to pass a tip to the cops, anonymous like, about DiFaro? Where'd you and your Nazi friends be then, eh?" Suddenly, Bruno found his head drawn back and a dagger at his throat. The tobacconist drew the blade gently along the skin. Beads of blood appeared where it had tracked.

"Do that and I would deal with you, my little jambiya and me."

"Stop it! Both of you. This is not helpful."

Silence fell on the shop. Sounds of traffic rushed in to fill it. Halliday stepped to the counter and picked up a packet wrapped in brown paper, then started for the door. The tobacconist let go of Bruno's hair. Bruno wiped his neck with his pocket handkerchief, all the time glaring with cold eyes at the tobacconist, who returned the stare with a kind of mocking leer.

"Do not come here again," he commanded. "We will not otherwise have peace."

***

Laura stood in the alley, bereft but resolute. She would give Halliday's warning no quarter. She had a thought. What if Halliday were in the neighborhood to buy tobacco? With firm steps she directed herself back to the shop. She turned the door handle, began to push the door open, but stopped just as it touched the bell. Bruno was talking, accusingly, of Nazis and DiFaro. Shocked, she stood rooted with her hand on the doorknob. "So it's all true," she thought. After Halliday ordered the men to stop their fighting, Laura began ever so slowly to pull the door closed. Suddenly it was jerked from her grasp. The bell jingled.

"Miss van Duyn. I see you have not heeded my warning."

Laura found herself once again in Halliday's grip, to be pulled inexorably into the shop. When Halliday had got the door locked, she reversed the Open sign and stood regarding Laura with cool eyes. "You would do well not to make me your enemy. I could do you much harm." Her voice took on a harsh, grating edge, in some clipped north-European accent.

Laura had regained her faith, her resolve, and her gaze did not waver. "I don't believe you." Astonished, the two men laughed, the tobacconist's a sunny ring, and from Bruno, a threatening rumble.

Watching closely, Laura saw in Halliday's eyes, just for a moment, in the way they wavered and lost focus, confusion and irresolution. "It's Bruno," she thought, "Halliday can barely manage him." She pressed her case. "If you killed Tony, why was there no body when Detective Hardy went to investigate?" Now Bruno's eyes narrowed. "Yeah," he said, "what happened to the body?" Halliday's discomfort increased but only in the eyes, Laura noticed, and still almost imperceptibly. Laura admired her despite herself.

"You saw him fall, Bruno, you felt for the pulse and it was not there. He was dead to you. Do you think I would let the body lie, for the police to find it? Knowing that because of you, they are breathing down our necks? I had it removed, of course."

She paused, drew Laura's gaze, and gave her a cool once-over. "So, Miss van Duyn, you have made me into your ideal? Tell me, when you were a girl, did your mother read you stories, fairy tales? Fill your head up with romance and adventure, knights in shining armor come to the rescue? Is that what I am to you, someone to rescue you from your dull little life?" While she talked, she stepped carefully backwards until she leaned against the counter beside the tobacconist. "Do you think I am not capable of murder, Miss van Duyn?" Her hand moved up, almost too quickly to follow, to rest for an instant against the tobacconist's neck. He fell to the floor. Halliday came up to Laura -- that voice in her ear again. "If you follow me, I will do the same to you." She went on towards the door. "Come, Bruno, we have work."

***

Fenton rubbed the back of his neck and glanced around the shop, taking in the blanket-covered body behind the counter. "Coroner says he's dead all right, some kind of fast-acting poison the way you described it." His eyes came to rest on Laura. "How are you doing?"

Laura raised red-rimmed eyes. "A man dies to prove to me what the evidence showed all along. If I'd listened to you, he might still be alive. I am not doing well, Detective."

There was a commotion outside the door. The patrolman standing guard stuck his head into the shop. "Detective, guy here says that's his brother, he wants to take him away for the funeral."

"Tell him he's got to be autopsied first. He can pick up the body down at the morgue tomorrow."

"Detective," Laura said, "it's their tradition to bury their dead as soon as possible. I saw him die, the coroner has given his opinion. Can't you make an exception?"

Fenton took his time, mulling. Finally, he said, "Yeah, let him in Collins."

Collins stepped aside and two men entered single file, carrying a long, wide board between them. The first, his brother's very image, bowed to them, and they proceeded to the back of the shop, where they knelt, placed the board on the floor, and gently lifted and then lowered the body onto it. As they passed Laura and Fenton with their burden, the two men murmured words of gratitude for showing them mercy and called down Allah's blessings upon them. Laura's eyes began to fill again. Fenton looked on, concerned.

"Feel like a cup of coffee? Might help to talk this out."

"No, thank you, Detective, I know what I have to do. I'm going to bring her to justice."

"How?! Where will you look, who will you ask? Miss van Duyn, I understand you feel responsible, but you need to leave police work to the police. Go on back to your paper, you're good at that society page stuff, and that's where you belong."

"Don't patronize me, Detective."

"Patronize! She's dangerous, you're going to end up just like Difaro and this fellow." He jerked his thumb towards the door. "Look, if I think you're going to impede my investigation, I can put you into preemptive custody, and I ought to for your own good."

She held out her arms. "Go ahead, Detective. Then explain to the press why you've put one of their own into jail. You'll have every newspaperman in the city impeding your investigation."

Fenton huffed, frustrated. "I don't want to arrest you."

"No, you just want me to obey you, but I won't. Detective, we don't have to be adversaries. I promise, anything I find I will share with you. And I know what she looks like and not to get close to her. I will be safe." She stood firm, her eyes locked on his.

After a minute, he said, "All right, but you owe me something, you said you'd share anything you found out. Well now you know what she looks like, and you owe me a police sketch so I can put up some posters."

"You saw her yourself, you don't need me."

"That was three nights ago, which I mostly spent in a fight with the big guy, or in the dark after she turned out the lights. I can't remember what she looked like."

"You should have made your posters while you still remembered."

Exasperated, he rattled off half a dozen things he'd done since Friday night, "...besides you having me half convinced she was innocent."

"I was only testing your police work..."

"No, Miss van Duyn, you weren't. You were defending her, she has some kind of hold on you. I haven't figured out what yet, but it's not hard to see."

He was riled and didn't notice she'd wilted a little. "She has."

"Who has what?"

"Halliday has figured out her hold on me."

"...And?"

"She was my knight in shining armor, my rescuer."

He snorted. "From what?"

"My dull life."

"That's nonsense..."

Laura, interrupting, "No, it's not, she was right. I hadn't a clue, but she was right. How could she know me better than I do?"

"I can't answer that, I'm not a psychologist." He straightened up and she saw he took up a lot of room when he did. "I'm a cop, and you owe me a sketch. In exchange, I won't arrest you. Is that OK?"

She nodded, tremulous, with that same look of distress the City Editor had seen.

"Oh, come on, Miss van Duyn, don't just go limp on me, you have a backbone, I've seen it. This woman's killed two men and she could be gone tomorrow. You know what's right. Just straighten up and do it."

She cleared her frown. "Yes, of course, Detective. Let's go."

He took in the shop once more. "Guess I'm finished here. Collins," he shouted, "let's lock this place up."

CHAPTER 14
ASSEMBLY

The big Packard moved slowly down among the tenements baking in the August sun. From time to time, Bruno would stop the car and call out to a man loitering on the sidewalk or nursing a beer on his stoop. He'd hold a short interview, and if the man suited him, would hand him a card. The man, as often as not, would immediately leave, set off up the sidewalk with a spring in his step. If he didn't, he'd go inside and re-emerge with his jacket over his back on a crooked finger and his cap set jauntily on his head. To the lucky few, Bruno offered work. Just a few days, but with food and a place to sleep and one hundred dollars to boot -- a year's rent! Down there among the baking tenements, that was something to set a spring in a man's step.

***

When she returned from the precinct where she had given a description of Halliday, Laura found a note on her desk, "Your mother called, please call her back. Janine." She picked up the telephone and dialed her mother's number, hearing her answer on the first ring.

"Hello, Mother, it's Laura."

"Laura, thank goodness I finally ran you down. Since your father read the papers this morning, it's been all I can do to handle him, he's that upset. He wants to come right down there and bring you home. He thinks what you are doing is frightfully dangerous. I've wondered myself what any of this has to do with the society pages, but they said you'd been moved to City."

"Yes, Mother, just this morning. The City Editor asked for me personally."

"That's wonderful, dear! But your father won't like it, he thinks City is grubby, and you're too high-minded for it."

"Reporting about parties doesn't take a high mind. I think City is where high-minded reporters belong."

"Of course, you're right. The problem is making him see it that way."

"First, Mother, you must steel yourself for the afternoon papers. There will be more to upset him, I'm afraid. But tell him I'll come to dinner tonight and explain everything. He'll just have to hold his horses until then; you make him understand that."

"You're sure you don't want to come home?"

"No, Mother, I've started something, and I need to try my best to finish it. I don't know yet how I will, but I won't come home."

"Well, I can accept that. I don't know if your father can. Is seven all right? For dinner?"

"Yes, that's perfect. I'll see you then."

"Goodbye, Laura, we love you."

"Goodbye, Mother, I love you, too."

***

She typed her story, her telling of the morning's events, for the evening edition, and Mr. Hirsch took it for editing. After he read it, he called her in.

"Sit down." She sat. "Tough morning. Need a belt?"

The odd question distracted her. "I'm sorry, Sir? Danny, I mean?"

"Scotch. Calm your nerves."

"What?" The offer of liquor at work further flustered her, although instead of frantic, she seemed vague and unable to comprehend the conversation. "Oh, no thank you."

"Don't you drink?"

"Well, yes, sometimes, my mother's family owns Bushmills."

"Good brand. Too expensive." He held up her pages. "This is a fine story, and it will sell papers. Nobody gets a hundred here, though. You got a couple of things to fix. Then we'll send it down to the typesetter, OK?"

"Thank you." She took the sheets from him.

"What have you got planned for the afternoon?"

"I hadn't thought."

"Take it off, you've been through a wringer today."

"All right."

***

Back at her desk, the telephone was ringing, with Gertrude on the line. "Please," she said, "if this is an imposition, say so. Fen called, said you'd had a bad morning and wondered if I could keep you company. I'm seeing Joe tonight, but would you like to have lunch tomorrow?"

An unexpected gratitude possessed her. "Why yes, Gertrude, I would. Thank you."

"Fine, I'll meet you at your office, I've never seen a newspaper office before. One o'clock OK?"

"Yes please."

"I will see you then. Good-bye."

"Good-bye."

Laura fixed her edits and handed the story off to Mr. Hirsch. She gathered her bag and her jacket over her arm and turned to leave. A fellow typing madly across the way called out, "Nice story, van Duyn." She smiled all the way to the elevator.

She stood in the lobby, suddenly struck by this gift of free time and not sure how to use it. Halliday was uppermost in her thoughts of course, but hadn't she followed every possible lead or trail? Despite her brave words at the tobacco shop, Laura knew she stood little chance of finding Halliday, let alone bringing her to justice. No witnesses, no locations, no information, not even a hunch. A ship would come, that's all she knew, but it could come anytime and anywhere. How many dozens, maybe hundreds, of ships would enter and leave New York harbor in just the next day, and this ship could land just as well on Long Island, too? No, there was no possibility in simply guessing where it would be. Maybe the wanted posters were the last straw, their only hope that they would bring someone forward before Halliday left. She sighed to herself. Well, she did want to have her nails done and a change of clothes. Then it would be time for dinner with her parents.

CHAPTER 15
DINNER WITH HER PARENTS

Charles van Duyn stood in his darkened study high over Central Park, whiskey over ice in his left hand, the glimmering lights of the nighttime city shining upon his face. He wore a dark, crisply-pressed banker's suit. From its vest pocket hung a golden watch chain. He stood stern and solid with his iron-gray hair firmly in place. He sipped the whiskey and grimaced as it burned his throat.

"God damn it, Colleen, I won't have some no-account, irresponsible, jackass newspaper editor ruining my daughter's life. I want her to quit and come home."

Colleen van Duyn floated up behind him, placing an earring. "Oh, Charles, don't be rude," she scolded. "You don't even know it's the editor's fault. We are going to hear our daughter out before we decide anything. Now go and dress. I have to see Cook about dinner." She swept out of the room, leaving behind the hint of Fleurs de Rocaille.

Charles sipped again from his glass. "I mean business," he growled to himself, "so I'm going to stay dressed for business." He heard the apartment's doorbell and the maid's shoes tip-tapping across the foyer's marble floor, then voices.

"Good evening, Miss Laura. It seems so long you've been away. Please, let me take your coat."

"Thank you, Moira," came his daughter's reply. "Am I early?"

"Oh no, Miss, the table's just been set."

Charles determined to get down to business. He straightened his tie, drained his glass, set it on the windowsill, and walked out to meet his daughter.

Laura caught the motion out of the corner of her eye, turned and came to meet him offering a stiff hug and a peck on the cheek. She stood back and said in a low and wary voice, "Hello, Father."

"Hello, Laura." He gazed steadily into her eyes. She gazed back.

"Oh you two, knock it off. We're a family, let's try to be civilized." Colleen came forward. "Laura, sweetheart, I'm so glad you're here. It seems an age since we last saw you. Has it been only since Thursday?" She took Laura in her arms and hugged her long and deep. They stood back, holding each other at arms' length. Colleen took Charles's arm. "Let's go to dinner, shall we?"

Charles stalled, saying he needed another whiskey. "Pour one for me, too," his daughter ordered. "No ice, please, just a little water."

Charles rounded on her. "What will it be next, cigarettes? Have you utterly lost your sense of propriety?"

"No, Father, I've lost yours and found a different one. May I please have my drink?"

He turned to Colleen, flustered, speaking with real heat, "What am I to do with her? What has she become?"

"She grew up Charles, and you are to do with her exactly as she asks you to. Now please, get her a drink, she's an adult and is entitled, and let's go in to dinner. It's getting cold." She pulled open ornate double doors, and, putting her hand across the small of Laura's back, ushered her into the dining room. The wallpaper was gold and black, but not garishly so. The room had, in proportion to the table it held, a long and narrow aspect, the more so because of the substantial sideboard along the left wall, arrayed now with the evening's dishes. Colleen had asked that the table be set for family, with three places clustered at its near end. The women sat opposite each other. Charles arrived a moment later with two glasses. He took the end chair and placed a glass before Laura and one before himself. Laura nodded her thank you. The butler approached with a tureen and began to ladle consommé into the bowls set out for it.

"Just put it all on the table, Quinn, we'll serve ourselves and you can have the rest of the night off. I need to talk to my daughter."

"As you wish, sir."

"Charles, that's not necessary."

"I'll still pay him, Colleen. I just don't want his ears to turn blue if the conversation gets a little agitated."

Colleen sighed. "Very well, if that's the way you think this evening will go. Quinn, you may have the night off."

"Very good, Madame." He briskly removed the dishes and platters to the table, sliced the roast, and was gone. As he worked, Charles and Laura sipped their whiskeys. Charles moved his soup bowl aside, and filled his plate with roast, potatoes, and gravy.

"Have some salad, Charles."

"I don't want salad, Colleen." He sliced off a piece of roast, and started chewing. "Your mother told me I could stop holding my horses when you got here. Well, you're here, so I'm not holding them anymore. I moved you downtown as you asked, paid for that apartment, got you a nice respectable lady's job, and you end up with your name in the paper, connected to common criminals and now a murderer? May I remind you, despite the disregard with which you seem to hold your own welfare, as your mother has determined you're an adult, you may do as you please, but a bank's reputation is its most valuable asset." He shook his fork at her, with a piece of roast beef impaled on its tines. "Any whiff of scandal can bring it down. I am not about to risk my customers' money and sending your mother to the poorhouse without a good explanation. Your mother said you would explain everything. Well go ahead, let's hear it."

"What your father means, I'm sure, Laura," Colleen broke in, glowering at Charles, "is that you're our only and very much loved child. We don't understand what you're doing, except that it seems dangerous. Can you understand how barren our lives would become were anything to happen to you? It's not that we don't want you to do these things, it's that we fear what might happen if you do."

"Yes, Mother, I understand, thank you." She turned to her father. "I have done nothing wrong. In fact, I was doing what I was trained to do, what you agreed I could do, I was gathering news. By flushing this woman out, by putting her on the run, causing her that distraction, we have interrupted her sinister plans. We have, I have made the city safer by what I did. Father, there are brave people out there protecting us, and I helped them. Now how could that harm your bank? Give your customers some credit, Father, they will understand what I am doing and why. And so should you."

Charles exhibited the van Duyn wilt under Laura's onslaught. He swallowed, cleared his throat, and gazed across the table. "Guess I'll have some salad."

"Is one of those brave people that Detective Hardy?" Colleen asked with concern. When Laura nodded, she continued, "I would hate for him to come into harm's way."

"You needn't mother. He takes very good care of himself."

"What's he like? We know he's brave, but is he handsome, too?"

"I hadn't noticed, Mother; please don't play my matchmaker," said Laura, heading her off.

Colleen came as close as she ever would to a pout. "But you haven't had a date in so long. Aren't you lonely, dear?"

"For a man? No. Mother for the first time in my life, I'm doing something interesting, something important. It's all I need right now."

"Maybe I'll interview that detective," Charles mused, "get another perspective."

"Oh, Father, please don't. This is nothing to do with him. Both of you need to understand: I am fine, let me live my life, and don't worry."

Charles had finished his salad and returned to the roast. "Well, I do say, daughter, there's more color in your cheeks than I've seen in months. To be honest, you'd grown fidgety, but you seem to have put it behind you, and I am thankful. Your mother and I will worry about you every day. Nothing, I'm afraid, will ever change that." He took another bite of potatoes. "Now we've settled that, you might as well give us the whole story, all we've seen is the papers. Go on, give us the, what's that new word, skinny?" Laura nodded. "OK, then, what's the skinny?"

Laura related everything she had seen and done since her decision to attend the detective's press conference. They gasped as she described being shot and asked to see the bullet's mark. Laura cried at the tobacconist's death, and at her story's conclusion, they both sat back seeming exhausted. Charles puffed up his cheeks, then let the air burst out.

"I didn't see that much action on the Marne. But you've kept your wits admirably and watched out well for yourself. I'd be afraid if I was that woman and damned glad to have you around if I was that detective. Good job, Laura. Keep it up." He pushed himself back from the table. "Mother, thank Cook for dinner. I need a cigar. I shall be in my study." He arose and left.

***

Colleen caught her daughter's eye. "Laura, I am proud of you."

Laura patted her hand. "Thank you."

"I mean I'm proud of you right now, of what you're doing. You remind me of fond memories."

"What do you mean, Mother?"

"I had my own adventures when I was young, before I met your father."

Laura leaned towards her. "What do you mean, Mother?"

"I mean, Ireland at that time had any number of agitators to choose from if one wanted a...political life. I stood with the workers. We needed information about the other groups, so I got it -- that was my job."

Laura was bemused. "How did you do that?"

"I had quite nice ankles and wasn't afraid to show them off to young men, for a price. Sometimes they found out what I was up to, and I had to run for it. I learned to be a very fast runner. Sometimes, still, they caught me. For that I carried a shillelagh, and I was feared for it. It wasn't always fun, there were riots, awful riots, with people killed. But we were proud of what we did, we were doing good, whatever sorrows or obstacles we faced. That pride carried me a long, long time, and it made me strong and alive."

"Why did you stop?"

"I began to feel a little nag, a lack, something in my life that I wanted, and I realized it was the most fundamental of all, I wanted a child. I was, I had been relegated by then to simple money-raising, an endless round of meetings, convocations, and benefits, formalized begging is what it really was. I found it dull and easy, which gave me plenty of time to think and plan. One day your father came, an American taking an interest in Ireland. He wanted to give us some money. I still don't know why."

He came from a banking family, but a modest one, nobody rising higher than vice-president. His inheritance had left him well-off, but he was not a shirker, so he went to work, began to build on that foundation and now, at 32, stood as president of the second largest bank in New York.

"I looked at him, friendly and generous, prepared to spread his beneficence over us out of simple kindness, and handsome, too. I realized, in our times, only a capitalist could afford the kind of life I wanted for my child. And so I proposed to myself that I would marry him."

"You married him for money, so I would have a privileged life? Mother, that's horrible."

"Oh dear no, I was already in love with him, the minute he walked through the door, before ever I found out anything about him."

"And he was worth your ideals and your pride?"

"I admit it was a compromise. I lost adventure, but I gained you and so a new kind of pride. I have never, never regretted that decision." In her turn, she patted Laura's hand. "Now you know why I am proud of you. You have made your own chance at an adventure, and I want you to take it, I can't help but think you will be enriched by it. Just don't ever forget what you learned today: enriched does not always mean happy."

Laura sat back, dismayed.

"That's my skeleton, out of the closet." Colleen smiled. "And it must remain our secret."

"Father doesn't know?"

"That his wife threw rocks and bottles in the streets of Dublin? Dear me no, he takes Capitalism very seriously, and anything that might threaten it. If he knew, he would know there is nothing to be done, and that would agitate him. For his peace of mind, I can keep this little secret. And I still have my memories."

Laura stood to leave. "Thank you for dinner, Mother, and for taking me into your confidence." She came around the table and hugged Colleen. "I don't know when I'll see you again."

"I'll say a prayer for you every night."

"Thank you. I'll say good-night to Father on my way out."

***

As the cab she'd taken from her parent's home approached her building, Laura saw Garrity again loitering outside her door. She told the cabbie to drive on and got out two blocks later. She stood wondering where she could just be alone to think, away from the jangle of interruptions, detectives and parents, telephones, and snooping reporters. Another cab came along and almost reflexively she called it down. The cabbie asked where she was headed. She had to stop and catch up to where her mind had already gone before she could give the address. Twenty minutes later, she alighted at the Royal Arms Hotel, begged the key off the landlady, and retreated to that spare and polished room. She raised a window to let out the heat. A cooler breeze blew, perhaps a harbinger of autumn six weeks hence. She took off her shoes and stockings and jacket and lay on the bed. She curled onto her side and drew her knees up, drove her nose into the mattress and breathed deep, but got only a sneeze for her trouble, no hint of anise, pine, or jasmine. She thought of the shirts in the closet, then remembered the detective had taken them. So she pondered instead how it had felt with her arms pinned to her sides and that voice, amused, at her ear.

CHAPTER 16
A FATEFUL DAY

The sky glowed pink with the dawn. Bruno stood solid as granite at the entrance to the old warehouse. He turned as the door behind him opened inward, screeching on metal hinges. An acrid smell washed over him, man sweat, cigarette butts, and warm beer. Halliday emerged, in work shirt and dungarees and white sneakers. Her supple hair, lustrous as polished wood, swung as she shook her head. She stood next to Bruno and rolled a cigarette. "Light?"

He pulled a Lindy's matchbook out of his pants pocket and passed it to her. She lit the cigarette, shook the match, and dropped it. She stood gazing across the dock to the slip, dragging off the cigarette, and squinting against the smoke.

"The ship is still on schedule. Is your crew ready?"

"Yeah, I'll make them ignore their hangovers. Don't know if that was a good idea last night, that beer."

"It bought their loyalty and put them to sleep, out of trouble. They'll feel better after breakfast. I will need a ride downtown this morning. I need to arrange a distraction to keep the police off our trail."

"How about that woman, that reporter? You worried about her?"

"She has no way to find me."

"You thought that before."

She smoked. "Even if she finds me, what can one woman do? I don't worry about her." She dropped the cigarette and stamped on it hard, ground it into the cement. She spoke as she reached for the door handle behind her. "Watch your back. Expect some surprises."

"Thanks, I'll keep that in mind."

***

Laura woke early to the sound of pigeons cooing on the window sill, as if they expected breakfast. She felt refreshed and surprised at how well she'd slept. She smiled and stretched, yawning. She pushed herself up from the mattress and tried in vain to smooth her wrinkled skirt. She went to the bathroom where there was a mirror over the sink and removed her blouse. She ran some water and took a small jar of cold cream from her bag. She cleaned off yesterday's lipstick and rouge and splashed water on her face. There was no towel, she realized, so went to lean against the wall next to the window and let her skin dry in the fresh air.

The neighborhood was awake with people leaving their buildings and traffic rushing on the street. Laura's stomach rumbled, and she roused herself. She had enough cash in her purse for either a cab home or subway fare and breakfast. Her stomach rumbled again.

She put on her jacket and shoes, stuffed her stockings into a pocket, and went downstairs to surrender the key to the landlady, who was already up and serving breakfast to a few tenants who paid her for board as well as room. She invited Laura in for something to eat, and Laura gratefully accepted. She introduced Laura to the people around the table as, "...that reporter was there when that poor shopkeeper got bumped off yesterday." They were all immediately interested and crammed over to make room for her at the table. When she sat, they began to pepper her with questions and she started to quail, but found her backbone.

"Please," she said, "I really can tell you nothing more than has been in the papers, but perhaps you can help me. Can you tell me anything about Halliday, the woman who lived here, or the men with her?" The people glanced at each other around the table, then as a group shook their heads. The landlady spoke. "We have discussed this matter. She attracted no attention to herself. In my country there are people like her."

"Are they with the government?"

"No, not government, some other group."

"Who? What do they do?"

"It is very hard to tell because they call no attention to themselves. The poor people know them best. The poorer you are, the better you will know them."

"Did you see the blade of grass in her room?"

"Yes, Miss, I did."

"What does it mean?"

"I don't know, my family was not so poor, we did not know them so well. This woman, she is as near to me as I have ever been to any of them. And to me there is no trace of her. I can only tell you one thing, she was not from my country." She raised her eyes upwards with folded hands and said, "And from You I ask only that You give me another tenant like her."

It had taken a moment for a thought to click with Laura. "So this group exists, these people are in other countries besides yours?"

The woman nodded. "Yes, Miss, it seems so."

Laura pondered this new information a moment, then, seeing she would get no more from them, made her excuses to the gathering and stood to leave.

"But you haven't eaten anything," protested the landlady.

Laura plucked two pieces of buttered toast from a plate at her hand. "May I please just take these? You have been so kind, you have been helpful to me. Thank you." She left, and realizing she still had cab fare, hailed one just passing by and took it home, collecting toast crumbs in her lap.

In her own kitchen, she made tea, sweet with milk and sugar, and more toast with butter and some jam. She showered, gave her teeth a good brushing, dressed, and left for work.

***

Horace opened his eyes, staring up into the dusty network of iron beams that supported the roof of the old warehouse. He had not slept well, given the rancid smell and the snoring, and his own racing thoughts. He reached to the cot next to his and grabbed Gus's shoulder.

"Hey," he whispered, "you awake?"

Gus moaned and rolled over, irritated. "I am now!"

"Think Bruno's gonna bump us off as soon as that ship is loaded?"

72

"That's what I'm thinking. What do you want to do now?"

"We gotta get Bruno back on our side somehow."

Gus snorted. "Yeah? How?"

"I'm working on it. He's dumb, that's to our advantage, and all he cares about is getting paid."

The heavy warehouse door screeched. Bruno lumbered through and began pounding rhythmically with a massive fist on the sheet iron wall. "All right, you guys, time to rise and shine. Breakfast in five minutes, and then the trucks'll be rollin' in. You gotta unload 'em and then you gotta load the ship. Let's get ready for work and no complaining, 'cause it's your fault if you drank too much beer and I'll dock you if you don't do your job."

A general stirring and complaining arose from the sleep-shrouded but loyal crew, among whom there were, in truth, few hangovers. They weren't about to jeopardize a job by overindulging in liquor. Bruno had chosen well.

Before it rose out of control, their grumbling surrendered before the smell of brewing coffee. Men randomly flung their legs over cots' edges, sat up hawking, and rubbing sandpapered eyes. The scents of flapjacks and bacon mingled with that of the coffee, inviting the men to breakfast.

Horace sat up. "One thing you can say about Bruno, he ain't spare with the grub." He stood, Gus joined him, and they went in to breakfast.

Two men with spatulas stood over a long griddle heated by bottled gas. They scrambled eggs, and flipped rashers of bacon and thick pancakes. At the back of the line, Gus and Horace picked up trays, knives, and forks. They filled mugs with coffee from an urn. Gus took his black and Horace ladled in the sugar. The cooks passed them plates of eggs, bacon, and pancakes. Gus went to sit down while Horace slathered on butter and dowsed his pancakes in maple syrup.

One of the men looked up as Gus went by. "Say, fellas," he yelled, "I hear it was girls against the boys...and the girls won!"

Guffaws filled the room, but Gus ignored them and went to sit on an unoccupied bench. As Horace sauntered past, he turned to the joker and snarled, "Shut your trap, Pignoli, or I'll shut it for you."

Pignoli leaped to his feet, fists ready. Horace slammed his tray onto the table. Pignoli leaped in with a quick jab to Horace's rib cage.

Horace staggered and coughed, but as Pignoli wound up for the next punch, Horace heaved a great sigh to restore his breath and delivered quick one-two punches to Pignoli's temples. Pignoli's head snapped right and left, and he dropped to the floor like he just fell asleep. A huge hand grabbed the back of Horace's neck and twisted him around.

"Lay off," Bruno growled, "or I'll break your neck."

Horace went limp and whined, "Yeah, sure, Bruno, I'll never lay another hand on him."

Bruno picked up the bucket of water he'd brought and upended it in Pignoli's face. Pignoli sputtered and sat up. He jumped up at Horace, but Bruno grabbed his shirt front, hauling him in before he could throw a punch, and pulled him off the floor. He turned to face the rest of the men while Pignoli gagged in his hand.

"You guys gotta behave. If that ship ain't loaded on time, you're all fired, and you don't get your pay. You all signed to that when you hired on here. Get back to your breakfasts if you know what's good for you."

Bruno opened his hand and Pignoli tumbled to the floor groveling. Bruno shoved Horace over next to Pignoli and lowered a size sixteen shoe across both their chests.

"I got my eyes on you two," he hissed. "You let it go or I'll crack your heads and dump you in the river."

Horace and Pignoli, gasping, nodded agreement and Bruno let them up. He turned to the cooks and yelled "More food." The men cheered. The cooks began to crack more eggs and ladle pancake batter.

Bruno hauled Horace and Pignoli to their feet. "Eat!" Pignoli returned to his plate. Horace sat down opposite Gus, bowing his head to shovel food into his mouth.

"Thanks, Horace," Gus grinned, "I was hungry."

***

Gertrude raised her hand and knocked firmly on the flimsy door. It opened to reveal an exhausted, coughing woman, a child in her arms, his spit-up strewn across her shirt. She stared at Gertrude as if mute.

"Mrs. Varga? I'm Gertrude Hardy from the relief society. Your neighbor, Mrs. Santiago, told us that your husband recently began drinking again. I'm here to offer help to you and your children."

Mrs. Varga nodded slowly and stood aside so that Gertrude could enter the apartment. As she looked around, Gertrude saw the reason for Mrs. Varga's exhaustion. The living room was spotlessly clean and neat. It smelled of cinnamon and beeswax. Two girls and a boy sat at a trestle table in the kitchen, reading attentively. The boy also scribbled math formulas onto a piece of slate at his side, his lips moving as he solved them. Gertrude turned to Mrs. Varga and lifted the baby from her arms.

"Here, I'll hold him while you change your shirt."

Mrs. Varga sighed and sagged. "Thank you," she murmured, and went down the hall to her bedroom. Gertrude stepped into the kitchen, pulled out hand towels from a cupboard above the sink, laid the towels in the sink, and ran warm water over them. She put the baby onto the towels and began to unpin his malodorous diaper. He was not, fortunately, soiled. Gertrude pulled the diaper from his bottom. She wiped his backside with one of the towels, rinsed the vomit off his chin and chest, pulled a dry towel from the cupboard, and wrapped him in it. She turned to the three children at the table. "You, girl, what's your name?" she asked.

The girl looked up from her book. "Anna," she said.

"Anna, please find me a clean diaper."

"But my mother says I am to study," Anna objected.

Gertrude snorted in annoyance, but replied, "Very well, then tell me please where I might find a clean diaper."

Anna pointed to a closet door behind her. "In there," she answered, as her eyes dipped back to the book, "the linen closet."

Gertrude strode to the closet, pulled open the door, and withdrew a clean cotton diaper. She laid the baby back in the sink, unwrapped the towel, and pinned on the new diaper. As she raised him to her shoulder, Mrs. Varga returned to the kitchen in a fresh white blouse. She took the baby and stood, staring shyly at the floor, murmuring thanks.

Gertrude turned to the older children at the table. "Children," she said, "please go out to the living room while I speak with your mother."

The children looked to Mrs. Varga, who nodded. They stood and left the room. Mrs. Varga sat on one side of the table and Gertrude the other.

"Mrs. Varga, please look at me." Mrs. Varga raised her eyes to Gertrude. "Mrs. Varga, how long has it been since your husband began drinking again?" she asked in a quiet voice.

Tears started in Mrs. Varga's eyes, but she stilled them and spoke firmly. "Three weeks, Miss Hardy. And just yesterday his boss found out and fired him. He said you cannot be drunk and be a good butcher at the same time."

"Your husband's boss is right, Mrs. Varga. Has your husband hit you or the children?"

"No, he is still a gentle man with us. The drink does not make him mean. It just makes him sleepy."

"Very well, then. Have you got any money?"

"Just what I could save from Antal's last pay. I hide it in different places, but some of it he finds and spends on drinking. He is out spending some of it now. I don't have enough to pay the rent next week."

"Mrs. Varga, I can give you money for the rent and for food for one month, if you can keep it from Antal, and here is an address. This is a meeting place for men like Antal who cannot control their drinking by themselves. It has worked wonders for other men. Mrs. Varga, Antal does not have to tell about himself, even what his last name is. That is the rule, so he doesn't have to feel ashamed about going because nobody will know who he is, and everybody there will be just like him. But you must see to it that he goes every week."

Gertrude opened her purse and pulled out an envelope. "Here," she said. "Now, are you sure you have a safe place?" Mrs. Varga nodded and took the envelope.

"Mrs. Varga, you have to get him to that meeting. It will do him a wonder of good. It might even bring him back to the Lord."

"Oh, no, he is a Socialist. He does not believe in God."

Gertrude hmphed. "Well, I will check on you next week to see how you are doing. Can I get you anything else?"

Mrs. Varga shook her head. Gertrude stood up. "Okay then. Please bring your children back in so that they may continue their studies." She looked around at the spartan but spotless kitchen. "Mrs. Varga, you are going to be fine. I will see you next week." She let herself out.

***

All morning fourteen-wheelers drove onto the wharf. Halliday's men just had time to unload one and send it on its way before the next pulled in. The name of a fictitious business enterprise adorned each trailer, "Anders Meat", "Cosmopolitan Shoes", "Blue Stripe Cigarettes", so, according to Halliday, nobody would become suspicious seeing too many unmarked trucks going down the highway together. In reality, the trucks were loaded with heavy wooden crates, stamped "Rifles, "Cartridges", "Caution: Explosives". Halliday's crew worked furiously in the hot sun, none harder than Horace and Gus who, wary of Bruno, hauled crate after crate without pause. Finally Horace sagged and asked Gus if he'd mind taking a break. Gus lowered his end of the crate to the ground and sank to sit on it, panting, head hanging. Horace sat next to him. He pulled off his wool cap and wiped it across his brow.

"Gee, Gus, I'm wrung out."

"Me too," Gus panted, "and we ain't got a lot of time. Any bright ideas?"

They saw Bruno pull up in a new Packard. The warehouse door opened and Halliday came out and got into the passenger seat. Bruno made a U-turn, came up on Horace and Gus.

"You two get back to work."

Horace and Gus stood slowly in the dead, heavy air, and each grabbed a crate end. Bruno pulled away. As soon as the car left the dock, Gus dropped the crate.

"I'm gonna make a run for it," he hissed.

"No, wait Gus, I just got a plan. We're going to nab the payroll."

Gus just laughed and stooped to get the crate again. When Horace didn't pick up his end, Gus straightened. "Aw, come on, Horace, you have to be kidding."

"No listen, Gus, it has to be here, she's paying us tonight, and she's not someone to take her money to no bank. Bruno, he has to know where it is. And like I said, he's dumb, I can convince him to come in with us, and then he'll tell us where it is. When nobody's watching, we'll just stroll in and take it. Come on, Gus, I can take him. Have I ever let you down?"

"Yeah plenty, but I ain't got so many friends, I guess I should just stick with you."

"There you go Gus. Trust me, by midnight we'll be rich." Horace bent for a handle and Gus did, too. Together, they hauled the crate off down the dock and stacked it on top of the growing pile.

***

When Laura arrived at her desk, Hirsch was waiting for her.

"Listen, van Duyn I know you're on this other story, but something's breaking, a two-alarm fire in a theater off Times Square. You up for that?" He watched a little anxiously for her lip to tremble, but she only said, "Of course," and left. She returned, wrote, edited, and handed in her story. It was nearly 1:00 o'clock and time to meet Gertrude. Laura waited at her desk, assuming Gertrude would come up to see the City Room, since it was her first time at a newspaper office, but at 1:15, Laura decided Gertrude must have meant the lobby. She stood in the lobby another ten minutes, then thought maybe they'd crossed in the elevators and went back to the City Room. Gertrude wasn't there and nobody had seen her. More than a little concerned now, Laura returned to the lobby, then went out to the street but Gertrude was nowhere. Truly alarmed, she went back to her desk and called Detective Hardy.

***

Bruno dropped Halliday off in the meat-packing district on the lower west side of Manhattan. Bruno hated it -- the smell -- as much as he liked meat. He told Halliday he had an appointment with his wife, his euphemism for a tryst, and said he'd be back to pick her up in an hour. Before she left the dock, Halliday had changed. She was dressed now in heavy work shoes, baggy slacks held up by suspenders over a t-shirt and a worn tweed jacket twice her size. She'd stuffed her hair under a cap, and adopted, surprisingly in a woman, a swagger as she walked down the street. Nobody gave her a second look, so nobody missed her when she slipped into an alley and, striding now, went about two thirds its length. She stepped into an alcove. Ten feet ahead of her a closed door marked the building's back entrance. She pushed on the wall to her left and a narrow panel swung back on silent hinges to reveal a tunnel formed by the construction of a false wall against the building. She entered the tunnel and closed the panel behind her. She stood in total darkness now and proceeded, counting, down the passage. At eight, she stopped and, raising her right hand to the wall, felt for a metal box attached to it. She took a key, a special key, from a pocket in her coat and, by touch, found the keyhole. A door swung open on the front of the box. Had there been a light, it would have looked like a perfectly normal police telephone box, painted black, on a black wall. She reached in and lifted the receiver.

A man answered, "I'm here, baby."

"Jake?"

There was silence long enough for a double-take. "Halliday?"

"Jake, have you told someone about our telephones again?"

"Aw, Halliday, just one, she went out of here crying last night, she's got man trouble, and I was worried about her, she doesn't have a phone, and I just wanted her to call me and let me know she was OK."

"So you gave her your key?"

"Yes, and now I have an excuse to visit her and get it back."

"Probably your plan all along."

"I wouldn't deny that."

"Get it back! Now, have you got a pencil and paper?"

"Sure."

"All right here is my plan." She began to dictate to him. It took little time because her plan was simple, and he understood her immediately. When she was done, she reminded Jake about the key, closed and locked the box, and felt her way back to the alley. Waiting for Bruno, she began to be impatient after about two minutes. Bruno was just across town, she could walk and meet him when he'd finished his assignation. Her pace was quick, and she soon got hot, so about at the Bowery she shed her coat, leaving it in the arms of an indigent man. She found the big Packard easily enough. Bruno had left it unlocked and the keys in the ignition, such was his power in the neighborhood. She sank into its back seat, kicked off her shoes, and let her hair down. After five minutes, the apartment door banged shut. Halliday looked up to see Bruno at the top of his stoop shaking out a pant leg with a big grin on his face. He yelled at the kid sitting on the bottom step and flipped him a nickel, then, as big as he was, descended shuffling like a soft shoe dancer. His smile vanished when he saw Halliday. He climbed into the driver's seat.

"Have I spoilt your mood?"

"You ought to try it sometime. Might improve yours."

"With you, I suppose? Would you make the earth move for me, Bruno?" Before he could answer, she sat up and skittered across the seat, her face nearly touching the window as she gazed over the sidewalk. At the foot of the stoop, glancing first left, then right, stood Gertrude Hardy. She went right in her sensible shoes, swiftly through the crowd.

"Bruno, that was Detective Hardy's sister."

"Yes, Miss, I know." Bruno glanced in the rear view mirror. "Back to the warehouse?"

"Bruno, I think we might need some insurance. A hostage, perhaps. I want you to pull up next to Miss Hardy and abduct her."

"Miss, that ain't in the plan,' Bruno rumbled, "You never said nothing about no abductions. This ain't no time to let complications get in the way of what we gotta do."

"Bruno," Halliday purred, "I have other insurance, too, I know about that craps game you run at the IOOF. I could have it raided. Doesn't it keep your kids in that Catholic school uptown?"

Bruno grumbled, but accelerated past Gertrude and into the next available parking space. He got out of the car and stood mountainous against the pedestrian tide. Gertrude went so fast, she came up on him only just as she recognized him. He grasped her forearm and bent to her ear.

"You and me's going the same direction. Why don't I just offer you a lift?"

Gertrude tried to pull away, but Bruno tightened his grip inexorably. "I insist."

She grabbed at her bag with her free hand. Bruno took it. "Sorry, Miss, your piece ain't gonna be available this time. Not like when you done Gus in that alley. And before you start thinking about yelling, you oughta pay attention to this."

Gertrude felt the blunt end of a pistol at her ribs and stopped struggling.

"That's right, Miss Hardy, you just climb into that big black car over there. It's got a nice comfortable ride."

Bruno guided Gertrude to the Packard's rear door, his arm tight around her waist. He opened the door, thrust Gertrude inside, closed the door, and locked it. Gertrude scrambled to find the door handle and escape, but Halliday collared her, held her until Bruno got in and pulled away. When she'd been loosed, Gertrude reared back against the door. "What do you want with me?" she demanded. "You don't just grab citizens off the sidewalk. I ought to punch you in the nose."

Halliday smiled. "Not so ladylike for someone of your standing."

"My standing doesn't mean anything when my well-being is at stake." She raised tiny, nut-hard fists.

"You're quite brave, but…" Halliday glanced at Bruno looming in the driver's seat.

"I'll split your lip before he grabs me."

"Split it if you like, it will not get you out of this car. You are captured Miss Hardy." She took a handkerchief from her pants pocket. "Now, I apologize, but I am going to have to blindfold you. If you will promise not to escape, I will leave your hands free, but if that is a lie, just remember, I am a very fast runner, and I will not be so kind if I have to run you down."

∗∗∗

At 2:00, Laura sat in a cab heading towards Greenwich Village, where Gertrude's relief agency had its headquarters. Her call to the detective had been fruitless. When she had confessed her worries to him about Gertrude, he passed them off, said his sister had probably just gotten wrapped up in her work and forgotten.

"That's more likely than that she's been kidnapped by Halliday. Did you try calling her office?"

"I haven't got the number." He gave it to her. "You call, she'll be there. Listen, I have to go, I got a tip, and I'm taking a squad down to Battery Park."

"Why Battery Park?"

"That's what the tip said."

"Said what?"

"Said if I was interested in catching Halliday, I ought to go down to Battery Park."

"But that's just outlandish. She's not going to dock her ship at Battery Park."

"Are you saying I'm being set up?"

"It would make sense to keep you distracted."

"So instead she's kidnapped Gertrude and hatched some elaborate plan to keep me out of the way. Now who sounds outlandish?"

"But what if it's all true?"

"Miss van Duyn, I don't have a choice. This is the only lead I've got, and I have to investigate. If the lead is true and Gertrude has been abducted, then following the lead is the only way to find her. I'm sorry, I have to go." He rang off.

She sat looking at the slip of paper with Gertrude's number on it. She should just call, she thought, the detective was probably right, but she was too anxious. She had to be doing something more than wait, so she left, with Hirsch's permission. Now she sat in the cab's back seat, hands squirming, glancing from side to side, trying to raise some hope. The cabdriver swerved into an open space at the curb. He turned to Laura.

"This is as close as I can get you lady. That'll be seventy-five cents."

Laura got out of the cab and handed the driver a dollar. "Could you wait please? I'll just be a minute." The driver nodded, and Laura turned and walked half a block to a narrow townhouse. A small sign mounted on its doorway read "Samuel L. Clemens Presbyterian Relief Society". She climbed the ten steps to the door and walked into the building's foyer. A pert young woman greeted Laura from behind a large oak desk.

"I'm looking for Gertrude Hardy." Laura explained, "She was supposed to meet me for lunch, but she never came."

"You are that reporter, aren't you?" the girl interrupted, wide-eyed. "Oh, Miss van Duyn, Miss Hardy's told us all about you, how you nabbed those two crooks. All of my friends and I, we can't talk about anything else!"

Laura looked up, startled. "Well, I didn't, I didn't do it on my own," she stammered, "I had help, you know…". She stopped. "But, please, that's not why I'm here. Can you tell me where Miss Hardy is? Otherwise, I'm afraid something has happened to her."

"Miss van Duyn, you think that gang's kidnapped her don't you? Wait…" She pulled a clipboard from the desk in front of her and ran her finger down the attached schedule. "She did come in at 7:45. She was here until 9:10, and then she went out to visit a family. She left a note, she thought she would be back by 11:00." She looked back to Laura. "And here it is 2:00 o'clock, and no sign of her."

"Is the family's address there?" Laura asked.

The girl looked back at her schedule. "Yes." She scribbled the address on a notepad, pulled off the page, and handed it to Laura.

"Thank you," Laura replied. She bent to the girl's desk and wrote her name and the newspaper's telephone number on the notepad. "Please, if you hear from Miss Hardy, call me immediately."

The girl nodded solemnly at Laura. "Miss van Duyn, don't you worry. I'd do anything to help you." She rested her fingertips on the notepad. "Miss van Duyn?" she asked, suddenly shy, "Could I have your autograph? My friends will be so jealous."

Laura laid her hand gently over the girl's and smiled. "I'm flattered that you and your friends think so highly of me, but I'm not a movie star. Just please keep a lookout for Miss Hardy. I'm sure your friends will be just as jealous knowing that you helped me."

The girl smiled at the thought. "Thank you, Miss van Duyn. It was ever so nice to meet you."

Laura thanked her and left. The cab still waited at the curb. Laura gave the driver the address. He frowned. "That's a pretty rough neighborhood, lady. You sure you want to go down there?"

Laura assured him she did. The driver shrugged and pulled his cab into the traffic. A few minutes later, he pulled up at the apartment building where the Vargas lived.

A band of t-shirted boys in ragged trousers loitered on the stoop. As Laura approached, they moved aside to let her pass. She smiled and thanked them and asked if they knew where the Vargas lived. A boy gave her directions. She climbed the steps and entered the building's dim first floor. The vivid tang of too many people living too close assailed her nostrils. She paused to let her eyes adjust to the light. To her left a staircase mounted to the next floor. She began to climb. From above came random shouts, doors banging, thumping footsteps, and children laughing. She found Mrs. Varga's apartment on the fourth floor.

In answer to Laura's questions, Mrs. Varga said that Miss Hardy had visited her earlier, and no, she didn't know what had happened to her after she left. Dejected, Laura returned to the stoop outside. As she walked down the steps, one of the boys spoke. "There was another lady here this morning visited the Vargas. You looking for her?"

Laura's heart leaped. "Yes, yes I am. Do you know where she is?"

"Might be. That guy, Skolimowski, put her in his car, drove away with her and some other dame in the back seat. He hired my old man a couple of days ago for some work, loading a ship or something, over in Brooklyn. He could have taken her there."

"Did your father say where?"

"He told me where the dock is."

Another boy spoke up. "Skolimowski, he's a tough guy. I saw him beat up another guy once because he said somethin' bad about Pollacks. That guy still don't walk straight. Skolimowski ain't nobody you want to tangle with on your own. You ought to tell the cops."

Laura stood lost in thought, contemplating the mote and coalescing wisps of a plan. The boys eyed her warily. "The police would be loud. That might get Miss Hardy hurt. I need stealth. You all know that she is in danger. The longer she's with them, the greater the chance she will come to harm. But you are right, I cannot rescue her alone." She stopped and quickly gazed into each boy's face. "Would you like to have an adventure with me? Would you help me rescue Miss Hardy?"

After a moment, a tall boy stepped out of the group. "My name is Miguel. I will help you. Just tell me what to do." Miguel's offer proved the group's catalyst, and the other boys rushed forward to offer their help, Vitale, Franz, Andrzej, Rasheed, Levi, Jim. With brimming eyes, Laura smiled her lovely smile, and gathered the boys around her to plot Gertrude's emancipation.

***

Gertrude, blindfolded, felt the car slow and stop. A moment later the door next to her opened and Bruno's hand closed heavily on her shoulder and drew her out. She stood swaying a little, head tilted slightly upward. Without warning, Bruno hoisted her over his shoulder and she lay slung down his back as he walked, stopped, opened a door on screeching metal hinges, stepped across a threshold, and set her down on a concrete floor. He fumbled at the knot behind her head, and then suddenly she stood blinking in dim, dusty warehouse light. To her right a group of men hunched over sandwiches and bowls of soup. With a start, she recognized Horace and Gus, actually looking better off than they had two days before when she'd seen them hustled into a paddy wagon. A scuff behind her signaled Halliday's entrance. She tossed a key to Bruno.

"Take her to my quarters." Bruno put a hand at Gertrude's back and steered her to the rear of the building and up an iron staircase. At the top, he used the key to unlock a heavy padlock that secured a hasp. He slid the door aside and waved Gertrude in ahead of him. She stepped through and blinked at suddenly bright light flooding through skylights set in the pitched roof above. This room made of hangers and girders and corrugated steel was bolted onto the warehouse's frame up under the roof, which formed the ceiling as well, angling up from left to right. The room ran for a quarter the length of the dock, fifty by twenty feet along the back half of the building. It had held offices, but the interior walls had been removed, leaving just one long room. The walls were white above a wood floor, sanded down and waxed to gleaming. The white was sullied a little by dust. Light fixtures hung on conduits from a wire channel halfway up the ceiling, just plain industrial shades and bare light bulbs. Against one wall, some felt blankets lay pulled tight across a thin mattress. Farther on, hangers on a pipe bolted to the wall held articles of clothing, another beat up men's jacket, a cardigan sweater, a cocktail dress, a trench coat and fedora, the linen blouse, aglow in the sunshine, a couple of pairs of overalls, and a nurse's uniform. A shelf next to the pipe held neatly folded stacks of dungarees and work shirts. On the floor beneath was a pile of hats, caps, scarves, and shoes. Past the wardrobe was a wood-paneled screen, through whose gap at the bottom Gertrude could see the lower part of a commode and a sink pedestal.

"Well, at least it's plumbed," she thought.

On the wall opposite the mattress, was a makeshift kitchen -- a counter built from two-by-fours and plywood, a gas stove, a sink, and a ten-year-old icebox.

Halliday stepped in behind Gertrude. "Would you like some tea?" she asked. A Scandinavian lilt. She kicked off her shoes (she wore no socks), and stood there, still in her slacks, t-shirt, and suspenders.

"I'd like to use the toilet."

"Of course."

"Tell him to leave." Gertrude nodded at Bruno.

"Yes, Bruno," Halliday ordered, "Put the key on the counter and leave us alone."

"I ain't sure that's a good idea. You two ladies start gabbin', pretty soon you're friends, and this operation's shot."

Halliday stood to face him. "You are no longer required, Bruno. I shall count to ten." Gertrude knew a Polish grandma when she heard one, and smiled in spite of herself.

With his eyes fixed on hers, Bruno pulled a cigarette from his pack of Lucky Strikes, struck the match, lit the cigarette, took a long slow pull, and turned the match upside down to let it die on his fingers. He dropped the cinder onto the burnished floor and ground it into dust with a Florscheimed toe, then turned on his heel and left, trailing a cloud of bluish smoke.

As the door slid shut behind him, Halliday walked to the opposite wall where she pulled open a concealed panel, revealing a black electrical switch. She counted to ten, then reached inside to flip it. She turned to Gertrude.

"Now there is enough electrical current flowing across those stairs outside to incinerate anyone stepping onto them. That will keep Bruno out, and should eliminate any thoughts of your escape."

Behind the semi-privacy of the wooden screen, but otherwise as vulnerable almost as she could ever be, Gertrude took stock and decided there was nothing she could do for now except take things as they happened and watch for an opportunity to escape.

When she had finished washing her hands and restoring some dignity to herself, Gertrude went out to confront her captor. Halliday was setting out lunch, slicing tomatoes, a salami, a dark and sweet-smelling loaf of bread. A teakettle had just begun to rumble.

"I was perfectly serious about the tea. Help yourself to food." Gertrude hesitated, wondering if she should worry about poison.

"Miss Hardy, the food is perfectly safe." Halliday laid a tomato slice and some salami on a piece of bread and ate. "You see? I'm not uncivilized."

Gertrude, who hadn't had lunch, and who needed her strength, made herself a sandwich. Halliday offered tea, which Gertrude took with milk and sugar. Although her expression did not betray her thoughts, she reveled in the tea's heady essence, redolent of her Virginia girlhood, an anchor to which she could make fast her fear. She drained it, set the empty cup on the counter, and faced Halliday.

"I don't consider murder civilized."

"Miss Hardy, you and your brother and Miss van Duyn are mixed up in something you cannot begin to understand. If you stop my plans, you will guarantee harm to thousands of innocent people. I would like to ask you please, when your brother arrives, as I'm sure he will, to intervene and let me finish my task here."

"You tried to have us killed."

"No, I did not. That was Bruno. He is difficult to control."

"Yet you work with him."

"I required his help, Miss Hardy. I knew he was dangerous, but he got me what I needed. Sometimes I must work with men like that."

"Well, you both make a fine pair. What makes you think I'll give any credence to your story? Give me some proof."

"I cannot tell you my plans. Too much rides on them. Maybe I prefer to have faith in your compassion, Miss Hardy. I know you helped Tony even after he betrayed you."

Gertrude stiffened. "I'll not aid a murderer."

"I envy you your upbringing, the certainties it gave you. I have seen many people killed, for many reasons, some I thought were good ones, but everybody did not agree with me, and when I listened to them, I was no longer so sure myself. I weighed Tony's life against my plans, and judged my plans more important. Even to make my case to Miss van Duyn, bringing a man down before her eyes, that man would have said I did the right thing. You do not agree, and maybe if I talked to you a while, I would no longer be so sure, but I haven't any time left. I promise, Miss Hardy, although I hope and prefer that I don't have to, I will use you in any way that I can to ensure my success. If I finish my work and if your brother does not appear, I will release you tomorrow morning. Now, I must go down and see what progress my workmen are making." She opened the concealed panel, flipped down the switch, and left. Gertrude walked over and tried the door, but it was locked as she suspected it would be. Which left her standing there chewing her sandwich.

***

Battery Park was crowded. Fenton had sent his men out across its expanse to look for anything out of the ordinary, but that was two hours ago and – nothing. He considered the possibility that Miss van Duyn was right. Someone, a teenaged boy, tapped his shoulder. "Detective Hardy?" Fenton nodded.

"I have a message for you from Miss van Duyn," and he described the Brooklyn dock's location. "Your sister's there." Fenton considered tactics. He'd need more men and some shotguns, he'd have to go back to the precinct first. He thanked the boy for the message, asked if Laura had gone back to the paper.

"No, she's going to rescue Miss Hardy," and he was gone through the crowd, leaving Fenton to shake his head in disbelief at her audacity. It took a while for him to assemble his men and return to their cars, where they found traffic hopelessly snarled. Fenton found a call box and asked for an explanation of the delay. He was told that someone had let open a bunch of fire hydrants and flooded the streets. And there was a big truck stalled across Trinity Place at Fulton. Fenton knew it was not Miss van Duyn's story that had been outlandish. He weighed his options. Wait for the traffic to clear or ride the subway uptown? He figured in the end it would be six or half a dozen, but if he rode, at least he felt he was going somewhere.

***

Bruno sat brooding over a cup of coffee in the mess hall. Shouldn't trust a woman, he decided. Except his wife. She understood a dollar, a payday. Now Halliday does something stupid, kidnapping that Hardy woman. And for what, a chance to get kidnapping added to his rap sheet? What's she gonna do when the cops show up anyway, kill her? He shook his head. Just adds up to more complication, more risk. A shadow fell across him. He looked up to see Horace, eyes everywhere but on him.

"Whaddaya want?"

"I seen you bring in that Hardy dame. It don't seem like havin' her around makes things any easier."

"What's your point?"

"Listen, Bruno, you should get paid for the job you do, right?"

"Yeah, go on."

"Bruno, you do all of Halliday's heavy work while she sits up in her apartment. If the men complain, you take the heat. Every time there's a dustup, like that little fracas between me and Pignoli this morning, you're the one has to put himself in the middle. It could be one of these days you get your nose busted."

Bruno started up. "You threatening me? You better watch your mouth."

"Bruno, relax, you got the wrong idea. I'm on your side. I'm just sayin' you're the real power here. I know Halliday, she pays you good, but now she brings in that dame against your better judgment. Bruno, she ain't givin' you the proper consideration. And when it turns out you was right, who's gonna pay for her mistake? Her? Are you kiddin'? She'll be long gone. So, Bruno, you got to forget about her, and consider your own interest. You got a wife and a couple of kids. If this operation falls apart, what's gonna happen to them?"

Bruno sulked. "I don't know, I never thought about it."

"Well, I did, and what I thought was, they're gonna be on the street. Now, I know all these other guys here, they think they're depending on the money, too, but if all they want to do is haul stuff and load stuff they can find lots of jobs doing that. They'll be all right. But you're the guy that runs the operation and you deserve extra for that. Here's Halliday bringin' in that Hardy dame, ignoring your consideration. That don't seem fair. Seems like Halliday should pay the price for her mistake. So here's what we do, and I'm only including myself because I was the one had the idea, but what if we was to take possession of that payroll? Those other guys are gonna miss a payday, sure, but they ain't got the responsibility you got, and they can find work somewhere else, but you got a family to support, and if this operation falls apart, who's Halliday gonna blame? You. Bruno, you're the one should get that payroll, except for just a little cut for me because I had the idea and I intend to take the risk, then you sell Halliday up the river for takin' advantage, and you and Maria, you're set."

It sounded good, but something didn't add up. After a long count, Horace shuffling and shrugging, Bruno snapped his fingers. "Hey, wait a minute, it ain't gonna be no easy walk gettin' that briefcase. How we gonna do that?"

Horace paused. "You know where it is, Bruno?"

"She's got it hid up there somewhere." He slid over. "Sit down, here's a story. One time she had me drive her out onto Long Island, way out, almost to Aquebogue. There was an abandoned barn. She went in, came out with a banged-up suitcase, looked that way anyway, but I carried it in and it was strong and some kind of lock I never saw before. I was going to take it up for her, but she took it herself. Next time I went in there, I couldn't see it, I figure she hid it and that's got to be the money. But she's either up there with her stairs turned on or got it locked. How we gonna get in and look for it?"

"Don't worry, Bruno, I said I'd take the risk, didn't I? You just got to make sure nothin' happens to me or my pal Gus." He held out his hand. "Friends?"

***

Pandemonium gripped the precinct-house meeting room. Fenton stood at the podium, wildly waving his hands for attention while a dozen policemen shouted questions and snapped answers at each other. Finally, Fenton roared over the hubbub, "Sit down and listen!"

The officers gradually quieted, and Fenton continued.

"I realize I'm a little short on details at the moment, but please remember that this woman Halliday has no idea we're coming. The element of surprise is worth twice your number."

"How do you know that, Hardy?" an officer shouted. "Halliday's had her cronies back for hours. You know she'd put the screws on those goons 'til they talked." The other officers shouted their agreement, reigniting the babble.

"Listen," Fenton pleaded, "all Halliday wants is to get that ship loaded. The longer it's in port, the more vulnerable she gets. She won't be wasting her men looking out for us."

"Okay," blurted another officer, "say you're right. What do we do, go in shooting, raise a big ruckus? That'll get a lot of people hurt, maybe killed."

The men raised their objections to an even higher pitch. Fenton realized he had no choice but to let them run out of steam, so he stood back. One by one, they stopped talking and turned their attention back to him. When he had them all, Fenton spoke quietly. "If we pull this operation off, we'll all have commendations. Let's stop bickering and settle on a plan. If my ideas haven't satisfied you, let's hear some of yours. You there, Hargety, and you, Davis, push those chairs aside." Fenton descended from the podium into the midst of his men, into the open space where the chairs had stood. He unfurled on the floor a wall map showing the area around Halliday's dock. Kneeling beside it, he gazed up at the men. "Gather 'round boys. We've got work to do."

***

As darkness fell, a taut young man leaned against a dockside warehouse in the western part of Brooklyn. Rooftop floodlights did not reach under the building's eaves, and so he stood shadowed and unobserved as Halliday's crew cursed and stacked and occasionally howled in pain at a stubbed toe or smashed finger. One figure the youth recognized, Bruno Skolimowski, dishing out kicks, knocks, and assorted threats, keeping the men in line. The boy heard a harsh sound to his right and looked to see a door open. Halliday herself stepped into the glare. She went to stand with Bruno among the crates and rushing men. While they talked, the boy slipped along the warehouse and into the open door. He stood a moment to let his eyes adjust and then began to prowl, into the mess hall, back through the jumbled cots, and finally up the staircase at the back of the room. The padlocked steel door barred his passage. He held his breath, listening for sounds of occupancy below and, hearing none, beat on the door with clenched fists. The door, slung loosely on a horizontal steel rail, stopped a body from entry or exit but provided no similar barrier to sound. His knock provoked a flurry of steps in the room beyond and a tense, whispered reply, a woman's voice. At her prompt the boy answered.

"Are you Gertrude Hardy?"

"Yes, who are you?"

"I'm Miguel. Miss van Duyn sent me to find you. Me and my buddies are gonna help her spring you. I'm going to go now and bring her back. You just sit tight."

"Miguel, wait. When that woman Halliday is here in this room, those stairs are electrified. If you step on them, you'll be killed. Don't come up here unless you know she's not here."

Miguel thanked Gertrude for the information and assured her that he and his friends would get her out. After he descended and crept up to the door, he was startled to see all work stopped and the men gazing across the water. Moments later a spotlight's long beam sliced through the darkness, falling across the bow of a ship drifting almost imperceptibly towards the dock. Lights extinguished, no engine thrum, signals of a purposefully stealthy approach and a wily captain. More spotlights erupted, illuminating the slip's length and forming a path for the approaching vessel. Although he longed to watch it dock, Miguel realized his opportunity to slip away while Halliday and her men attended to the ship's final arrival. He went out through the door and crept silently along the building with the ridged iron plates rippling the skin on his back and arms. As he turned the building's corner, the behemoth began its final approach. It drifted into the slip, and men appeared on deck to cast off thick hemp ropes. With practiced precision, the workmen on the dock hauled them up and formed into long lines, adding their effort to the ship's inertia, dragging it inward to its final rest. At the last moment, the unseen captain backed the engines hard and, tilting the wheel, let the ship drift to a stop beside the dock. The men began to secure the lanyards to cleats that lay along the dockside.

Around the corner in darkness, Miguel sprinted a block back from the waterside, rounded another corner, and came to a stop in front of Laura and the rest of the boys. They crowded around, impatient for him to catch his breath.

"Miss van Duyn, she's there, Miss Hardy is there. And that ship you talked about, it's here...." He knelt and sketched the warehouse layout with his fingers in the thick soot and mortar powder that covered the sidewalk. At the end, he looked up at Laura, pressing his index finger to one particular spot.

"...and Miss Hardy, she is here, and one more thing you must know, that Miss Halliday, she has electrified the stairs to her room, and we must not walk on them unless we know that Miss Halliday is not there."

The boys pounded the air, indignant, announcing their intent to smash, break, and enter. Laura, charmed by their bravery and recklessness, felt her heart swell with pride in them and with unbounded faith in their humanity. She hadn't even known these boys four hours ago, yet here they stood ready to risk themselves for the sake of one imperiled woman. On both knees next to Miguel, she looked up, fixing each boy with fierce and flashing eyes. She caught Miguel's arm and stood with him. Words caught, husky in her throat and furious with emotion. "You are my steadfast friends. You have made me proud, and I will not lose one of you. You must swear to me that you will not sacrifice yourselves, and I promise I will make you such men, men to make the world proud."

The boys shuffled their feet, eyes to the ground, but began to smile shyly, casting sideways glances, each finally looking up to meet Laura's eyes and affirm his oath, and Laura smiled and, gathering them in, knelt once more on the sidewalk and drew her own sketch.

"Now, here is my plan."

***

"Hey Mister, you got any work?"

Bruno rounded on the boy tugging at his coat sleeve. "Get outta here, punk, before I give you the toss myself."

"You don't understand, Mister," the boy pleaded, "my old man left, and I got six brothers and sisters. My mom, she says I gotta be the man of the family and get some work so's we can eat."

Bruno spun the boy around, hauled him up by his collar, march-timed him on tiptoe around the corner of the warehouse into darkness, and tossed him into the street. "And don't come back!" A sharp jab to his ribs, a .38 it felt like, stopped Bruno's return to the dock.

"Keep moving, Mister Skolimowski. I will not have you making a run for it." Laura prodded with the gun, urging Bruno along the dark street. Halfway down the block, a semi-circle of boys blocked his progress. They each held a club pulled from the detritus of the ruined block, a wooden beam, a sharp-splintered hockey stick. One boy hoisted an empty, dented, five-gallon gasoline can.

The boy ejected by Bruno drifted out of the darkness to stand at Laura's shoulder. "He hurt you Rasheed?" Miguel stepped forward, a baseball bat drifting from shoulder to palm, "Hey, Skolimowski, you roughin' up my friend?"

"Why, you little…" Bruno grabbed at his jacket, feeling for the oiled wood and steel, let the little wiseacre feel the pain of a chunk of lead… "Skolimowski," Laura snapped, "enough! Give me that gun."

Bruno, finally sizing up the odds, carefully pinched the gun between thumb and index finger, and dropped it into Laura's palm. As several boys stepped forward clamoring for possession, Bruno tensed to jump away, but Laura checked him by jamming both guns into his ribs. "Boys, none of you is old enough to handle a gun responsibly. They both will stay with me. Now please tie up Mr. Skolimowski."

Bruno spat in the dust. "Wait a minute, lady, this is too much. No way you and a bunch of kids is gonna knock down this organization. Now why don't you all toddle home to bed and forget any of this ever happened, or else you're gonna get hurt real bad."

"Mr. Skolimowski, you're not in any position to negotiate. Vitale? Levi? Let's get started."

As Bruno's eyeballs scrolled skyward, Vitale and Levi stood forward with a length of stout manila rope, wound it in several loops around his ankles, and tied it off. Rasheed , at Bruno's back, began to pat him down, all the time growling, "Now, Mr. Skolimowski we're small, but we're wiry, and we hit pretty good. So unless you want us beatin' you up, I suggest you sit down on the sidewalk here and let Miss van Duyn ask you a few questions." He turned back to Laura. "Nothin' on him, Miss van Duyn."

"I ain't sittin' in the dirt and I ain't answerin' no questions." The boys surged forward, taking aim. "All right, all right," and Bruno sat in the dirt. The boys circled around.

"Mr. Skolimowski," Laura began, "since you haven't got it on your person, please tell us where you keep your copy of the key that unlocks Halliday's apartment?"

"I ain't got no key."

Miguel raised his bat. "You tell Miss van Duyn the truth."

"I'm tellin' you the truth, I ain't got no key. Only Halliday has a key."

Miguel loomed over Bruno, who, finally raising a forearm to shield his face, softened his voice. "Look, kid, I don't wanna get my face broke. I'm tellin' you the truth."

"Miguel, that's enough. He hasn't got the key." Miguel stepped away, and Laura turned back to Bruno. "Mr. Skolimowski, does Halliday carry the key with her?"

Bruno looked up, puzzled. "Yeah. Why?"

"Where does she keep it, on her person, specifically?"

"Depends on what she's wearing. Wherever there's a pocket."

"Does she always wear something with pockets?"

"Yeah, near as I can remember."

Laura nodded at the boys. "Well, that will make it a little easier."

"Hey, wait a minute, what you got in mind?" Bruno asked.

Laura wagged a finger at Bruno. "Mr. Skolimowski, our plan is a secret."

"Listen, I want that Hardy dame outta there as much as you do. She's only gonna foul things up. And when things get fouled up, I don't get paid."

"Mr. Skolimowski, you will not be paid anyway. You will be

arrested and stand trial for murder."

"There ain't any evidence that I killed somebody. Listen, lady, if I really wanted to escape, there's a hundred ways I coulda dealt with you and the kiddies here, most involvin' you gettin' your necks broke. I'm just goin' along, seein' what you come up with. Better Halliday's mad at you for bustin' her out than me."

Laura replied evenly, "Mr. Skolimowski, your bravado is faked, I think. In any case, your failure to detect us and your capture are likely to incense Halliday just as much, not to mention that the police want you in connection with two murders. So even if it is not faked, your bravado is misplaced. Boys, tie his arms and gag him, please."

Bruno began to struggle as they swarmed over him, but he could not fight them all off. When they finished, he was belly down, squirming and sooty, unable to go anywhere.

***

A cry for help caused several of Halliday's men to raise their heads. Two boys came down the dock, one with his arm around the waist of the other, who hopped on one foot and grimaced in pain. When they drew near the men, they stopped and lowered themselves to the ground. Halliday stepped out of the crowd and knelt next to them, speaking in the cultured tones of a Park Avenue matron.

"This is not a place for boys. Please get up and leave now."

Pete looked imploringly into Halliday's eyes. "Lady, you gotta help my friend. I think his leg's broke." He strove to haul Andrjez back to his feet. To hurry them along Halliday put her arm around the small of his back and lifted. Andrjez resisted, feigning intolerable agony, also snaking his arm around Halliday's waist. His act distracted and delayed Halliday, giving him time and the opportunity to pat the large pocket on her skirt front, and then to insinuate his fingers into it and withdraw a key. He sneaked Pete a thumb's up, and immediately stood, shaking out his leg, then putting weight on it, hobbling a bit and breaking into a brisk walk towards the end of the warehouse. Pete trotted after him, tipping his cap at Halliday over his shoulder. "Must've been a miracle, Ma'am. Thanks." As they disappeared around the corner, Halliday reached into her pocket. "Thieves," she shouted, "they have stolen my key. Bruno..." She looked around. "Where is Bruno?" she demanded. The gathered men shrugged their shoulders. She picked out the first familiar faces she saw, "You, Horace, Gus, get those boys, and watch out for the police. The rest of you, get back to work." As the men moved off, she strode to the warehouse. Inside, she went immediately to the staircase, reached underneath it, and retrieved a key that hung hidden on a hook behind it. She turned to climb the stairs, but Laura was there. With a pistol she gently prodded Halliday.

"I thought you might have a second key. Give it to me, please."

"Miss van Duyn, once again you flout my warnings. You are becoming reckless." She dropped the key into Laura's outstretched palm.

"It's for a good cause. I can stand the risk."

"And your cause?"

"Bringing you to justice."

A loud whisper came from over towards the door. "Miss van Duyn?"

"Yes, Andrjez," Laura answered, "we're back here."

Andrjez stepped up to them. He cast an appreciative eye over Halliday before turning to Laura and holding up a key. "Here's the other one."

"Thank you, Andrjez." She took the key and sent Andrjez back out with his friends. "They have your men on a goose chase," she told Halliday, "and I have both your keys. We are going up the stairs, you in front. When we get to the top, I will hand you a key, and you will unlock the door."

"Or you will shoot me?"

"Not to kill."

Halliday smiled a soft, small smile. "You think of everything, Miss van Duyn." She stepped around to the foot of the stairs and began to ascend. Laura shadowed her two steps below. At the top, Laura handed her a key and she opened the padlock. Laura took back the key and called out, "Gertrude, it's Laura. I'm coming through with Halliday. Please stand back from the door." She nodded to Halliday who pulled the door aside, catching Gertrude just backing away, fists loosening, arms dropping to her side. Laura urged Halliday into the room and they stood there.

"The next step in your plan, Miss van Duyn?"

Laura asked Gertrude, "Have you seen any rope?"

"No."

"Cut up those blankets, then."

Gertrude took a blanket and stepped to the counter, found a large kitchen knife, and stripped off a long narrow piece, then cut it into three shorter lengths which she handed to Laura, and left the blanket in a heap against the counter.

Laura bound Halliday's arms behind her and asked, "Gertrude, where is the switch that electrifies the stairs?"

Halliday's jaw clenched.

Gertrude pointed to the panel on the wall. "Behind there, but you need a key."

Laura stopped to rummage along a shelf under the counter and came up with a twelve-inch cast iron skillet. The panel itself was just stamped sheet steel, so the heavier frying pan made short work of it as Laura wielded it like a club, and behind it the switch's parts, Bakelite mostly, a kind of plastic, yielded to Laura's efforts, scattering bits of themselves across the counter and onto the blanket. After a moment, two bared wires made contact, sending out spits of blue and white sparks. Laura stood back alarmed.

"Gertrude, what should I do?"

"I don't know. I didn't study electricity."

Laura spied a wooden spoon among the other kitchen utensils. Grabbing it, she thrust it between the two wires. The sparks stopped but, Laura saw, the hot wire began to char the wood.

"Gertrude, we've got to get out now." She hurried back and untied Halliday. She and Gertrude each trained a pistol on her.

"Well, and now what have you got in mind?" Cool, no distress.

"We'll go downstairs," Laura said. "When that spoon burns through, the stairs will be impassible."

"Not to mention an almighty fire," Gertrude declared.

Halliday went first, Gertrude and Laura behind, pistols leveled at her back. At the bottom of the stairs Halliday turned. "My men, you've got to let me pay them. Regardless of what you want with me, they have families to support. They will starve if they don't get their pay."

Before Laura could react, Halliday turned and raced up the stairs. Laura gave Gertrude a helpless look. "Save yourself," she cried, and then turned after Halliday. As she regained the apartment a shower of sparks signaled the spoon's demise, except that it proved good tinder, and a blinding flame shot from the panel and engulfed the blanket that Gertrude had tossed down. The flames quickly spread to the wooden cupboard. The blazing light bulbs above Halliday's head burst in a shower of sparks leaving only the dull glow from the spreading flames to illuminate her as she hoisted a heavy case over her head. As Laura started towards her, she came on the run, slamming the case into Laura's midriff and knocking her to the floor. The pistol flew backwards out the door and Halliday was on her like a cat, scratching at her eyes, her blouse, her arms and shoulders. Laura raised a forearm, sweeping across Halliday's onslaught, slamming her backwards onto the floor. They each rose on haunches, orange glare alight in their eyes, and circled, Halliday with crooked fingers foremost, Laura ready to spring, fingertips touching floor. A sheet of flame erupted from the wall behind the cupboard at Laura's back.

"You might have killed the both of us," Halliday rasped. "The circuit is closed again. The stairs are impassable."

Laura answered, "If I give my life, I will have saved others from your clutch."

"Did you think I hadn't planned another escape?" Halliday darted at Laura, knocking her backward and out of breath, then back along the room to the shadowed far wall. After a moment, a shaft of yellow light appeared, and a shadow slid down its length. Laura heaved herself onto hands and knees and picked her way among the shards and sparks, flames snaking at her heels. At the back wall, she found an opened trapdoor through which a chain link ladder hung to the floor below. She swung herself over, fingers and toes clutching at shifting rungs, and found her way down amid the smoke and flame. A shadow on the wall beside her betrayed Halliday's presence, but, beginning to cough, Laura directly sought the warehouse door. On the dock, she stood, regaining her breath and blinking in the glare. At a touch on her shoulder, she turned, and she and Gertrude collapsed into a deep embrace, and murmured thanks, each for the other's safe deliverance.

Several workmen gathered around them. "Who are you," one asked, "and why is the warehouse on fire?" Laura glanced at the gathering pall of smoke drifting out of the warehouse and then at the labels on the boxes stacked beside her.

"Sir, you must get off of this dock. If these crates explode you could all be killed."

"But Miss, we got to get paid. If we put in a good day's work, Bruno said we'd get a hundred dollars. We need that money for rent and food."

"Precisely, and I have no intention of sending you home without giving you what you're due." Halliday stepped out of the group to stand beside Laura and Gertrude. Gertrude brought her pistol to bear on Halliday's heart.

"Let's avoid any possible misunderstanding," Halliday murmured, withdrawing the second pistol from her breast pocket and passing it to Laura.

***

The boys had given them the slip, so Horace and Gus picked their way slowly back towards the dock, not anxious to report their failure to Halliday. They looked up at the sound of a moan and a rustle ahead. As they hurried forward, Horace's toe caught something soft, and he pitched forward across Bruno's chest. Bruno arched his back and tossed Horace off. Horace stood up and casually brushed dust from his clothes.

"Gee, Bruno, looks like you're in kind of a jam." Bruno glared. "All right already, I'll help you out. But listen, you gotta recognize I'm givin' you a hand here. No funny stuff, okay?"

Bruno still glared, but he sank back onto the sidewalk Horace reached behind Bruno's neck and undid the rope that held the gag in place. Bruno loosed a profane and vulgar indictment at his attackers and their ancestors. When Horace had freed him, Bruno leaped to his feet and bounded off towards the dock, Horace and Gus sprinting to keep up.

"Say, Bruno, what happened?" Horace panted, "Whatcha' gonna do now? Is that van Duyn broad behind this?"

Bruno snarled at Horace to keep quiet as they rounded the corner onto the dock. Horace's next question died on his lips as he surveyed the chaos ahead. Smoke and flame licked out of the warehouse at its eaves. The work crew, like a routed army, scrambled here and there, fearing the conflagration, but unwilling to leave unpaid. The men took shelter in whatever parts felt safe, crouched behind boxes or on the ship's deck. Centered in the shifting crowd, a trio of women stood pinned by a spotlight, one holding aloft a briefcase, the other two training pistols on her.

Bruno started through the crowd, shoving workers out of the way as he went, passing through the gauntlet to stand finally before Halliday. He jerked his thumb at Gertrude.

"Lady, I told you snatchin' her was a bad idea. Now give me that payroll, and me and the men, we'll get out of here, and you and these other ladies can sort out what's what."

Halliday leveled her cool gaze at Bruno. "Bruno, my ship still is not loaded, my quarters and my facilities brought down. Thanks to a couple of women and some boys. This failure I lay at your feet, and I do not let failure go unpunished."

Bruno stepped closer, menacing, but Halliday stood her ground. Laura aimed the gun at Bruno. "Step back Mr. Skolimowski. I am arresting you both and charging you with the murders of Anthony DiFaro and the tobacconist."

Bruno spat on the ground at Halliday's feet. His left hand lashed out, swatting away Laura's pistol, and with his right he aimed a roundhouse at Halliday's cheek, but Halliday was already moving, ducking in under the massive arm, right hand arcing upwards, the minute and glittering needle at Bruno's neck. She spun away and Bruno fell with staring eyes onto the pavement, convulsions already subsiding, his great chest stilled.

Halliday, hair streaming, eyes flashing, and wreathed in smoke and bright light, darted among the men as they parted in wonder. She passed into the open thinking herself assured of escape, but again, Laura blocked her way. Halliday laid down the case. "Pay my men," she said, and unencumbered, she was gone, flitting back through the crowd and into darkness.

A rhythmic throb shook the air as the ship's engines came to life. Sailors bounded down the gangplank to cast off the hawsers. Laura called for the workmen to bar them, and fistfights broke out as the sailors, shouting, tried to drive through.

The warehouse's roof collapsed. Sparks and hot cinders cascaded across the dock and among the bundles and stacks of crates that littered it. Realizing their peril, the workers and sailors scattered, melting away into the streets and the night.

Away down the dock Fenton and his men crept into the light, astounded by the chaos and unsure how to proceed. Spying Laura and Gertrude, Fenton started towards them. Just as he drew near, a quick and silent shape dashed against his back, sending him tumbling. Horace danced across Fenton's prone form, snatched the briefcase and ran cackling back towards the warehouse, thinking to steal away through the shadows. A bullet out of Fenton's pistol whizzed past his head and he crouched, whispering thanks not to have been hit. A moment later, Fenton's bullet, having pierced the iron wall of the warehouse, ruptured the copper pipe that fed bottled gas from the massive holding tank to the mess hall griddles. The greedy flames welcomed this new fuel, igniting a mighty cloud of flame that vaporized the iron wall and enveloped Horace where he crouched. Its force picked him up, carrying him across the dock and over the ship. Searing fragments of iron and smoldering slivers of wood broke after him across the ship's bow. Billowing flames engulfed the crates along the dock, igniting ordnance and explosives in a second fireball. The shock wave buckled the ship's weakened gunwale and lit the cargo already stowed, breaching the hold's far side. The harbor water rushed in and the ship settled onto the muck at the bottom, then slowly listed outwards until the seawater, in uneven ballast, caused it to heel, groaning, onto its side. Diesel pooled on the water, and bits of wood and canvas spun lazily through random eddies. A rain of clanking shards rattled across the gunwales and the dock, and a hissing great cloud of vapor rose, concealing for a time the dock and ruined building, and then slowly dissipated with the noise and the smell, leaving, except for one man screaming, silence, and clean air and darkness.

***

With his toe Captain O'Malley shoved a bit of charred wood across the dock where piles of wreckage still smoldered. He'd been there all night, he'd seen the warehouse go up from his precinct and had been the first one on the scene.

He squinted at the wreckage. The warehouse was more or less a complete loss. At headquarters he knew, they were having trouble identifying its owner. There would be insurers, no doubt, who'd want to be notified. He spun around and faced the slip. It was going to take a marine wrecker to right the ship, assuming they could plug up her holes and pump the water out. Might have to go straight to salvage. At least there'd been no bodies. The main force of the explosion had been upward and so the police squad, Detective Hardy and his sister, and some lummox they'd found dead to the world, slumbering in the muck left behind by the Fire Department, had been spared its heat and shock. They were all cut up a little by the shards of corrugated steel and copper pipe raining down from it, and had been dutifully hauled off to local hospitals for observation, all except Hardy, who'd insisted he was all right. He'd grilled every officer and firefighter on the dock, said he was looking for two women, but nobody had seen them. O'Malley figured they'd got caught in the explosion, carried into the water or, O'Malley shuddered, cremated, but Hardy wouldn't have any of that.

"When the rest of us came out with just a few scratches? That's ridiculous."

"I ain't a detective, I guess, like you." He gave Hardy an eyeful of disapproval and walked away. Now here he was back again, jabbing at O'Malley's shoulder. O'Malley rounded on him. "Yeah!? What do you want?"

Fenton was holding out his badge and revolver. "Take these, I quit."

"But I can't..." and then he could only sputter at Hardy's heedlessness.

"Look, they're going to ask for it anyhow, they'll need a scapegoat, and I'd rather quit than be fired. I think I have better things to do anyway." He grabbed O'Malley's hand and thrust the objects into it. O'Malley stared after him as he walked away and whistled. "I don't envy that man and the devil's own load of grief he's got coming."

CHAPTER 17
SOUTH

Laura came from darkness into darkness, weeping, cradled in someone's arms. A quiet voice, almost a whisper, said, "Hush now, you're all right, everything is all right. You're in shock, and you need sleep, I'm just going to put you back to sleep." A warm hand gently smoothed her hair. She felt a pinch along the side of her neck, and the voice came again. "Just go to sleep."

***

She awoke with a ferocious headache. Transfixed, she lay still, eyes closed, breathing deeply, willing loose every tendon, every joint, every knotted muscle. The pain receded, leaving room for other sensations: stiffened and bruised muscles, straw prickling her neck, cool breeze across her face, body gently rocking, a tapping sound echoing her pounding heart. She opened her eyes to see sunlit pasture and cornfields sliding by through the boxcar's open door. She turned her gaze inward and found a young man, a bulging cap on his head, sitting with knees drawn to chin, barefoot, dressed in baggy dungarees and a flannel shirt, staring out the door. He turned as Laura stirred.

"It's good you all are finally awake. Please accept my apologies for the headache. It is an unfortunate side effect of the drug. As you should already have found, however, it does not persist once consciousness is regained."

It took Laura a moment to recognize Halliday's voice, pitched low in a languorous drawl. She tossed Laura a bundle.

"Here are some more appropriate clothes, more practical than that skirt and blouse."

Laura reached warily for the bundle, found shirt and trousers like Halliday's, and coarse woolen socks.

"I have declined to wear the socks while the weather is warm. I find their itch to be intolerable."

Laura nodded and glanced around the boxcar for some cover.

"I apologize that privacy is wanting. I shall avert my eyes while you undress."

Halliday edged to the door, swinging her legs over to dangle, and sat in the sun watching the countryside approach and recede. She took off the cap and shook her hair free. The breeze played with it, dark locks afloat and falling.

Laura unbuttoned and shed her blouse. She pulled the flannel shirt across her shoulders, pushed her arms through the sleeves and fumbled to button it, a man's shirt she realized, with buttons on the right. She stood and unzipped the dark skirt, letting it fall to the floor. Balancing first on left foot, then on right, she gathered and pulled on each pant leg, finally hoisting the whole lot to her waist, tucking in the shirt's tails and sliding the trousers' brass buttons through the hemmed buttonholes. She stuffed the socks into the pockets.

She faced Halliday's back. "What shall I do with my clothes?"

Halliday gestured to a corner of the car. "Put them in my knapsack."

Laura found the knapsack. As she pushed her clothes inside, tendrils of memory gathered and then a sudden deluge, fire and smoke, Gertrude's round eyes and the detective reaching for her, the percussion that brought darkness, and now, in sudden panic she wondered, were they gone? And her parents' terrible uncertain fear, not knowing if she, their only child, was gone, too.

Halliday spoke without turning. "Your parents will be informed that you are safe. Your friends survived, even that rabble you drafted to destroy me. I fear that detective will bear the brunt of it, his bullet sent the whole place up. Floundering as his career apparently was, it likely will not survive. He would have done well to have listened to you."

Laura rose up, indignant. "He is a decent man. He doesn't deserve being made fun of."

Halliday's cool eyes settled on her. "I have no quarrel with his decency. I'm just saying you were the better detective."

"That was mostly luck."

"No, it wasn't. You have a sharp eye for opportunity, Miss van Duyn. You took me down in less than three days. Nobody outsmarts me like that, ever." Her courtly speech had disappeared and she stood, looming now over Laura, who reared back in alarm and confusion. Halliday half-smiled, marveling, and shook her head. "You don't even know." She knelt and held Laura by the shoulders. "You need to wake up to your potential, Miss van Duyn, and I can wake you."

Laura shook free, caught Halliday's eye, and held it. "So you would be my rescuer after all?"

"If you wanted me to be."

"I'm not going to smuggle arms to Hitler."

"That was just my front. Did you really believe that's what I was doing?"

Laura shrugged. "No."

"Then grant my revenge and make up for what you've done. Come with me and I will make you into someone you could scarcely have believed might exist."

Laura shook her head, more to clear her thoughts than to doubt. "You killed three men."

"No, I did not."

"But that tobacconist...I saw you."

"You simply misread what you saw, as I intended. I assure you, the tobacconist has returned to his shop. Tony Difaro and his brother are, if he took my advice, on their way to the Coos Bay CCC. I spared even Bruno, against my better instincts. I do apologize for causing you distress, but at the time, I'm afraid you left me little choice. Bruno was a handful, and I needed him."

"How can I believe you? Even the coroner said the tobacconist was dead."

"Besides having been the beneficiary of the very same treatment yourself, without having suffered, as near as I can tell, any permanent ill effects, when I had every opportunity and perhaps a fine motive myself to kill you, I can offer no further proof than to stick you in the neck again, which I would prefer not to do. If you choose to disbelieve me, and wish, on those grounds, not to accompany me any further, you are free to leave at the next stop, and we will never see each other again."

"How can you not be angry with me?"

Halliday, still kneeling, rested her forearm on an upraised knee and leaned towards Laura. "You have done far less material damage than you might think. The arms were lost, that is true, but we have more. I can pay the men from other sources. The dock and the ship will attract commercial interest, and can be bought for a song. The salvage and rebuilding will provide work for many men. There is of course, the psychic damage of my defeat, but if I have gambled well, I will have gained you, and on the balance, that will ease my disappointment. You will find, Miss van Duyn, that I am not an idealist. I take what is given me and make the best of it." She searched Laura's eyes for her answer.

"All right," Laura said. What else could she say?

CHAPTER 18
ALTERCATION AND A MEAL

A jab in her ribs from Halliday's toe jolted Laura awake. She sat up yawning, scratching her dusty scalp. Halliday stood at the boxcar's door, bathed in the dim glow from a nearby town, peering ahead into darkness.

"What's the matter?"

"Slowing down, train yard ahead. If we stop, we'll have company, passengers or railroad police." She turned to Laura, holding out a small black case, opened and bristling with needles, each capped with a tiny wooden plug. She drew out two and handed one to Laura.

"Do not stick yourself. You will be instantly unconscious. Now let's hunker down and wait."

The train jerked to a halt, sending them sprawling into a dark corner. Flashlight beams crossed the open door and men shouted.

"Reuben, you all check down that way. I was sure I saw someone hanging out the door a minute ago."

A nearer voice called back, "Yessir, Uncle," and a moment later, a fat young man began to haul himself, puffing, up onto the boxcar's floor. He got his belly hoisted over the lip of the door and scrabbled for a handhold in the scattered straw, his legs fishtailing behind him. Halliday darted out of the shadows, found the jugular vein, and slid the dart home. The boy went limp and began to slide backwards out the door. Halliday grabbed for his shirt collar, belaying his retreat, but making no headway. Then Laura was there straddling his bulk. She slipped her hands through his belt, and together they dragged him, inert, over the threshold and collapsed next to him on the floor.

Uncle yelled out of the darkness, "Reuben, did you find anything?"

Halliday stood and walked to the doorway. Flawlessly rendering Reuben's soft Virginia drawl, she called back, "Nothin' here, Uncle. I'll check on up the line, see if anyone's there."

"Fine," Uncle replied, "I'm goin' to head on back to the station house, finish my drink."

Halliday returned to crouch by Laura. "I'm glad Reuben's a tenor." She bent over him and went through his pockets, retrieving a flashlight, a pistol, a wad of bills, a pint of bourbon, and a pocket-sized New Testament.

Laura's eyes widened. "You can't steal his things."

Halliday, who had begun counting the bills, didn't look up. "These private cops make too much for what they do, rolling hobos, beating up on them, or worse. He'd just gamble the money away or buy himself a woman. We'll make honest use of it, and," she held up the pistol, "we can defend ourselves." Tilting the Bible toward the light, she ruffled through it, tore out a page, and shoved it into Reuben's pants pocket. "There, maybe he'll turn over a new leaf."

The train jerked and began slowly to move forward again. Halliday grabbed Reuben's shirt collar and tugged at his slumbering form. "Give me a hand," she gasped. Laura pulled until they got him alongside the door. "Now roll him." They heaved Reuben over onto his side, and momentum carried him out the door.

Halliday wiped her forehead on her shirtsleeve, pulled off her cap and tossed her hair. She grinned at Laura. "You all are stronger than you look." She twisted the cap off the bottle of bourbon, took a short pull, and passed it to Laura. "Have a little reward for your hard work."

Laura took the bottle gingerly between thumb and forefinger and sipped. Though more raw than her father's Irish whisky, the draught still bore the same warmth, first in her belly and then out to her arms and legs. She took another swallow and passed the bottle back to Halliday.

Halliday sipped again and replaced the bottle's cap. "I'm about to faint for lack of food in me. There's got to be something to eat on this train. Let's go find it."

Halliday swung onto the ladder outside the boxcar's door. She pulled herself up two rungs and, clinging by one arm, offered a hand to Laura, who took hold and swung herself over. They ascended to stand atop the roof of the car, swaying a little against its motion. Halliday stooped to crawl towards the rear of the train with Laura picking her way behind. Reaching the break between cars, they descended, passed over the coupling, and climbed to the roof of the next car. Halfway along, Halliday grasped the edge of the roof, swung over and down to land with a thump inside the car. Moments later her head reappeared as she climbed back.

"Only a couple of hobos sleeping. Keep going."

Laura led to the next car, and peered over its edge. "I think it's locked," she called to Halliday.

Halliday smiled slyly. "Then what's inside is worth protecting." She disappeared over the edge. A moment later Laura heard a gunshot and the door slide back. She climbed down the ladder and followed Halliday into the car. Halliday pulled the door closed after them and snapped on the flashlight. They both gave low whistles, and Halliday breathed, "Jackpot."

Before them stacked floor to ceiling were crates of provisions bound, according to the shipping labels, for the Georgian Terrace Hotel in Atlanta. Halliday pulled the bundle of cash from her pocket. "Eat. I'll pay for it."

They fell to prying open crates with a crowbar they found nearby. One held tinned Norwegian sardines, and another, English crackers. They made crunchy sandwiches until their fingers grew slick with oil. They found tiny jars of Beluga caviar and glistening slabs of pâté de foie gras, Belgian chocolate truffles, cherries preserved in syrup, and saucer-sized rounds of Camembert cheese. Fizzy Perrier water and a bottle of Burgundy wine quenched their thirst. Surrounded by their meal's leavings, lying cushioned on piles of excelsior they had pulled from the crates, they drowsed in the sable darkness, the air close and warm, perfumed with herbs and garlic, salt fish, and the sweetness of rendered grapes, and Laura's wine-loosened tongue ventured a question.

"Did you really never kill anyone?"

A long moment, ten slow heartbeats, and then Halliday's voice out of the dark, "I never told this until now. I let a man into my life once, he said he loved me. He promised we'd go someplace nice and he'd take care of me. I thought I loved him, but maybe it was just his promise I loved. He sold me out for five hundred dollars and a bottle of Scotch whiskey, put me in a his-life-or-mine situation. He was already a walking tragedy, bound to be done in by somebody. He climbed as high as he ever would, and I let him out of his life before he started down the other side, and he did me the only favor he could, he left me a little bit of sorrow I could use to carry on."

CHAPTER 19
WEST

Laura awoke when the train jerked to a stop. Halliday stood at the door, slid open a crack. "Our stop. Nobody around. Let's go."

She slapped a twenty dollar bill on top of the nearest crate, weighed them down with an empty Perrier bottle, then quietly slid open the door and jumped to the ground. Laura followed her, yawning. The gravel on the rail bed was cool and damp with dew, and poked at her bare feet. Halliday strode down the track ahead of her, using the ties like steppingstones. Laura followed, glancing around as she went. Grayish dawn light outlined buildings backed up against the rail yard. Farther on, in silhouette, office towers several stories high marked the downtown section of a small city. Laura caught up to Halliday and asked where they were.

"Raleigh."

Halliday stopped and pulled herself into the car where they had started the day before and returned a moment later with the knapsack. She pulled out two pairs of tall, pale leather work boots, handed one pair to Laura, and squatted to put on the other pair.

"I hope I got your size. I'd hate for you to get blisters. Don't lace them too tight."

Laura took the wool socks from her pants pockets, crouching on the track to pull on first the socks and then the boots. She stood, took a few tentative steps, and nodded towards Halliday that they fit.

"Good. Let's go." They set off up the track. The sky brightened and birds took to singing in the trees.

The women had occasionally to wait at a crossing for a delivery truck, bus, or taxicab to pass. Always, Halliday bowed her head or crouched behind some bush or tree, pulling Laura down with her until the vehicle disappeared around a bend or over the crest of a hill. Within an hour, the city began to give way to farmland and woodlots, swamps, ponds, and meandering streams. Halliday relaxed, venturing whistled imitations of the bird calls that surrounded them.

They entered a woodsy thicket, and Halliday turned from the track onto the meager trace of a path that ran down through the trees and bushes. Laura plunged after her, crossing a low meadow through thick, dew-drenched grass, thrusting aside willow stalks and papaw seedlings hung with spider webs rent by the weight of the water they carried. Her feet caught on strands of Virginia creeper running along the ground. After five minutes her trousers, soaked to the knees, slapped at her ankles, the armpits of her flannel shirt dripped sweat, and she panted in the clammy air. Insects clung and bit.

Halliday strode on, heedless of discomfort or Laura's distress. Gradually the path widened and climbed out of the meadow into a dry and open woodland of pine and oak trees. The mosquitoes thinned, the air lightened, and Laura breathed easier. Halliday stopped abruptly, crouched, and swept aside accumulated detritus, revealing the brass-grommetted corner of a green canvas tarpaulin.

"Help me," she said, and they pulled the heavy, diesel-infused cloth aside, uncovering the black-enameled lid of a fifty-five gallon steel drum buried in the ground. Halliday picked up a heavy stick and dug a shallow groove around the drum's circumference, leaving room to snap open the fastener and lift off the lid. She pulled two saddlebags and a shotgun out of the drum's dark interior, laid them aside, and fastened the lid back in place, packing dirt around it and covering it with the tarpaulin. Laura helped spread twigs and leaves until the cloth was once more disguised to Halliday's satisfaction.

She stood and brushed the dust off her hands and asked, "Can you ride a horse?"

"Yes, I hunted foxes with my grandfather."

Halliday looked her up and down. "Can you ride western?"

Laura nodded.

Halliday grinned. "Well, come on, then, let's see what you've got." She slung a saddlebag at Laura, picked up the other bag and the shotgun, and led the way over the crest of the hill and down into a grassy-floored dell where two horses grazed. A crooked barn stood just at the meadow's edge, its cladding buckled and silvered. A creek, dammed to make a pool beside the barn, trickled through the meadow in a wandering bisect. Halliday knelt at the pool's edge and cupped her hands in the water, then lifted them to her mouth to sip. She motioned Laura down beside her.

"Go on, you'll need it." She stood and walked off towards the barn.

Laura lowered herself onto both knees and bent over the water. She inhaled a primordial scent, of moss and moldering wood and algae over damp stone. Water skimmers fled, mayflies darted, and caddis fly larvae cloaked in grit and tiny pebbles picked and stumbled across the rocky bottom. Laura dropped her shoulders, let out a ragged sob, and leaned sideways until her cheek rested on the sharp rocks. She was grateful for the pain because it helped the tears to come.

After a while, the sobs ran themselves out. An ant crossed her forehead. Sweat trickled down her neck. A mosquito danced before her eyes. She sighed, pushed herself upright and unbuttoned her shirt, shrugged it off, and laid it on the rocks beside her and plunged face first and neck deep into the glimmering pool. She came out sputtering, the sting of water up her nose, and sneezed, cupped her hands and filled them, splashed her face and scrubbed at the corners of her eyes and behind her ears, slicked back her hair, cupped her hands again and drank. She soaked her shirt and wrung it to dampness and it felt good, clean and brisk, when she pulled it back over her shoulders. She stood, refreshed, and followed Halliday to the barn where it backed up against the woods.

She peered through the open door. A narrow aisle led between two stacks of fragrant hay to a board fence that divided the barn in half. Laura heard Halliday rummaging off to the left behind the stacks of hay. The fence began to swing aside, and Halliday appeared, walking it to the barn's far wall. Looking up, Laura saw frame and rafter leaning off kilter, but braced by sturdy poles. From the outside, the barn had looked tumbledown, liable to collapse, but that was an illusion. She walked on around the barn and shoved hard up against it. It did not budge, confirming her observation that someone only wanted it to look decrepit and abandoned. She continued to the front of the barn in time to see Halliday opening another, wider door.

Catching sight of Laura, she called her inside.

The front half of the barn was a single large stall with a straw-covered floor. Halliday had opened a cabinet spiked to a support pole. Inside, one above the other, two saddles sat on crossbeams with blankets draped over them and bridles hanging from the saddlehorns. Halliday took two nosebags from hooks on the wall next to the cabinet, opened a bin underneath, half-filled each bag with oats, and stepped back to the front door. Her quick, high whistle brought the horses trotting to the barn, both mares, one black with white stockings and blaze, the other a roan with ginger mane and tail.

Halliday strapped a nosebag onto each horse and, while they ate, she and Laura flung blankets over them and hoisted on the saddles, cinching them tight under the belly. Halliday tossed on the saddlebags, detached the nosebags, let the horses finish chewing, and fitted the bridles. Laura picked up the reins and led the horses outside. Halliday pulled closed the wide door from the inside. A padlock snicked. A moment later Halliday came around the barn with the shotgun and the knapsack. She stopped at the pool to fill two canteens then came on to where Laura stood with the horses. She slid the shotgun into a leather scabbard fitted to the saddle on the black horse and stuffed the limp knapsack into the saddlebag. She took Reuben's purloined revolver out of her hip pocket and handed it grip-first to Laura.

"Can you shoot it?"

Laura shook her head.

"Well most times you'd only have to wave it around to make your point, and even if you did have to shoot it, that would be more than adequate even if you didn't hit anyone, and even if you did, it's only a .22 so most likely he wouldn't die." She showed Laura how to put the safety off, "But don't do that unless you really mean to use it. I trust you to have the good sense to know when."

"You do?"

Halliday smiled. "I've seen you work. I trust you."

Laura nodded and slid the pistol into her left pocket. Halliday mounted the black horse and motioned Laura onto the roan. She gestured with her foot through a stirrup.

"Those heels aren't too thick, mind your feet don't slip through." She tugged the reins against her horse's neck, turning her towards the opposite edge of the meadow. With Laura following, they crossed a dense line of oak and pine seedlings sprung up at grass's edge and struck a track, two uneven, stone-clotted furrows running uphill through the trees. Halliday steered the horses to the verge between the ruts and let them have their heads, which they bowed occasionally to snatch at clumps of grass. Over the crest of the hill the ruts disappeared, and the track meandered, apparently randomly, sometimes all but gone, then reappearing as a mere smudge on the forest floor. After an hour and a couple of miles or so, they struck a regular road made of packed red dirt, just wide enough for a cart and horse, and running straight along. Shrubs and young trees crowded hard against its edges and the forest stood up behind.

With no cover, the sun fell full on Laura's neck. Sweat trickled between her shoulder blades and beneath the heavy denim trousers. She rolled up the sleeves of her now-dry shirt, which brought a little relief. She drew back gently on the reins to stop the horse, dropped to the ground and turned to rummage through the saddlebags. She found a bandanna, tied it around her neck, and pulled out bundles of jerky and dried apricots wrapped tightly in cellophane and a packet of salt tablets and thrust them into her trousers pocket. She took a long pull at the canteen, upended it over her head, and climbed back onto the horse to jog it into a trot and pull even with Halliday.

"Where are we going?"

"A place I know."

"When will we be there?"

Halliday glanced sideways. "In a few days."

"We don't have any food or shelter."

"We'll manage. I'm not worried."

Laura gnawed a strip of jerky. "It seems inefficient to put your factory back here in the woods and then take your products all the way to New York to ship them. I suppose it makes your network harder to trace. Can you really manufacture steel gun barrels all the way out here?" She turned to face Halliday directly.

"Yes, there is iron in the mountains and coal..." She stopped, eyes narrowed. Laura held her gaze with mischievous eyes. Halliday pursed her lips and kicked her horse into a canter to spring ahead, but Laura quickly followed, and so they went up the road together, wordlessly, side-by-side.

CHAPTER 20
AMOS

They went at a steady canter through the heat, stopping whenever they crossed a stream to let the horses drink, and to fill their emptied canteens. The road ran seemingly straight west because the sun never ceased to beat on them save when a small cloud passed before it -- tiny, shaded respites made even more refreshing by their rarity and brevity. By noontime, they were both utterly exhausted and bone sore, so that Laura breathed a deep sigh of relief when they came abreast of a log cabin set back in the trees and Halliday pulled into the bare dirt patch in front of it that served as a yard. A bare old hound lifted his head off his blanket to sniff and went back to sleep. A man came out the door beside it, whipcord-thin and wattle-necked, dressed in a dingy tee shirt, overalls, a shock of silver hair, and a shotgun held loose in the crook of his left arm. "Hey there, Amos," Halliday yelled, "you got anything to eat?"

"Miss Halliday? That you?" He squinted out at the women on their horses, then pulled a pair of steel-wire glasses out of his bib pocket, and draped them behind his ears.

"Yes it is, Amos, and this is my friend Miss van Duyn."

Amos looked Laura over. "You takin' her back into the mountains?"

"We're not discussing where I'm taking her, Amos."

"I understand, Miss Halliday, sometimes you do is all. I got some stew on the stove and a panful of corn bread. Your horses need feedin'?"

"You still got the pasture out back?"

"Yep, sure do. Grass is up fine, and there's water, too. Help yourselves."

Amos went back inside to lay out lunch, and Halliday and Laura rode past the cabin, up a short hill and out into a meadow where the grass was up knee high. They climbed down stiff-legged, pulled off saddles, blankets, saddlebags, and bridles, then pulled water out of the well to fill the cistern standing beside it. They hobbled back to the cabin. Inside, it was dim and cool. Amos had laid out tin plates on the table and set a Dutch oven and ladle amongst them. He was piling cubes of cornbread onto a platter when they came through the door. He turned to Laura.

"You can wash up there at the sink if you want to," he said, and nodded towards a hollowed out half of a tree trunk fitted with a cast-iron hand pump set against the wall. Laura crossed to it, pumped water into her cupped palm, and lathered up with a big bar of yellowed soap set beside the pump. Halliday joined her and when they had scrubbed and rinsed both returned to the table. Amos hadn't waited for them, was dipping chunks of cornbread into the stew heaped on his plate. Laura ladled stew onto hers, and lifted her eyes to Amos.

"Mr., um, Amos, I don't think I've ever smelled anything quite so good. What's in it?"

He smiled, seemed pleased at the asking. "Last of the carrots and potatoes. Some deer meat and some squirrel and some rabbit. Couple of wild onions. Bacon drippings and salt. It's a tad strong in the mouth. I like to cut it with a bite of cornbread."

Laura dug in, and found that Amos was right. She needed the bland cornbread to offset the meat's musk and the bitter onions. The hunger in her belly soon overcame any misgivings of taste, and when she found herself mashing cornbread into the last of the gravy to clean up every bit, she realized Amos's cooking was delicious. She looked up for seconds and found Halliday and Amos grinning at her.

Amos chuckled. "Reckon Miss Halliday'll have you turned into a country girl soon enough." He winced as Halliday poked him with her fork, and changed the subject. "You gals mind if I smoke? I usually take some tobacco after lunch, do a little reading while the food settles."

The women shook their heads to show that they didn't mind.

Halliday, in fact, withdrew a pouch and a packet of rolling papers from her hip pocket. She filled a paper from the pouch, rolled it with precision, like a graceful machine, and sealed it. She offered the cigarette to Laura, who declined. Meanwhile, Amos took an ancient, scarred and beat up Meerschaum pipe out of his hip pocket, opened a wooden box that sat in the middle of the table, pulled out a ragged shred of tobacco, and stuffed it into the pipe. A tin tube sat next to the tobacco box, filled neatly with wooden matches stood on end, heads up. Amos and Halliday each struck one and lit up.

Amos sniffed the air. "Puts me in mind of a box of licorice drops."

Halliday smiled, exhaling. "You'll have to go to town for those, Amos."

When Amos had his pipe going he stood and walked across the room to a shelf nailed on the wall that held two books, a King James Bible and a threadbare, dog-eared copy of The Adventures of Sherlock Holmes. He picked up the Holmes and settled himself into a chair underneath the bookshelf. He opened the book to a random page and began to read, puffing slowly at the pipe.

"Which is your favorite case, Amos?" Laura asked.

Amos looked up. "Oh, it's got to be The Speckled Band. The first time I read that one, I hadn't got a clue how a man could be murdered all shut up in a room like that. Mr. Doyle was a fiendish clever man to have worked out all those puzzles. You got a favorite, Miss van Duyn?"

"Yes, I like A Study in Scarlet. I was intrigued by its premise. A secret society established in some out-of-the-way place, yet with a reach that went right around the world. I would hardly have thought that possible."

Amos sat up, was going to say something, but Halliday headed him off. "Not a word, Amos."

He waved her away and went back to his book. Laura's eyes went mischievous again. Halliday finished her cigarette while Laura filled their canteens at the sink. Amos's chin had sunk onto his chest, and his pipe had gone cold, the result of neglect. He snored, not loudly, but with persistence. Halliday brought their dishes over to the sink. She motioned for Laura to follow and they tiptoed out onto the porch. The dog's tail wagged idly, and his eyes stayed closed.

"I'll do the dishes if you get the horses," Halliday offered.

Laura walked up the hill to the pasture. The horses dozed in the shade at the edge of the grass; Laura walked right up to them. They stood, docile, while she fitted the bridles and saddles, and trailed obediently behind her as she led them by the reins down to the cabin. Halliday waited for her on the porch. As Laura came alongside the cabin, Amos emerged carrying several small bundles tightly wrapped in cotton cloth and bound with twine. "Here's your supper, Miss van Duyn," he said, and began to stuff the bundles into the saddlebags. Halliday came out, and she and Laura climbed onto the horses. Amos stood back and glanced up at the sky through the trees.

"I feel there'll be a storm this afternoon. It'll cool things down mightily, but you all are going to get wet. How far you aim to get tonight? Ain't no shelter between here and Abel Grissom's place yonder, and that's a fair thirty miles. Abel ain't home, neither, got sent out..." he glanced quickly at Halliday, "...uh, to run some errands."

Halliday climbed onto her horse and looked down at Amos. "We'll manage. I know this country well enough. You'd best worry about who's right outside your house and the questions they're asking rather than where we're spending the night."

Amos hung his head. "Yes'm, I reckon I will. Didn't mean no offense."

Halliday reached down and patted him on the shoulder. "Don't give it a second thought, Amos. I never knew a truer man, and I want to thank you for the hospitality you offered us, and the fine table you set. Here's a little something for your trouble." She dug into her pocket for Reuben's cash, stripped off a twenty dollar bill, and handed it over to him. Amos broke into a wide grin.

"Why thank you. I've been saving up for a used Model A Ford they got on the lot down in Raleigh. I reckon this'll put me right over the top. I'll take my leave of you now, and go dig up my coffee can." He turned to Laura. "It's been a pleasure meeting you Miss. Will you come back sometime? We can have a little talk about A.C. Doyle."

"The pleasure was all mine, Amos, and thank you for the wonderful lunch. I will look forward to seeing you again."

Amos set off up the hill behind the house, whistling. Laura turned her horse after Halliday's, grimacing as her sore thigh muscles protested. "Serves you right," Halliday remarked, "for trying to weasel old Amos."

Laura glared. "Since it was my fault, I hope you weren't hard on him."

"Didn't even come up," Halliday replied, and turned her horse back to the road. "Come on, we've got a long way to go."

Halliday pushed the pace all afternoon, never slowing below a bone-shaking trot and frequently kicking the horses into a full gallop. The road began a slow, steady climb upward out of the coastal plain and onto the Piedmont plateau, and it grew less straight, winding around hills and up twisting canyons. The sky gradually filled with clouds, foreshadowing the storm Amos had predicted. Although the air remained hot and heavy, not having the sun on their backs brought a little relief. Laura began to hear thunder grumbling in the distance and watched the sky expectantly, hoping for a cooling rain. It finally came late in the afternoon. One minute the air was still. The next a fierce breeze kicked up carrying a few fat raindrops that thickened quickly into a steady deluge. Halliday slowed the horses to a walk and let them have their heads and they did not stray from the road. Laura wrapped her reins around the saddle horn, spread her arms, and tilted her face to the sky. The lashing, icy water raised goose bumps along her skin, but she reveled nonetheless in her release from the oppressive heat. The horse jumped at a burst of nearby thunder. Laura grabbed madly at the saddle horn to avoid being thrown. She sheepishly picked up the reins again and rode after Halliday.

The storm's main outburst passed over them within fifteen minutes, but the rain continued more slowly for another half-hour before drizzling away. Behind the storm came cooler, drier air. Laura would have taken a serious chill had not Halliday again galloped off up the road. The exertion warmed Laura up, and the rushing air dried her clothes.

Early in the evening they passed a dirt track leading off the road. Halliday waved at it. "Abel Grissom's place. We've made good time, but there's more than an hour of daylight left. We'll keep riding for a while."

Laura's heart sank at the prospect of another hour in the saddle, but made no show of her disappointment for Halliday, who, in any case, galloped away without looking back. That last hour was the most grueling that Laura had ever endured. Her legs ached, her back ached, her head ached, her stomach ached. Exhaustion covered her in a numbing cloud, which might have brought relief but for her need to stay awake lest she fall off the horse. Her head continually dropped to her chest as she drowsed, to jolt her awake and renew the fierce pain. Halliday grew impatient at having to turn constantly to nudge her horse into a trot. She persisted through the hour, but covered only a few more miles. Finally, she gave up and turned off the road into a grove of trees. Laura followed, fending off low-hanging limbs that showered her neck with bits of dried bark and grit that worked their way inside her shirt where they stuck and scratched and itched. The women emerged after a few minutes into a meadow, and Halliday pulled up and dropped to the ground. Laura eased one leg over the saddle horn and slid gingerly into the grass. She took one step and crumpled to the ground, her legs trembling, all their strength gone.

"Get up," Halliday commanded, "you've got to get that saddle off."

Laura glared, but grabbed the stirrup hanging next to her head and hauled herself to her feet. She got the cinch strap undone and the saddle off.

"Where shall I put it?"

"Back under the trees. It's less damp there. And hang your blanket over a tree branch so it'll dry out some. More comfortable to sleep on."

After Laura had stowed the gear, she rejoined Halliday who sat at the edge of the meadow, leaning against a tree. Halliday had pulled Amos's bundles out of the saddlebags. She began to open them.

"It's not the 21 Club," she said, "but it's better than going hungry."

There were biscuits, a little stale, spread with honey, several handfuls of withered apples and carrots, and a large chunk of smoked ham, enough of everything that, together with a piece of jerky and a few apricots, Laura's hunger was fully sated. She finished with a long pull at her canteen, and then sank back against the tree. The muscles in her legs twitched and jumped, but the pain had receded now that they were not subject to the constant jarring of a moving horse. She closed her eyes, and immediately fell asleep. She saw a quantity of billowing smoke and as she walked toward it in her dream, Halliday's face loomed and called to her. She felt a sharp poke in her side, and awoke to find Halliday jabbing at her with her finger, telling her there was toilet paper in the saddlebag if she needed it during the night, and to get to bed. Laura stood and pulled her blanket off of its branch and spread it neatly on the ground. She sat and pulled off her boots and socks and pants. She rolled back onto the blanket, ignoring the strong smell of horse, and fell asleep.

CHAPTER 21
IN THE MOUNTAINS

Dawn's light, bird songs, and a morning chill drew Laura gradually awake. She opened her eyes and watched the sky as it brightened, turning from gray to pink to blue. She stretched, her arms, then her legs, and gave a sharp cry that brought Halliday instantly alert and reaching for the shotgun.

"What's wrong?"

Laura groaned, "My legs, I didn't think anything could hurt so much."

"You've just got to massage it out. I aim to make fifty miles today, and I can't do that if I have to turn around every five minutes to hurry you along."

Halliday stood, hung a saddlebag over her shoulders, and walked away across the meadow to disappear into the trees on the other side. When she returned, Laura was standing, gingerly bending her legs.

"How do they feel?"

"Better, but...there's something else..." Her faced reddened.

"Well?"

"It's my time...of the month."

Halliday dug into her saddlebag. "Here, ever use these?" She handed Laura a flat gray box with *Wix* in raised script written across the top.

Laura accepted the box gratefully. "Thank you."

Halliday grinned. "About the only part of civilization I like. I brought about a year's supply along." She waved across the meadow.

"There's a creek over there, you can wash up. Got cramps?"

"No, I don't always get them."

"Well ask if they come. I have some herbs I picked up in Brazil, they work wonders."

Laura went looking for the creek. When she returned, they breakfasted on the last of the jerky and apricots, with biscuits left over from Amos, saddled the horses, and set off.

After that second day out of Raleigh (they made their fifty miles, Laura's protests notwithstanding), Halliday slackened their pace. For ten more days, they rode easy over back roads and trails, a network that seemed to Laura purposefully constructed to lie out of the mainstream, hidden from the ordinary flow of travel and commerce. The land gradually folded itself into hills, and finally, into rounded mountains cloaked in dark forests of pine, oak, and hickory, interrupted by plunging gorges and rising, granite outcrops.

The women foraged for food, Halliday taking a rabbit or brace of quail with the shotgun and pointing out to Laura the plants that bore roots and tubers for roasting, puckery wood sorrel, and the mushrooms they could safely eat. They caught fish off the line Halliday had coiled in her saddlebag. Yet their wild harvests were not always sufficient. Many times they would have gone hungry had not the people of the land welcomed them into their homes. Laura quickly grew accustomed to their rough ways and homely food, and in that remote country their companionship and conversation gave her welcome respite from the trail's monotony.

Halliday held unerringly toward her destination. Never did she hesitate over which fork in the trail to take. When they felt overwhelmed by accumulated sweat and grime, she found a deep pool for bathing. When the skies threatened a downpour, she turned to a nearby sheltering cliff or deep fissure in the rock. If she came onto a lush meadow, she would stop for the day even if it was early, so the horses could eat their fill and rest. She and Laura would hunt up some food, gather firewood, and doze in the shade. It seemed to Laura that the bracing, clean air and the isolation were a tonic for Halliday, a restorative. She eased up and relaxed, smoked less, laughed more, lost a caged-in feeling that had seemed to haunt her in the city.

For a couple of days, Laura tried to glean clues from her, details of her life or where they were going, but after the ironworks slip up,

Halliday would not be drawn out, not even to give her full name. Bored without conversation, Laura sought a different tack. Noting Halliday's knowledge of the land, she asked every question she could think of regarding geography, plants and animals, weather, history -- all subjects for which Halliday had ready answers and which she never tired of relating. One day, as the horses ambled up a long, sun-dappled slope, Laura asked about a particular bird call.

"That is a pine warbler," Halliday replied and mimicked its trill.

"You're good at that. Not just birds."

"It's a convenient talent. My voice is often the only disguise I need."

"Why do you need to disguise yourself?"

Halliday put her off. "You've seen what I do. It's just necessary."

"Do you let it down for anyone?"

Halliday rode on a while, brushing away low-hanging branches. "Evelyn," she said, "Evelyn Frances Halliday."

Laura, laughing, said, "What a grand name."

Halliday smiled back, quiet, reflecting. "It was the only grand thing my mother could give me."

Laura's laughter evaporated. "I'm sorry, I didn't mean to make fun."

Halliday waved aside her concern. "You didn't know."

"Will you tell me about her?"

Again with that quiet smile, she said, "OK."

Her mother had been a maid in a rich household, taken by the master and turned out, penniless, by the mistress. She bore her daughter, a strong, healthy child, in a mission house, and gave her that grand name. They survived together in an unrelenting world, their only goal, not to die.

"She was good at surviving. She nearly always could find food or shelter. Our life had vexations and uncertainty, but considering our circumstances, it wasn't utterly bleak."

"Vexations and uncertainty! You almost make it sound pleasant."

"Some of it was pleasant. Yes, we went hungry, and we were frequently cold and uncomfortable, but there were compensations. Summertime. My mother loved me, she was loyal, she was like a tiger if anyone threatened me. And we were free, we had no ties to governments or families or history. Our life was limited, but we could make of it what we chose."

"But surely you would have been better off with a home and at school."

"Perhaps. I can never know, so I see no reason to speculate. My life still has vexations and uncertainty, the very things most people avoid. But it suits me. I am satisfied that it is the best I could make it." She turned to Laura. "If I had lived a different life, you and I would not be here together, and I think in the end that will be more valuable than any schooling might have been."

Laura was stunned to find tears starting in her eyes. To calm herself, she turned the conversation. "Where is your mother now?"

"I don't know. She died when I was 12, of the flu, and she was placed in a pauper's grave. They would not let me come to her burial."

"There must be records, her name must have been noted."

"I never knew it. Just that it wasn't Evelyn or Frances or Halliday."

"She didn't tell you her name?"

"Mother was all I needed."

"But you were only twelve, still a child. How did you survive?"

"I was well-prepared, I would have been fine on my own, I think, but I was lucky, a circus took me in when she died." She smiled at the memory. "Although maybe the luck was in having my mother. She read the papers. She knew many people were dying. As she grew ill, we followed that circus. She set us up right next to it the night she died. She made me promise to find the ringmaster when she was gone. I did, and he did not seem surprised to see me."

"Still, you must have been devastated."

"I missed her terribly. I cried myself to sleep for months. But I loved the circus. I was taught magic and to tumble. I had a pretty costume and applause every day. And as I grew older and able to reflect on her death, I began to understand sorrow, what it meant to me. I gained strength from it, it was like the heat that tempers steel. When, inevitably, other misfortunes came, I could endure them."

"You make it sound like everyone should feel a loved one's death."

"Everyone does."

Laura made a startled cry of wonder.

"I do understand," Halliday responded, "I don't believe that, if only because my mother was cheated out of a long and happy life.

And of course, I still miss her every day. I've seen many people beat down by tragedy. They succumb to addiction or cruelty, to madness. I don't wish it on anyone. But my life, who I am, is made up of everything I have experienced, even her death and the sorrow I feel because of it. They are both fully part of the legacy she left me, to be free, to be self-reliant, to be resilient. To deny my loss would dishonor her and her legacy." She pulled up her horse. "I know it's early yet, but this looks like a comfortable spot. Let's make camp."

***

That was their last full day on the trail. In the evening, the two women sat before a small fire, letting supper settle, remarking on the night's sounds and the stretch of nice weather they'd had, no rain for three days. Halliday pulled Reuben's pint, still half-full, out of her hip pocket, unscrewed the cap and, handing it to Laura, said, "Let's have a little celebration."

"Of what?"

"Tomorrow we'll ride up this mountain and be there."

Laura sipped at the bottle. "It's funny, I had a home and I went to school, and here I seem to be ready to throw all that out and any advantage it might have given me to become like you."

Halliday pulled a glowing twig from the fire and squinted through the smoke as she lit her cigarette. "Would it be a fair trade?"

"I don't know. I'll have to see it first." She stood. "We need firewood. I see you got your boots off awfully fast tonight. I can take a hint."

Halliday grinned. "I saw a bunch of windfallen oak down the hill."

Laura walked out of the illuminated circle, paused a moment to let her eyes adjust to the moonlit night, and then wandered away. She stooped occasionally to gather a piece of wood. She went along for a half an hour or so, not picking a particular path, until she found herself back at the foot of the hill gazing up at the campfire. She considered those she would leave behind, her mother and father, Gertrude and Detective Hardy, Mr. Hirsch, and her boys. They would have no choice but to go on. Her parents were assured of her safety, if she could trust Halliday, and she realized that was no longer a question. The Hardys she wondered about, had she even made an impression on them? Certainly she had, but how deep had it gone, how long would it last? Gertrude had become a friend, but Gertrude was practical, she dealt with what was before her. She decided for herself what was true. She would accommodate, with aplomb, Laura's absence.

The detective was a harder read. He had mostly provoked her and she him; he might go as far as saying good riddance, but she didn't think so. He might, perhaps, treat her absence as a puzzle, something to figure out. If Halliday was right about his career, she almost hoped that's what he would do, something to keep him busy. Mr. Hirsch, well, she'd run out on him just as he put his neck out for her, a debt she vowed she'd make up to him. And her boys? She felt sorriest about them. She could see them losing direction and once again congregating on stoops and street corners with nothing to do. She worried about boys with nothing to do.

She lifted her eyes to the forest's dark canopy and the high ridge looming behind it, and considered New York, the place she used to live, tall and proud, busy and familiar. She lowered her gaze back to the campfire and the horses, a blanket to stretch out on and a companion to share small talk with as she fell asleep, a blaze of stars to keep her company all night. She would miss New York, but there would be compensations.

She climbed back to the camp and dumped her armful of wood by the fire. She sat, took off her boots, and lay back on the blanket. Halliday wished her a good night.

"Sleep tight," Laura replied, "See you in the morning."

CHAPTER 22
THE LOST VALLEY

The next morning, Laura and Halliday climbed the mountain. Laura could see, running along the ridge that topped it, a massive stone face. As they climbed, the cliff loomed until it seemed to become the whole world. At its foot, Halliday turned off the trail to ride alongside, picking her way over the talus gathered at its base. Laura could not make out a path, but Halliday seemed to have a specific destination in mind. They rode for more than a mile, with the cliff ever towering. They came, at last, to a cleft. Halliday got off her horse, took the reins, and led it down the cleft. Laura did the same and followed after. The cleft narrowed as they went and the sheer walls seemed to close above them, blotting out the light and the sun's heat. Ferns and mosses carpeted the stone. An occasional drop of water landed on Laura's neck. The smell of the earth rose around them. The mountain eventually closed over the fissure, leaving a passage through the rock.

"It's going to get tight in a minute. I hope it won't bother you. It doesn't last long."

"No, I'll be fine. What about the horses?"

"They live up here. They're used to it, they've been trained."

Only a dim light illuminated the cave, and that for only fifty feet or so. Without the heat outside, the air was cool and clammy. The walls quickly closed in around Laura. In the darkness, she put up a hand to run it along the rock, anticipating skull-cracking projections.

They went on through a timeless void, slow and steady, picking their way through blackness, feeling along the smooth floor for outcrops that might trip them up. The walls soon fell away to an arm-spanning distance. Sometimes water trickled underfoot. They crossed patches of loose stone. No sound came except for their footfalls, their beating hearts, and, eventually, a rumble from Laura's stomach, emptied of its breakfast. She wiped away the dampness from her forehead and realized she could see her pale hand glimmering. Looking down, she saw rocks silhouetted on the floor, and then, before her, a triangular slice of blue sky. They passed from the cave trailing their horses into the country beyond.

They stood in the midst of a wooded slope at the bottom of a draw that ran down between two faces of bare stone. Laura glimpsed through that narrow gap a strip of green and open land rising in the hazy distance to a high, forested ridge.

"Yo, Eve. Eve Halliday."

The women turned and spied a young Negro man, maybe 20 years old, standing on an outcrop that capped the cave's entrance. He wore a rifle slung over his shoulder by a strap that ran from barrel to stock.

"Good morning, Smith. Were you waiting for us?"

"I been out on the ridge, saw you coming up the mountain."

"Anything else to see?"

"Not this morning." He nodded at Laura. "Who's your friend?"

"My name is Laura. Laura van Duyn."

Smith tipped his floppy hat. "Pleased to meet you."

"And you, too, Mr. Smith."

"Ain't no mister. Just Smith."

"Well, Smith, pleased to meet you, too."

"Would you dance with me tonight?" Smith was from New Orleans.

Laura blushed and Eve laughed. "Why Smith, you've gone and embarrassed her."

"I didn't mean it. I just like her bones. She could cut a rug."

Eve looked Laura up and down. "Yes, Smith, I believe you're right. Ask her at supper. Maybe she'll say yes."

"All right, Eve, I will." He tipped his hat again and turned to climb the hill.

The women mounted their horses and nudged them into a walk. The path led steadily down and the draw gradually widened so that Laura began to see more of the valley into which they were descending. It wasn't much, just a slip of a valley, an aerie in the mountains, high and alone. Its slopes were covered in an open forest of hardwoods and pines with a thick duff and chunks of rock stuck up out of it and ending in a bottomland as big, Laura estimated, as Central Park. She saw it contained a settlement clustered at the edge of a pond, a motley collection of portable, ad hoc shelters. Laura was astonished to see among them a teepee, and what the National Geographic called a yurt. Most of the rest were variations on tents, although there were a few rudimentary structures, lean-tos and huts, and three more substantial buildings, one of them some kind of factory, it seemed to Laura, given its chimney. Another was small enough to be a house, perched back from the edge of the pond opposite the factory. Laura could not discern the function of the third from its look. A straightened and squared water course, a canal, emptied into the pond, which extended down the valley and gave way eventually to marshlands, above which flocks of birds wheeled and dove.

Around the edges of the settlement, they rode through plowed or dug up plots of land lush with vegetables. Laura recognized tomatoes, pumpkins just starting to set, cucumbers and zucchini, an assortment of cabbages. One patch was piquant with garlic, leeks, ramps, and onions, and the next one aromatic with herbs. Beanpoles stretched everywhere. Flocks of chickens ran loose in and around the legs of grazing livestock – horses, donkeys, and sheep.

There were two roads. One ran the valley's length until it got too marshy to continue. The other, at a right angle, went out to the opposite edge of the valley where a mineworks, like a blood-red scar on the land, climbed to the top of the ridge.

They passed women at work in the gardens, scrubbing laundry, tending flocks, kneading dough, picking blackberries from masses of vines strung up on a network of poles. A passel of children whooped and ran through them, playing at some game, a combination of tag and hide-and-go-seek.

A pen built on a band of fallow ground that separated the gardens from the settlement held a half dozen pigs nearly submerged against the day's heat in a pit of mud. Women trooped around it hauling water from the pond. Some of them balanced two buckets off the ends of yokes, bearing them across their sturdy shoulders; another group, dark-skinned, with graceful long necks carried buckets on their heads in no apparent discomfort, chattering and laughing as they walked. Laura noticed there was segregation among the groups, by race Laura saw, and also by language, she guessed, because even groups with similar coloring kept apart. She asked why they didn't plant closer to water and their homes.

"They used to and used the soil up, planted it too many times. The soil is still good up there."

"Where are the men?"

"Off doing man things." Eve grinned. "Posting lookouts, hunting and fishing. Running the mine and the steelworks."

They ended up at the house. It had the aspect of a chalet, built of stout logs and with wide eaves. They tied their horses to a crossbar. Eve led Laura under an arbor entwined with wild roses and down a flagstone walk to the front door. Through it, Laura saw that the house was set into the ground.

"Watch your step." Eve pointed out a short flight of stairs. She walked from window to window, reaching up to fold back shutters and throw open the casements, letting in the sun to reveal a single, neatly kept room. Laura was reminded of the nun's quarters from her childhood. She took a tentative breath and smiled, for there it was, anise, jasmine, tobacco, something not quite pine.

The floor was laid with rough-hewn wood planks. The walls were glazed to ground level with a dark-red clay, the same color as the road and the mine scar. Log walls continued upward another four feet and held the deep-set windows. The furniture -- a table, a few chairs, and a dresser -- was likewise of wood, but sanded smooth and varnished. A wide low bed covered by a multicolored quilt stood out from the wall midway along. A wood-fired clay oven sat in a corner at the back of the cabin. Next to it, a trestle, running the cabin's width held a cast-iron basin painted a cheerful yellow. An iron pipe stoppered with a wood plug stuck out a few inches from the wall above the basin. Several oil lamps hung from hooks the length of the ceiling.

Eve pulled out clean clothes from the dresser and gave them to Laura. "These should fit. You can bathe in the pond if you like. I'm going to stake out the horses."

Laura welcomed a dip in the pond. Eve had returned by the time she'd got back to the house and changed. Eve went for her own bath. Afterward, she took Laura sightseeing. The valley floor was not uniformly flat. They climbed to the top of a hill that offered a panorama across the gardens and animals and down to the little village.

"It was swampy. The people who found it drained this northern end. Many of these hills are built from the soil they excavated."

"Who were they?"

"Pacifists, descendants of refugees from the Thirty Years War. They refused to fight the British, so your Congress confiscated their farms. They came west in search of land, and this was where they ended."

"And the mine and steelworks?"

"Started after your civil war. At first, just a couple of blast furnaces to refine the ore. They made iron nails and horseshoes. Then they built a small Bessemer convertor and began to make steel."

Laura gazed over the valley. "And who are these people?"

"They are refugees, too, from persecution, war, poverty."

"Do they all get along?"

"The children do. Everyone else mostly does. We get an occasional fanatic in here trying to stir up trouble or a freeloader. Given how these people have lived, they're wary of power, so the fanatics don't gain any traction and leave frustrated. Freeloaders are pretty quickly isolated from the food supply by general consensus, and they either learn to work or they leave, too. Of course, there's always thievery, that's human nature, and sometimes a man will get his hackles up and start a fight."

"Does the thievery go unpunished?"

"Depends on how greedy the thief is. If it's minor, it's tolerated, they've all done it at some point to survive, and even though nobody goes hungry up here if they pull their share of the work, they understand habits don't break easily. If it's worse, well you saw they're divided up. As a point of honor, the family, the clan or tribe, whoever the thief is with does its own policing. Even though there's not a lot of mixing, they're all hungry for peace and tranquility after the turmoil they've come through, and on a basic level, their traditions, their ethics, their beliefs are similar. Almost all of them have been peasants, farmers, or small landholders. They've made do, got by, done what had to be done. They're close knit, they like stability, they like life to be lived as it has always been lived. Here, they live as they wish, with no governments, no arbitrary laws, no ruling classes. So they keep the peace as best they can and they make room for what differences do exist, in worship or custom, because they know if they don't, their lives will be in turmoil again."

Eve guided Laura down among the gardens and back into the village. When they met people, Eve presented her. Eve usually knew enough of their language to make an introduction. The people would smile and bow or offer a handshake and go back to their work. As they went among the dwellings, Laura once again marveled at the variety and ingenuity inherent in the buildings' construction. They came abreast of a lean-to. Even to Laura's eyes, it looked carelessly made, some sticks shoved crooked into the ground and some branches with dried leaves and needles scattered over the roof's cross members. A woman sat in front of it, absorbed in a thick book. She seemed about forty and thin, with severely short brown hair and intense, pale blue eyes in a narrow face. She looked up as they approached and addressed Eve in French, which Laura also spoke.

"This is your new friend, your acquaintance from Park Avenue?"

"I didn't live on Park Avenue."

"I might have known you would speak French. All the rich girls do. I hope you appreciate the kindness you are being shown. Given what you have done, you do not deserve it."

"What have I done?"

"You blew it all up. We could have defended ourselves with those guns, now there is going to be a terrible war and thousands will die because they do not have them."

Eve interrupted. "Nonsense, Dominique. That was only one shipment. There is time to send more."

"I didn't know," Laura protested, "and I had been shot, two men were dead, and my friend held hostage. Those guns might have been for Hitler himself. If I had known your plans, I would have acted differently. Still, I'm sorry, and I will do what I can to make up for it."

Dominique's eyes flashed. "You have much to learn. You are naïve. I insist, Evelyn, that you allow me to teach her."

"It's not up to me, Dominique. It's up to her."

"I don't want to be naïve, Dominique, so yes, you may teach me."

"Very well." Dominique returned to her book.

Out of earshot, Laura asked, "Is she a fanatic?"

"No, just a little rigid," Eve replied, "but she has a kind soul, and a deep concern."

Eve walked them around the pond to the steelworks. Along the way, they passed the tent Smith had built on a perfectly flat site he'd carved out of the slope. Deep channels ran around its circumference, meant to draw water away. It was made of white canvas, tight as a drumhead.

"He painted it with fish oil to make it impervious to water."

The front flap had been thrown back over the roof. Its frame stood revealed, tree limbs sunk into the ground, each one selected and placed where it would best complement its companions and lashed together with strips of cured hide. Inside, a few blankets lay neatly folded on top of a pallet built up from thick layers of felt. A pine bookshelf held a dozen books. A stone sill fronted the tent, tall enough to be a comfortable place to sit in the sun.

At the steelworks, Eve pressed up on an intricate latch, shouldered the door open, and waved Laura inside. A hissing and clanging racket assaulted Laura, and a hot, humid cloud of dust and steam enveloped her.

Ahead, a panorama: As did Eve's house, the building sat several feet in the ground. Daylight passed in and vapors out through tilted iron panels set in the walls. A wide, wooden platform skirted the room, whose far side Laura could just make out through the dim, hazy air. Steps descended from the platform to a pounded dirt floor. Eve described the equipment. The blast furnaces, cool now, stood to one side, brick vessels encased in iron sheaths with great bellows attached to them. Iron ore and refined coal went into the top while men operated the bellows, the blast of air heating the materials inside to 1,700 degrees. Then the liquid iron was let hissing out of drains in their bottoms into molds of sand. Beside the furnaces, in a large cleared space in the middle of the floor, stood an ovate steel vessel, twice Laura's height, spewing gouts of bluish flame.

A team of men, shirtless and shining, pushed at a horizontal turnstile set a dozen yards behind the vessel. A cable ran from the turnstile, up through a series of pulleys and back down to fasten onto the vessel near its base. As the turnstile went around, the vessel tilted on two massive trunnions to spill its molten contents hissing and sparking into a clay-lined, iron pot mounted on a rail cart. When they had emptied the vessel, the men pushed the cart along a row of molds, stopping at each one to tip the pot and fill it.

Eve led Laura down the steps to a boardwalk. As they crossed the factory, boys dodged around them pushing wheelbarrows filled with ore or lumps of coal. Past a thick door at the far end the noise dropped and the air cooled. There, workers at benches more precisely finished the parts and assembled them into implements or sculpted products from scratch out of steel ingots. Laura recognized plows, gun barrels, tools, and horseshoes.

Back outside, Eve said, "I'm starved. We'll eat at the hall tonight." She sat down on the grass and took her boots and socks off. "My feet are ready to breathe. You should try it," and so Laura did the same. They set out barefoot through the balmy evening air towards the hall, the third building, which Laura had been unable to place.

She marveled at the surrounding throng. Never before had she considered her city clothing, how solemn and confining it was. The clothes these people wore flowed and billowed in colors and decoration that spanned the rainbow. There were also, she thought, as many shades of skin and behavior. Some nearly bounded with confidence, but others walked at the fringes, heads hanging, glancing nervously at the crowd.

In the dining hall, everyone sat together at long tables passing platters and trays of food around. Some conversed together, often with halting attempts at another language and many hand gestures. Others kept to themselves, hunched over, furtively filling their plates, and passing the rest along without a word.

Food began coming past, and Laura eagerly dug in. It was plain food, boiled, baked, or raw. There was a corn and bean succotash with vinegar and onions. There was dried fruit, there was bread and honey. There were boiled eggs, ham, and bacon and some roasted chicken. Beer and root beer, or iced tea with honey and mint. Some tastes were new for Laura, tomatoes mixed with vinegar and onions and apples and cardamom and cumin, okra and peanuts in a spicy brown stew. She ate until her tummy stretched.

Eve stood. "Time to work off that third helping. Give us a hand."

They and the other women cleared the tables and washed the dishes at a split log sink that ran nearly the length of the hall. The water was only cold, but there was little grease, so the dishes cleaned up well. By the time they were done, the men had pulled the tables aside, leaving a wide space down the middle. Laura noticed for the first time a small stage at the far end of the room. A man sat on a chair, an old black man, a guitar settled gently across his thigh.

Eve bent over towards Laura. "I said there's not a lot of mixing here except, I forgot to say, when there's food or music."

The bluesman bent his head to the guitar's sound hole, plucked the strings with the thumb and forefinger of his right hand as their left-hand counterparts twisted the tuning pegs. He raised his head satisfied, stretched his fingers, and began to play, a slow picked rhythm and tune, heavy in the bass, and sang, and he sounded like smoke, thirst, and never-ending sorrow.

Woke up this morning,
you were so far away.
Woke up this morning
and you were so far away.
The sun kept on rising,
but it ain't my light of day.

That man took my children,
sold them way off down the road.
That white man took my children,
sold them way off down the road.
The sun shines down upon me,
But my heart is achin' cold.

My wife, she caught a fever,
shook and shivered all night long.
My wife, she caught a fever,
shook and shivered all night long.
When the sun came up this morning,
She was cold and dead and gone.

Someday I'll get to Heaven,
I'll find all my people there.
Someday I'll get to Heaven,
I'll find all my people there.
The Son up in Heaven,
take away my woe and care.

Woke up this morning,
you were so far away.
Woke up this morning
and you were so far away.
The sun kept on rising,
but it ain't my light of day.

A man, to Laura's eyes a Jew, one of those who had kept himself apart at dinner, stepped shyly onto the stage, dressed in skullcap, baggy black trousers, and a voluminous black coat from which he drew a battered clarinet. Putting it to his lips, he began to blow a sinuous melody, threading mournfully through the open spaces in the guitar's rhythm. As he played, tears fell across his cheeks, and trickled into his beard. The singer put down his guitar, stood, and wrapped the clarinet player in his big arms, holding him tightly until the man subsided. Then he took him by his shoulders, held him at arm's length, and smiled.

"Life's not all sadness and sorrow, my friend. Let's hear you pull a happy tune out of that old licorice stick."

He turned to peer at the crowd.

"Hey, Esteban," he called, "where are you, man, bring that guitarron on up here."

A black-haired, brown-skinned man in white cotton and rope sandals stepped up with an enormous, fat guitar hanging by a strap around his neck. He tilted it to face upwards and thumped out a fast rhythm, alternating major triads based on tonic and fifth. A smaller man jumped out of the crowd with a Spanish guitar and energetically strummed along. The bluesman pulled the polished neck of an old wine bottle from his trousers pocket and ran it up and down his guitar in merry accompaniment. The clarinet player riffed in counterpoint to the bass. The Spanish guitarist sang, a yelping, cackling, loping melody in Mexican, and a woman in polychrome skirt and white petticoats leaped from the crowd to dance and beat a tattoo on her tambourine. Soon the floor was full of swirling couples and spinning children, while a dog stood yapping at the door.

The music and dancing ran long into the night. Musicians came and went. Laura saw a fiddler, a trumpeter, a washboard and harmonica player, an African woman in a bandana with a big box of dried gourds, rattles, and shakers, and a man with a pencil-thin moustache playing a conga drum. There were any number of wind and stringed instruments she couldn't even name, although she knew the oboe and guessed, from the description she'd had of it once, what the dulcimer was. There were too many singers to count. Laura heard jigs and reels, horas, polkas and waltzes, even made-up-as-you-went-along pieces. Those who didn't play danced, and snacked on popcorn, as they quaffed beer and iced tea. During one particularly lively stretch, Laura leaned over to Eve.

"I believe I could jitterbug to this."

As if he had been there all along, Smith was at her elbow.

"Here's your chance, Miss van Duyn. Let's go," and he drew her protesting but smiling onto the floor where they twirled and leaped until Laura lost her breath. He was the best dancer she'd ever had, much better than she was, but he was so good, he made her look good, too, and even when she begged exhaustion and returned to her seat, still she sat flushed and smiling, waving her hand to cool herself down. Smith went on to find someone who could keep up with him.

CHAPTER 23
LAURA WAKES

Laura's education began. Smith taught her to dance, to build a shelter, and to shoot. A poet out of Siberia gave her lessons in Russian. A wisp-chinned, flat-hatted Korean gentleman taught her how to throw a man. A Sufi from Riyadh taught her to truly ride. Dominique, the former French nun, lectured on political economics. A little Cockney girl in ragged clothes showed her how to pick pockets. A Hindu fakir put her heels behind her knees and told her to breathe and to think only of breathing. A courtly gentleman in a white suit offered her hashish, which she declined, but she finally knew that scent, not quite pine. A Cherokee woman took her into the woods for a week with nothing but the clothes they wore. During their sojourn, she taught Laura to forage and explained to her the utility of free markets, viz., "When the government passed the Prohibition, I built myself a still back in the woods and sold some whiskey to my neighbors off the reservation. They always said I made the best whiskey. Even the sheriff liked a taste now and then. But they repealed the Prohibition. The sheriff come around, busted up my still, said he was sorry but the liquor companies told the government they didn't want no competition. Damn government ought to mind its business, let the poor people feed their children."

A slave, long escaped from Brazil and so wizened with age Laura was unsure whether a man or woman spoke, said, "If you learn never to want anything but only take what comes, you will never be poor. That is what scares the rich men in their banks and factories, that everyone will find out and never shop at their stores or eat at their restaurants, or buy insurance policies or talk on telephones, and then they will not be rich anymore or powerful. They will be just like everyone else. That is why they put pretty pictures in their magazines and clever songs on their radio shows so that we will think we never have enough."

Besides learning, there was work -- to put food by, chop firewood, care for the livestock, cook, clean, hunt, and fish. Laura grew hard and strong, her hands calloused, fingernails ground to the quick, skin browned by the sun. She cropped her hair to keep it off her neck in the late-summer heat. She rose early from Eve's bed to bathe in the pond before the morning's chill had climbed off it. The icy water closed her pores and rendered her skin smooth as chamois cloth.

Eve was ever there, Laura's companion and friend, her coaxer and cajoler. Evenings often found them sitting across a table in the dining hall where Eve would begin to talk. She revealed to Laura a secret history, how they moved people, and sent papers, money, and contraband. Their sign was a blade of grass, like the people it represented, strong in number, ubiquitous, humble, trampled underfoot. She enumerated way stations on the Underground Railroad that still ran. She taught Laura the value of hiding in plain sight and deception by appearance, how, for example, you could use a switch hidden behind a panel in an abandoned warehouse to make people believe that an iron staircase carried a lethal charge. In answer to Laura's questions, when and where did "they" begin, Eve replied, "We're not a they. We don't have power, we don't have money, we're not coordinated. We don't exist. Our invisibility is our advantage, and we use it to help each other, when we have to and we're able. We have a few sanctuaries like this one, where distraught people can have a reprieve for a few seasons. We collect castoff goods, repair them and pass them on. Sometimes we grift and con, sometimes we steal, and that is what gains us notice, the only times we're really seen, when we cause some supposed harm. Nobody ever asks why we did it to begin with, what was our objective. If we were asked, we could show them we were saving children or a whole village, but we are just shut up in prisons and silenced. We tried once to make ourselves known. We formed a guild, the Brotherhood of Beggars. But we were merely quoted the Bible and asked why God had forsaken us unless we were deserving of his scorn, so we weren't worthy of recognition.

We realized we were better off not calling attention to ourselves. We work in the shadows, spiriting people away from harm, acquiring bits of land, a few buildings here and there, off the map or in forgotten places, and they become refuges, like this one. You'd be surprised how often people forget who owns something."

Eve finished her own story.

One foggy night about a year after her mother had died, the circus's ringmaster had roused her, pulled her up on a horse behind him, and taken her into town along the riverbank. He gave her a key and a handkerchief, and pointed to a culvert that dribbled a noxious trickle into the river.

"Wet the cloth and tie it over your nose, it will help with the smell," he told her. "When you get to the end of the pipe, climb the ladder and knock three times on the grate with the key. Give the key to the person who comes. I am sorry to make you do this, but the acrobats all have colds and so you are the only one flexible enough. You can have a bath and a piece of chocolate when you are done," and he gave her a gentle push along the shore. After the bath and the chocolate, he gave her a hug and praised her bravery.

"Please, sir," she replied, "can I do more?"

He smiled and patted her on the head. "We'll see, little one, we'll see."

Of course she did do more and although, as Eve told the stories, she was ever the go-between, the errand runner, or left standing with the horses at the rendezvous, Laura sensed that as time ran on Eve had become their leader and chief plotter. She told exhilarating stories and tragic stories. Sometimes their plans had worked and sometimes not, and Eve still cried over the plans that had failed, because failures had usually ended badly. Yet they never considered giving up until that day when, betrayed for a pittance by Eve's erstwhile suitor, and on the verge of its unmasking, the circus disbanded.

"It was easy to disappear. I went back to the streets to beg, like a penance, and so I wouldn't forget how bad life was for the worst off. But I came out of that, eventually, and now I have this plan, I must get the rest of those arms shipped. It will be a long season of hard work. We will be cold. And tired."

Laura took a slow sip from the half a glass of beer between them and sat sketching aimless, unknown designs on the tablecloth with her finger. "Why did you bring me here?"

"Why," Eve stammered, "I thought I had told you…"

"Yes, yes, I know, my potential, but wasn't there anything more…personal? I felt like you knew me, you knew I needed rescuing before I knew it myself."

Eve took her own sip. "Just as you knew me, that I wouldn't kill, against all the evidence against me. Are you asking, did I bring you here because I felt a connection to you? I don't believe in fate, Laura, no force bent the universe so we could be together. It was only circumstance."

"When did you decide to bring me with you? If it was any time before that last night, you felt something, I know you did, we both did."

Eve emptied the glass, sat thinking for a long time, and finally smiled. "The first time you ran after me."

***

One morning, Laura reclined on the bed while Eve stood at the sink rinsing a teacup. Without turning, she said, "I have to go down south for a while."

Laura looked up, startled. "Why?"

Eve shook water from the cup, hung it by its handle from a hook on the wall, and came to sit on the bed. "You taught me a lesson. I won't ship this cargo through just one port. I'm going down to Charleston and Savannah to make arrangements."

Laura worried with her teeth at a hangnail. "It won't be dangerous, will it?"

"No, it's just business arrangements. Will you be all right?"

"Yes, I have some work. Maybe I'll knit you a sweater. When are you leaving?"

"In about an hour."

The hangnail bled.

"I'm sorry, I should have told you sooner," Eve said, "It's just for three weeks."

"Three weeks is a long time."

"I hadn't thought so, but now I've said it, you're right."

Eve left, and time passed. People asked Laura what was wrong. Laura, nonplussed, said she didn't know. At first, she fussed over the knitting. Something like a sweater did begin to appear off the ends of her needles. Seeing its imperfection, though, she tossed it down and took to hiking up the eastern ridges to sit and watch their approaches.

The evening came when Eve appeared, riding down the Main Road atop her trotting horse. Laura stood at the hitching post to greet her. Eve smiled as she swung down from the saddle.

"Did you miss me?" She gathered Laura in for a quick embrace.

Laura pulled back smiling. "Yes. Me?"

"Like part of me wasn't there. I'm starved."

"Let's go eat," and they walked arm in arm to the meeting hall.

After dinner, the band started up a ragged waltz. Laura stood. "I feel like dancing." She pulled Eve onto the dance floor. They came together to begin an unhurried circuit of the room. Used to following, they occasionally trod on each other's bare toes, provoking smiled apologies, although neither really minded. The fingers of Laura's right hand aimlessly wandered over the contours of Eve's back. Eve drowsed on Laura's shoulder.

"It's so hot in here," Laura murmured, "I need some air." She took Eve's hand and pulled her out to the porch that fronted the hall. It, too, was crowded with people laughing, drinking, smoking. Laura led Eve off the porch onto the cool grass and around the building's corner into darkness, where she leaned back against its rough siding. Her hand still held Eve's, and as Eve swung to face her, glided up past elbow and shoulder to rest finally at the back of her neck, drawing her gently in so that Laura could place a kiss, ever so light and quick, on Eve's lips. She fell back for a moment with wide eyes, and then took Eve again longer, slower, and more deeply. Her arms circled Eve's hips and Eve leaned in, her open right hand caressing the curve of Laura's breast.

"You don't mind?" Laura asked.

"Only if you stop."

"Just long enough to walk home?"

Hand in hand, they did.

***

Eve produced a tiny brass pipe and filled its bowl with crumbs of hashish.

"Will you join me?"

Laura nodded. Eve passed her the pipe. She flicked the wheel across the flint of a chromed Zippo lighter, and held the flame over the bowl.

"Just take a tiny bit. It will make you cough otherwise. You won't need much."

Laura pulled gingerly at the stem, drawing smoke into her mouth.

"Now breathe it down deep."

Laura inhaled. As it passed into her lungs, the smoke seemed to expand, becoming too much to hold in, and she coughed. The cloud's size surprised her; she did not think she had taken so much. Eve smiled. "Try again."

Laura put the pipe's stem to her lips once more, drew as Eve applied the flame. Laura began to inhale. It seemed after a while that she had been inhaling a long time. She could not remember when she had started. There was again the slow build of pressure in her lungs and the cough, from a deep place. She closed her eyes, fell back on the bed, and went into the place. A night bird sang at the window, and Laura listened to the song. There was only the song until the song ended, the bird gone. She opened her eyes. She'd been away, but she was back now. Her hands ran over the quilt beneath her, smooth and cool. She closed her eyes again and smelled the smoke that Eve exhaled, not quite pine.

The bed moved and Eve was beside her, slowly and with gentle fingers sliding buttons out of buttonholes, opening Laura's blouse. She bent and placed a kiss at the hollow of Laura's throat and another at the corner of her mouth. Laura's arms circled Eve, her fingers gliding through Eve's radiant hair. Their lips met. Laura went into the kiss, and it was only the kiss for a long time. She pushed Eve back and with fingertips traced the arc of lips, the downy curve of an eyebrow, a rounded ear. Eve stood to shrug out of dungarees, blouse, and underthings, to let her hair fall in a long cascade, and to blow out the single candle that lit the room, leaving only the ghostly glow of the moon at the window.

***

The next afternoon, Laura climbed partway up the valley's eastern slope to a meadow filled with fragrant grass and sunshine. She lowered herself to the ground and bent her legs into the lotus position. After a while the grass rustled softly at her back, and Eve leaned against her, cheek to shoulder.

"How do you feel?"

"Pins and needles."

"The yogi said you needed practice."

"That's not what I meant."

Eve fitted a squash blossom behind Laura's ear. Laura uncurled her legs and leaned back. Eve slid crosswise into the grass and they dozed, Laura's head resting on Eve's stomach, Eve's hand on Laura's smooth hair. When the sun had fallen towards the western rim, they roused themselves.

"Hungry?"

"Starved."

"There's a dance at the hall tonight."

"I feel like staying in. Can we just do that?"

Eve smiled. "Of course." She took Laura's hand and they strolled through the evening and the darting butterflies, down among the russet oaks and yellowed hickories, and into the throng-filled street, turning now and then to smile, one to the other.

CHAPTER 24
COLD

The valley steeped in October sunshine, made golden by the turning leaves. Laura basked in Eve's love and in the glorious light.

As a little girl, she had sung in her school's choir. Then she'd been shy, so that the choir mistress kept at her. "Louder, louder," she would demand, jabbing with her stiff finger, until she finally lost patience and drummed Laura out. Laura hadn't sung in public since, so she surprised herself, standing up one evening at the meeting hall to sing. The tune had run through her head for several days now, a jaunty love song brought over from England and molded through the years into something closer to home. Up there on the stage, after the band had tuned up, she hummed a couple of bars so the musicians caught the key, and swung into it after they played her an intro. She sung it plain, out of respect for the traditions from which it had sprung, in a fine, strong, almost husky, mezzo, and she sang it to Eve, sitting at a table halfway back, looking astonished and pleased, and when she had finished the song, Laura stood bemused as the audience showered applause down on her.

Eve went around flummoxed. How, in the name of all the turnings of her wandering life, had she ended up blessed and beatified in the arms of a woman? She had gone almost nunnish after that lone, sorrowful encounter with romance. She had needs, she knew. She felt stirrings, fitfully, and she'd seek to raise some enthusiasm for a shirtless and gleaming torso. Now and again she'd even engaged a torso and its appendage, but only to try to waylay and purge those stirrings she regarded as mere distractions, for there was ever work, never finished, forever more to be done.

The torsos had all been male, of course; she could not have imagined any other way, but the engagements inevitably left her vexed, even when they'd been conducted with a modicum of grace and generosity (not all had been, despite how those torsos gleamed). She felt only relief as they disentangled and parted. It wasn't his sex that prevented her attachment to a man, she'd say, it must only be that she remained skittish of the attachment itself. Now, here she would be, wrestling some dratted crate into place, sweating and gasping, and verily and inevitably the thought of Laura would find her, bringing calm (the crate slides miraculously into place) and, contrarily, agitation, for she must go immediately to wherever Laura was and embrace her. She tried to apply a little backbone, stand up to her desire, because still it was a distraction, an interruption of work that desperately needed doing and she was, after all, hardheaded. This should not stand. But she was possessed and intoxicated by love, delirious. And who could resist delirium?

Laura could, although not because her feelings for Eve were any less ardent. She was moved by a spirit of comity. Even if the valley's residents were kind and generous, so were they also conservative, their lives borne upon scripture and tradition. Two women as friends they could and did accept. But, Laura recognized, to have thrust upon them the notion of two women as lovers risked seeing their community ruptured and the two of them cast out. If she did not share her neighbors' orthodoxy, she still respected it as their source of strength and their right to its practice. She adored this town in its enchanting little valley nearly as strongly as she adored Eve, and so that it could remain protected and preserved, she chose not to reveal her feelings. A day would perhaps come, in a place where she and Eve could proclaim their love, but for now it must reside only with them (except for Smith, he knew right off, but then, he came from New Orleans).

So Laura prevailed upon Eve, and Eve accepted Laura's sense and tempered her impulses, but she still niggled at the how, turning the question over and over as she labored at her tasks. This she understood, that Laura had discovered and revealed the truth of her, what she had been unable to conceive in, of, and by herself. What she never could tease out of her own personality, though, was the

148

defining trait or need that would explain, that she could grasp and say, this made me vulnerable to Laura, this brought me inevitably into my loved one's arms. In the end, as she was a hardheaded woman, she let it lie, figuring love was a mystery she'd never figure out and she might as well just go with it, because it wasn't like there weren't other problems, mundane as they were, compared with her high-flown fancy for Laura. She stood outside the foundry and regarded the ever growing stack of crates she would have to drag fifteen miles down a mountainside in the dead of winter. Likely a thousand crates at three hundred pounds, more or less, apiece. Well, Amos could get her mules and wagons, she'd been down to his place to arrange it. She'd scouted the paths they'd use and for now, they were smooth and hard and clear, but one good storm could ruin them, that was the problem with mountainsides, they were exposed. She shrugged. At least they wouldn't have to worry about floods.

Laura had suggested to Eve, in her agitation, that as she couldn't sit still to meditate, she find some other occupation to settle herself. Before she had died, Eve's mother had taught her the fundamentals of drawing, and Eve had developed her skill, in her downtime waiting for things to happen, but she'd lost the habit someplace and, with one exception, hadn't drawn anything in years. As there was neither paper nor pencil in the village, she hunted up some old, bleached shingles, sanded them smooth with grit from the canal, retrieved a few blocks of charcoal from the foundry, and began to sketch. With her habit re-established, she did indeed derive calm from sitting and studying and transferring onto the boards what she saw, usually Laura, dozing, partially clad, amid ravelled sheets, stretching to pluck blackberries for the bowl she held at her waist, up on the stage full of song and her arms thrown wide, or in the woods walking, head back over her shoulder, smiling and her eyes shining. She stood the shingles when she'd done with them leaned back into the wall on a shelf opposite their bed where she could watch them, while Laura slept in her arms.

So autumn went, winding into winter, which settled on the valley like a thick and chilly blanket. Christmas Eve, Amos arrived with a string of mules and six Conestoga wagons. The arms had only just been got ready to haul, oiled against rust and crated. Eve shook her head at Amos saying she'd wished for his sake they could have gotten started sooner, he was getting too old to cross mountains, and he took crotchety umbrage at her judgment, actually shook his finger in her face saying his legs were fitter than when he was twenty. Eve waved him off, and promised if he went down, she wouldn't carry him nor waste a mule on him to get him out.

Pretty soon their tempers ran down, as tempers will between old friends. Eve and Laura took him to the hall that night, where celebration ran high, then settled down for a church service at midnight, with every branch of the Christian faith there represented participating as was its custom. Strangers to the faith stood and watched the rituals and ceremonies unfold, some not unlike their own, and others more foreign. Slowly the watchers joined in however they were moved to, and all felt godly joy that night, the saved and their newfound brethren, and that some kind of heaven was there for anyone who just cared enough to believe in it. For that night, anyway, there was no difference, God was just god.

The day after Christmas, Laura and Eve lay abed. The recent exercise of their passion had left the room considerably warmer. They'd thrown off the blankets, and now they drowsed together beneath just the sheet.

"I could lie here forever."

"Forever is a long time."

"Be romantic, I didn't mean literally."

Eve bestowed upon Laura a kiss. "Romantic enough?" When Laura nodded, she said, "Good, now we must work." She rolled out of bed and began to dress. Laura knew there was no protesting when Eve got that tone, and she delighted in that, she'd already learned to read her so well, they were tuned, balanced, like two cats dozing by a fire. She let her mind run on, she could see them, a couple of biddies fetched up in some shanty, their lives mostly lived, letting the days run down, their world contracting to just her and Eve, in rocking chairs, side by side on the porch.

She roused herself from her reverie; Eve was on her way out the door, letting in the wintry air. Soon, Laura was after her, down clamorous streets, an exodus out of the valley ahead of the weather in search of more hospitable climes, to the foundry building where the crates were stacked. Amos and Smith were there with the wagons all hitched, and a band of men standing around with them, hunched against the cold. Laura glanced at the sky, a uniform gray, could mean snow, it was cold enough. She hoped it held off a while.

She called the men over and then Eve was beside her, and four of them hauled up a crate and slung it across the gap into the wagon and slid it down the length. They moved aside and another crate came up between them, and they had a little sashay up and back until three wagons were filled, and then Laura, Eve, Smith, Amos, and two of the men stepped out on the Main Road. The Conestogas, in the interest of maximum freight-hauling utility, were not fitted with buckboards, so they'd be walking. They turned left onto the Mine Road and climbed the west ridge on a series of switchbacks out to the ridge top and headed south down the mountain.

***

They just about got it done, thanks to Eve, who had mastered logistics. She staggered the trips, three wagons at a time, with two days' rest for each team between trips, partly to forestall fatigue, and partly so they'd call less attention to themselves. Perverse as it seemed, that was also why she chose winter to do the work – it meant fewer people out to see them.

A good trip took two days, down and back, and they had a long stretch of good trips, well into January, before the weather caught up with them, when that meant breaking trail through ice-crusted snowdrifts with the ever-present threat of sliding off a mountain, losing the cargo, and injuring or killing men or mules. Then the runs stretched into three, four, even five days, and Eve canceled the rest periods at home, sending wagons back out as soon as they were loaded. Often, they'd have to hunker down on the trail, taking shelter in the lee of the wagons, wrapped up in blankets and waiting for a storm to break. They were all forever tired. Eve, in her wisdom, gave them a goal though, she imposed a deadline on hauling, the end of March, and if all the crates weren't moved by then, she'd live with it.

Near the end of their sojourn, they were into March, Eve noticed one of her companions limping, a man called Li. She asked him about it. In broken English and pantomime, he explained he'd stepped on a nail a few days earlier. Eve asked if he was taking care of it, and he shrugged, said it didn't bother him too much, so he'd just let it be. Eve made him sit, pulled off his boot and sock, and lifted his foot to eye level. The nail had penetrated his heel. The wound had closed and revealed itself only as a small black dot, but the flesh around it had swelled and gone purple and yellowed and was noticeably warm. When she pressed on it, Li grimaced, letting on that it bothered him more than he'd said. She put a hand to his forehead.

"You've got a fever. You should have told me."

They were at the bottom of their run, down a canyon where the railroad track hugged a narrow bank between the river and a stone face that rose sheer a hundred feet above them. There was a cave back in it where they had stored the crates until an available boxcar came by. Eve called Smith over and asked him to help her get Li into the cave, then asked Laura and Amos to gather up firewood. The sixth man, who had come down with Li, she asked to take his wagon and start back up the mountain, to rest up and wait for them to get back. She bedded Li down on some blankets in the cave. Now that he had no need to conceal his condition, he gave full rein to the misery he felt. He began to moan and shiver even as sweat stood out on his forehead. Eve got a fire lit. She turned to Laura and asked for some pans and a bottle of whiskey from the wagon, and some water from the river. She knelt beside Li.

"It's infected," she said, "and I've got to clean it out." She pulled up her box of pins. "I can put you to sleep and spare you the pain." He nodded, and so she put him out. She heated a pocket knife in the flame and with it punctured the wound on his heel and began to squeeze, wiping the discharge away with a handkerchief until it ran clear red. She put a pan of water on the fire and filled the other one with whiskey and let Li's heel soak in it. She boiled another handkerchief, then doused it in the whiskey and bound up Li's heel. Amos nodded at her ministrations.

"You done good," he said, "and all's you can do now is but wait. If it ain't got up into his blood yet, he may be all right."

Eve replied with a tired smile and thanked him. She went to sit slumped by the fire. Laura sat by her. She put her arm around Eve's shoulders and pulled her down and rested her chin on top of Eve's head. "You've done all you can. Try to rest some. We'll watch him."

Amos said, "I know he believes in his own Lord, but I don't see how it'd do him any harm to offer up a prayer to mine," and he bowed his head. Smith went out to feed and hobble the mules, and brought back tin plates and mugs, coffee and a coffeepot, a skillet, a loaf of bread, a chunk of bacon, and a block of cheese. He set water to boil in the coffeepot, flipped the skillet over on his lap, and began to slice bread, bacon and cheese with his fixed-blade knife. Eve was already back at Li's side, pressing a damp cloth onto his forehead. Laura bent down and took her hands and said, "I can do this, you get some rest." Eve relinquished Li's care to Laura, but continued to sit, contemplating him.

Even in sleep, Li still trembled and spasmed. He cried out, and Laura wondered if he was delirious. She stood and pulled Eve up, and they returned to the fireside. Laura sat and Eve leaned into her, and Laura began to sing a lullaby, softly. Amos and Smith sipped coffee. Li shifted and moaned. The settling fire cracked and hissed and cast their shadows and its own flickering upon the stone walls around them. Outside, darkness fell and silence, and Laura, staring into the flames, felt transported to a primitive time.

"This must be how civilization started," she mused. "People sitting snug by a fire in a cave while the wolves howled outside."

Smith flipped with his knife the bacon and cheese sandwiches browning and melting in the skillet. "Invite the wolf in, make him your friend, learn what he can teach you. Got to get along before you can have civilization. Fighting's just the opposite."

Amos grunted. "Way I see it Smith, you better ought to master the wolf before you invite him into your midst. You got things to teach him, too, who is in charge, first of all, else he might eat you up and your family."

"You accept the wolf on his terms, he accepts you on yours and there ain't no need to have a master."

"Given the history of your people, I can see your point, Smith, and I ain't saying slavery wasn't a God-awful business, it was. I say that even though my Grandad partook in it. But someone has to be in charge, otherwise there's just chaos."

Eve sat up. "The wolf sings to give thanks for his freedom. He already knows, whether tamed or mastered, he is still a slave. Neither one is worth his freedom. Then he is a dog, no longer a wolf."

Laura said, "But his freedom leaves him alone. Surely we have to give up a little freedom to have communities and be comfortable. A steady meal and a warm place to sleep might be worth a little freedom." Eve smiled at her. "There's some city girl left in you yet," she said.

Smith pulled the skillet off the fire and tipped a sandwich onto each plate. "Let 'em cool a little." He passed the plates around, and, so hungry were they that, contrary to his suggestion, they picked up the sandwiches right away, juggling them across fingertips, blowing at them, and nibbling gingerly until they were cool enough to devour in earnest.

Amos told a story. "I used to know a man down in Raleigh, kept a raccoon. Every year around springtime, it'd take off, be gone for two weeks, that man would wake up one morning, and there'd be that raccoon up on the kitchen table waiting for its breakfast. Like it wasn't going to be just a pet, it wanted that man to know it'd still got some free will left."

Smith said, "Likely that man respected that raccoon for it."

Laura said, "Likely there were a lot of little raccoons around afterward." The men grinned.

Laura and Smith gathered up the dishes and took them with a can of water off to a corner of the cave, where they began to scour the dishes clean with sand off the cave floor.

Smith, nodding towards Eve, said, "Times I was in love, I wanted to shout it out. Figured you might want to tell somebody about it."

Laura stiffened, started to stand up, and he put out his hand to forestall her. "I've seen it before. Ain't nothing wrong with it."

She settled back, still a little wary. "Does it show?"

He shook his head. "Only to someone knows how to look at it right. You kept it on the down-low pretty well."

Laura smiled, almost shy. "It was harder for her."

"Way she is, she don't have to justify herself to anyone. Someone objects, well, he can go hang himself. Shows how much she loves you she kept quiet about it. She ain't ever been quiet about anything before."

"That doesn't make me overbearing?"

"Miss van Duyn, I never in my life saw two people more suited to each other. She does it because she loves you, not because you tell her to." He piled up the dishes and stood with them. "I just thought you ought to know there's someone else thinks it's a fine thing and whenever you want to talk about it, even brag over it a little because you should, I'm here." He carried the dishes back to the fire.

When she got there, Laura saw that Eve had gone out. Laura went after her. At the mouth of the cave, she stopped to stretch, arched her back and tipped her head up at the moon and stars shining down upon her, and felt her hair gently brush against her neck. She wrapped her arms around herself against the chilly air, and spied the tip of a cigarette glowing, over towards the riverbank.

Eve was rustling through a wagon box. As Laura came up, she said, "I thought I saw an empty coffee can in here," then slammed the lid down in frustration, and took a savage pull at the cigarette. She leaned forward against the wagon, gazing at the water, calmer now. She dropped the cigarette, pressed the heels of her palms into her eyes, dragged them slowly down her cheeks and around to the back of her neck, and sighed.

"Couldn't he still be all right?"

"He could, but it's more likely he won't."

Laura took Eve's hands in her own, drew them down, and put her arms around Eve's waist. She leaned in and rested her cheek on Eve's shoulder, and they stood like that a while, front to back.

"He just barely escaped Manchuria. The Japanese would have put him down the coal mines. I said he'd be safe here."

"He was safe here."

Eve sighed again. "He was. You're right. He would already be dead if he'd gone down the coal mines."

Laura straightened and turned Eve to face her. "My lone wolf. You gave up your freedom for me." She pulled Eve in and kissed her lips. "You will never be lonely again." She took Eve's arm. "Come inside and get warm by the fire."

***

Back in the cave, Laura settled Eve and went to check on Li. His fever yet raged, but he was no longer agitated; he had gone listless and still. Even with no experience of serious illness to guide her, Laura could see his body was perhaps beginning to surrender to the disease, to shut down and accept its inevitable fate. She took the kerchief from his brow and soaked it with cool water, opened his shirt, and bathed him, thinking at least to make him comfortable for a little while. She closed up the shirt and dampened it, then returned to the fire and her friends. She poured herself a cup of coffee.

"It looks to be a long night," she said. She turned to Amos. "Tell me about A.C. Doyle."

***

Li died before morning. Eve improvised a funeral. She asked the men first to carry Li's body down to the river and then to go out and find a lot of wood. Eve and Laura undressed Li and bathed him, cleaned up his clothes and put them back on him, and wrapped him in a blanket. Amos and Smith were starting to build up a fire by then, and soon it was hot enough to serve as a pyre, so they laid Li carefully onto the flames, and stood watching while the fire consumed him. Laura sang a hymn, and Amos said a prayer for his soul. Smith talked about the man himself, his cheerfulness, his hard work, and his generosity. Finally, Eve stood forward to speak; to Laura it sounded like a recitation, a lesson, and it described how a man or woman could be reborn into the Pure Land, the place of Ultimate Bliss, filled with wonders, pools carpeted in golden sands, lotuses, luminous birds, and heavenly music. When she was done, she said, "By rights, he should be mourned for one hundred days. You can mourn him in your hearts if you like, but we have work to do." She knelt and lingered a while longer by the ashes. "This is a peaceful place," she told Li, "be at peace." She stood and addressed her company. "Let's hitch up these mules."

CHAPTER 25
BETRAYED

In April, Eve sent Laura and Smith to Asheville. She wasn't quite straight on what it was about. The last time she'd been down at the cave, a man she'd met in Savannah had accosted her, passed her a note about a "cashiered bureaucrat with a grudge" who said he could deliver some forgotten deeds out of the courthouse. That was about it, except for a place and a time to meet.

Laura and Smith left at midmorning, amid a raucous crowd of immigrants back for a season's work and refuge, with the spring sun warming their necks, the leaves unfurling, and swallows darting after mayflies. As the sun went down on the second day, they sat their horses on a hillside above the city. Smith pointed to a dark section of buildings off the downtown where a single red neon sign flickered.

"You go to where that light is, there's an alley around to the back. I'll meet you there." He nudged his horse downhill, turning with a smile before he disappeared into a thicket.

Laura waited five minutes and then descended a little to the right of where Smith had gone. She stopped a ways off from the city's edge and climbed down from her horse. From her saddlebag, she took a plain cotton housedress, a dark woolen overcoat, and a pair of low-heeled pumps. She changed from her traveling clothes, then tethered the horse to a nearby tree, and slipped cautiously and quietly onto the streets as darkness fell.

Although the way was not long, Laura took nearly an hour to reach the rendezvous. She lost her bearing several times and had to backtrack to find her way. Whenever she could do so without arousing suspicion, she stepped into the shadows to avoid groups of people coming towards her on the sidewalk. At last, the lurid sign flashed overhead. She stepped into the alley and paused to let her eyes adjust to what little light there was. Only shadows lay before her. She walked slowly down the alley to where it ended behind the tavern in a small, unlit square. Ahead of her, someone hissed, and a hand flashed dimly in the gloom, beckoning her forward. Laura hesitated, but seeing no alternative, walked towards it. She stepped through a doorway into a flashlight that dazzled her eyes. The door slammed behind her. A deep voice rumbled, "Is it Halliday?"

The man in front of her said, "No, it's the other one, that van Duyn dame."

A large and heavy hand spun Laura around and she stared up at Bruno's face, contorted with fury. Even as she watched, though, he relaxed into a wicked smile.

"Well now, this oughta be some fun."

Laura kicked upward, catching him hard in the groin, and he collapsed, losing his grip. Before she could grab for the door, the man behind her jammed a pistol barrel in her ribs.

"Now lady, I ain't gonna let you spoil Bruno's fun. Nor mine, neither. I never got any payback for that bullet in the alley. You know, I still got a scar?"

Bruno pulled himself up from the floor grimacing and backhanded Laura, sending her flying towards the wall. Her head cracked against a thick beam, and she slid unconscious to the floor. Bruno stood over her, fist raised.

"Careful, Bruno. He said don't kill her."

"He said don't kill Halliday. He didn't say nothing about her or that spook."

"You better wait. There's lots of time for killing if he says it's all right."

Bruno reluctantly lowered his arm, and then picked Laura up and slung her over his back. Gus shined the flashlight along the wall to reveal a light switch. He flipped it up, and a bare bulb came on to reveal a hallway running to the back of the building with an open staircase going up the left-hand wall. Bruno climbed the stairs ahead of Gus and stopped on the landing at the top, fumbling in his pocket for a key. He opened the door, and turned on another bare bulb that hung from the room's ceiling. Toward the front, heavy curtains hung. Two unmade cots and a double mattress lay pushed up against them. Several suitcases, a baby carriage, and a large footlocker stood in the center of the room.

Against the wall opposite the door sat Smith, bound and gagged but relaxed, his eyes alert to every detail of article and action. Bruno dumped Laura alongside him, and as she began to come around, bound and gagged her with lengths of cord and a bandanna he pulled from his pocket. Gus fussed with the baby carriage. He stood and wheeled it over next to her, folded the bonnet flat against the top of the basket, then crouched at the head end to turn a ratchet handle that protruded out the side. The wood plate in the bottom of the carriage began to tilt upward. Before Laura's eyes a figure rose, at first just a thin brown line, curiously humped and ridged, then a forehead, riddled with scars and knotted lumps of skin. Brow ridges arced across, on one side, a dark hole, and on the other, a lidless eye that drifted restlessly above a beak of bone. Beneath, from the mouth, shorn of lips, teeth gleamed in ghastly rictus, surmounting a skinless chinbone, white in the incandescent lightbulbs' glare. As the platform tilted past vertical, the figure came to rest, propping itself on what remained of its arms, blunted above the elbow, bones jutting, each tipped with a glittering stylus. Across its naked chest lay a rectangular imprint, as of a briefcase pressed into melting skin. The eye came to rest on Laura's face. Horace, what was left of him, drew breath and exhaled upon her the faint smells of ash and seared flesh.

"I expected Halliday, but you'll do," he rasped.

Laura struggled to remain steady, and she did mostly okay, but he saw her tremble anyway. "Yeah, you figured I was dead, didn't you, no way I could survive that fire, but I did, and I got that money, too. Trouble is, I'm a fright aren't I? I didn't figure on that." He drew a whistling breath and licked at a slick of something spread on a towel hung over his shoulder. "Petroleum jelly, because I got no spit left. No taste, either." He wheezed, and she realized he was laughing. He leaned closer in. "You, it was all your fault, yours and hers. So you go back, you tell her we're coming and there isn't anything she can do to stop us." He turned back to Bruno. "Hold her up."

Bruno seized Laura under the arms and hoisted her so she gazed directly into Horace's eye.

"Too bad you're not Halliday. Taste of her own." He raised a steel-tipped humerus. Laura felt a sting at her neck and sank back to unconsciousness.

CHAPTER 26
TOO LITTLE TOO LATE

Laura and Smith regained consciousness where they'd been dumped in a thicket on the outskirts of Asheville. After they'd found their horses, Smith wanted to go back into town and kill Horace and his henchmen.

"Smith, you heard him, they're long gone, and we have no way to find them. We have to try to get back and warn them."

Smith shrugged his shoulders, climbed onto his horse and rode off with her into the woods. They rode flat out, as much as the darkness and the twisting paths allowed. Smith said if they went hard at it, they could get home in eighteen, maybe twenty hours. They rode all night, stopping only to let the horses drink. The thought of pursuit, of not knowing what would come, left Laura both wide awake and exhausted.

Daylight found them many miles on, sore and weak, faces and arms tree-lashed. With daylight, though, they only quickened the pace, careering down valleys and lunging up the other side, spurring the horses ever faster. At noon, in the midst of a meadow thick with spring grass, Smith pulled up next to a stream.

"Horses got to eat and drink or they going to die. You sleep, I'll watch."

Laura protested, but Smith said, "One of us got to have some sleep. So we both don't nod off." He pulled a rifle from his saddlebag and began a slow circuit of the meadow. Laura slumped to the ground, asleep almost before her head came to rest. Smith gave her two hours, then shook her awake. Groggy, but feeling a little rested, she pulled herself into the saddle, and they went off again, speed redoubled. As the evening sun headed down the western sky, they climbed up to the high, rocky ridge that enclosed the valley.

"We're close," Smith said, "maybe we'll be in time."

A premonition caused Laura to glance east. A dark spot hovered at horizon's edge. She pulled a pair of binoculars from her saddlebag. After a moment, she slowly lowered them.

"It's a Zeppelin."

"Can we outrun it?"

"I don't know. I don't know how fast they fly."

"Let's try."

They turned their horses aside to navigate the treacherous slopes beneath the cliff. From time to time, Laura glanced eastward. The ship came on fast enough that she could see it grow, but not so fast as she had feared. It ran broadside sometimes, and at others end on, seeking the hidden valley. By the time they arrived at the cleft's entrance, though, they could hear its low, machine hum.

"We won't be able to see it now until it comes over the ridge."

"We still got to go on."

They climbed off the horses and descended into darkness. An anomaly in the grotto's shape amplified the ship's insidious thrum and sent it pounding down the tunnel after them. Laura's eyes brimmed with tears of frustration. In the lead, she strode forward and promptly cracked her head on a ragged stone edge. Blood mingled with her tears. She crouched, ran her hand along the wall, and stepped forward as quickly as she thought was safe. All the way through the mountain, the noise beat at them. It seemed hours had passed before Laura saw the exit outlined against the dusky sky ahead of her. They emerged from the tunnel and glanced fearfully upward. The noise died suddenly away. Moments later the ship drifted spiritlike over the ridge, its guy lines softly moaning, slipping like a black torpedo aimed straight at the village.

Laura and Smith put heels to their horses and galloped down the draw. By the time they reached the valley floor, the airship had turned south towards the settlement. Even as they watched, its engines came to life, propellers backing, and it hovered over the foundry in the still air. Frightened people streamed out of huts and tents, scrambling to get out from under the intruder. Laura and Smith galloped down the street shouting for them to run, to get up into the woods. There came an eerie moment of silence. The monster's engines idled. The people gathered under the forest's eaves and stood watching. Leaves tilted in a slow breeze, and swallows darted through the evening air. A puzzled dog whined.

A door opened in the ship's belly. The engines once more fed the propellers, and as the ship started forward, a bomb fell keening from the open bay to find its mark down the foundry's chimney. The detonation sent jagged pieces of mortared brick flying for dozens of yards. The ship continued its traverse, loosing an iron stream that consumed the factory, leaving only a blackened skeleton lit red by a smoldering glow. The Zeppelin flew slowly on, spent. Laura kicked her horse into a hard gallop to follow – but follow to what end? The ship gained speed, ran south down the valley, and departed over its rim. Laura, sobbing, nothing she could do, let the horse slow to a walk and finally reined it around towards home.

The valley was quiet now, save for the pop and snap of the lowering flames and the skirling birdsongs. Laura found the house collapsed, its back broken by a chunk of flying masonry. The door stood askew, pinched by the tilted frame, and Laura had to squeeze through to get inside. Late evening sunbeams shone through gaps in the jumbled roof. A light, warm breeze raised dust motes, glinting in the amber light, from the wreckage spread across the once tidy room.

Eve had been napping when the house fell. Its dislodged ridge beam caught her just above the waist, pinning her to the bed. She was awake when Laura knelt beside her. She managed a smile, despite the shock that threatened to overcome her. She found Laura's hand.

"I hoped you would come," she murmured, "Stay with me a little while."

Laura pushed back a strand of Eve's hair, brushed a smudge from her cheek with her coat sleeve. "I have to find the doctor and some men to get you free."

"Nobody can help me. Only just stay." She coughed and groaned. A bright trickle of blood rose at the corner of her mouth.

Laura's eyes brimmed and spilled. She pressed Eve's hand to her heart. "Does it hurt?"

"No, not anymore."

"Eve, what will I do without you?"

"You will never be without me. I will always be in your heart."

The coughing came again, and Eve grew agitated, her head thrashing on the pillow. "Laura, stay here, hold me while the darkness comes."

Laura lay beside her and pulled her close. Eve grew still. "Thank you, I am so warm now. I can't keep my eyes open. I think I will sleep a little." She relaxed, and her breath fell softly across Laura's neck, ever more slowly, until one time it did not come again.

Laura stayed until the night's chill drove her shivering from the house. At the factory, where a few residents picked through the remains for anything they might salvage, Laura asked for a can of kerosene. One was presently found. She carried it back to the house, poured its contents over the bed, and lit it with Eve's chromed Zippo lighter. She emerged from the house in silhouette against the flames to flag down a wandering horse, somehow saddled and bridled, and, as fate would have it, the very horse, ginger mane and tail, on which she came into the valley that day with Eve. She mounted and rode north into darkness.

CHAPTER 27
A SONG FOR EVELYN

Smith saved her. He tracked her through three days of aimless wandering and found her at the brink of a precipice, with all the long country, ridge beyond misty ridge, ranked before her, off to the edge of the world where the risen sun flared. She stretched her arms wide and leaned over the abyss, imagining the rushing air and the end of her pain. He stepped up silently behind her and got her around the waist and pulled her back. She fought him; if she'd been healthy, he didn't know that he could have taken her, but she was hungry and thirsty and exhausted, and even then she was an armful, but he managed to twist her around and hold her until her strength finally ebbed, whispering in her ear her name, "Laura…Laura…Laura…,". She sagged into him and he got her up onto her waiting horse, where she just about slid out of the saddle. He fetched a rope out of his saddlebag and cinched her in, knowing it was dangerous if the horse ever bolted, but he'd take that chance. He took her to Amos, down under the trees in front of his house, where he undid the rope and pulled her off the horse. He carried her up the steps, knocked the door open with an elbow, and bundled her into Amos's bed. Amos stood up from his table confounded. Smith took his arm, pulled him onto the porch, and closed the door.

"Eve Halliday is dead."

Amos said, "Hmmm…" a trembling, husky sound way back in his throat, "hmmm…hmmm." Tears ran out of his rheumy eyes and down along his old nose. He raised a finger, the same one he'd lectured her with when she'd said he was too old, raised it towards the heavens and began to exclaim, in the cadences of the country preacher he'd once been, "I heard a noise, an infernal howling out of the sky, and a shadow came onto my heart. I knew it would be bad, the Devil himself." He covered his face with his hands, and Smith let him weep a while.

"Amos," he said, "there's something I got to tell you, and you've got to understand it." Amos stilled under his hard stare.

"Miss van Duyn," he nodded at the door, "loved her, they loved each other the way any man and any woman would."

Amos ruminated on that thought. "You mean they shared a bed like a man and a woman?"

Smith nodded.

"It don't seem natural."

"You don't have any experience of it, Amos, that's why. When it happens, it's as natural as anything else."

"I recall the Bible takes a dim view of such relations."

"The Bible takes a dim view of a lot of relations, Amos, some for the better and some for the worse. What you ought to remember is working alongside of them, or sitting of an evening by the fire and sharing supper and some fine conversation. What you ought to remember is them taking care of Li and how hard they worked and how well they did their jobs. What was between them hasn't got any bearing on them being two fine people, and in fact their love improved the both of them. And now Eve's gone, it's for Miss van Duyn to take up her work. She's got to be saved Amos, she's too precious a soul to be let go of and get herself through this all alone. You're better than anyone I know at curing people, and you got to fix her broken heart. I'm asking you to put aside what the Bible takes a dim view of, because what it says more powerful is to love everybody as if they was your own." He stood and waited, to see if he'd said right what was in his heart. It was about the longest piece he'd ever spoken.

Amos drew a quavering breath and allowed as how Smith was right, and thanked him for his speech and for bringing him around to what was good and decent. Smith's knees nearly gave out, he was that relieved, but he turned and managed to walk to his horse and climb up into the saddle.

"Where you off to?"

"Going down to New Orleans, going to find me a freighter and ship out. Eve taught me there's a wide world, said I owed myself to see it."

"Ain't you even got time for lunch?"

"No, sir. I got to move, put this place of sorrow behind me." He tipped his hat. "I'll see you someday, Amos. I'll be back." Amos raised his hand, and Smith rode out of there.

For a couple of weeks, except for getting some food into her, Amos pretty much left Laura alone. He'd felt grief himself, first for a son six years old, and then for a wife and a new baby girl, both of them dead on the same day, and he knew there wasn't anything he could say or do. Despite what Smith had said, it was up to her to get herself out of it, that's how it had been for him, and either she would, or she'd spiral down into it and never come out, and there wasn't anything he could do about that, either. He felt it was encouraging that she'd still get up on her own and use the privy. One afternoon, she got up and fixed her own lunch, and he knew then she'd pull through.

Not that it got easy for her. She went for weeks when the merest nudge at a memory of Eve would keel her over and she'd lie doubled up wherever she happened to be until the crying wore her down to exhaustion. Amos had found her out in the yard like that a couple of times, in the damp and the spring mud, borderline hypothermic. He'd pick her up and wipe her off as best as his modesty allowed him to and put her to bed. She'd sleep twelve or fifteen or eighteen hours and when she woke up, she'd go maybe a day, sometimes two, until it happened again.

Summer came on the first week of June, some real power in the sun and the leaves out full on the trees. She'd sit out on the porch those days, pale and thin, wrapped in a blanket despite the heat, and sip the strong tea Amos mixed himself from bunches of herbs gathered wild and hung to dry over his kitchen counter. It took about a week for her to notice that some words had attached themselves together in her head, and imposed themselves on her memory so that she found herself reciting them. A week after that, she knew she was writing a song for Eve, when a melody attached itself to the words. And then, a wondrous manifestation of serendipity, the old black bluesman appeared coming down the path on a horse, his guitar strung up on a piece of rope at his back. He'd heard about the destruction up at the mine and Eve. He was headed back up to see if he could get started on rebuilding, he'd heard other folks were headed that way, too. He came onto the porch and got Laura up into a massive hug, her feet dangling, held her for a good couple of minutes, until she herself asked nicely to be put back. He set her on her feet and looked down into her eyes and said, basso, "You're going to be all right," and for the first time in weeks, the tears sparkling in her eyes were not tears of sadness.

He spent the night, rolled into a big blanket and reclining on the floor, beside Amos in his rig, a couple of benches shoved up against each other where he stretched out on the seats. He'd slept there since Laura arrived, and would stand no argument on the subject of returning to his own bed until she was better. The next morning, Laura made them both breakfast. Afterwards, Amos said he had to go feed the horses. Before he left, he said, "Miss van Duyn you ought to let this fellow help you finish that song you made up." The bluesman said, "Well, let's hear it."

He brought out his guitar, and, against the melody she hummed, he set out a finger picked accompaniment. Her melody was shaped by the high lonesome laments she'd heard often enough performed on the stage at the meeting hall in the valley, but there were hints of other musics in it. It began an octave over the root and slid up a step to make a minor seventh, but its impression, when it got matched to the guitar, was almost of parallel fifths, lending the tune an Oriental or maybe a native Indian cast. The bluesman listened and said she had a good ear, a talent she ought not to ignore, and she flushed with pleasure. They finished by fleshing out the lyrics and settling on phrasing, and he asked if she minded him taking it along to sing, and she said no, of course not. He said, "You know, Eve wouldn't want you to cast up here in this old corner of the world mooning over her. You got work to do, that's what she trained you for. You got any plans to go on?"

Though the ache still pressed hard on her heart, she knew he was right, and she smiled and said yes. When Amos came back, she told him she was leaving, she was ready, she thought New York, that's where she'd head, some boys she knew there needed looking after. He nodded and shook her hand. "Don't be a stranger."

She hugged him hard and thanked him, then rolled a few things up into a blanket, and went out to saddle her horse. She and the bluesman rode up onto the track together and parted, he to the west and she eastward.

23 ELM STREET, BAYPORT, JULY 22, 1978

Dearest Fenton,

You are delayed, and I cannot wait. I must leave tonight. I had hoped we could talk, but I have screwed up my courage, and I do not want to put off telling you what I was going to say, so I shall say it in writing instead of in person. Perhaps that will be better. I have never trusted myself to say exactly what I mean. I rehearse and I rehearse, but it never comes out quite as I had hoped. If I can gather my thoughts and put them down on paper, maybe they will be clearer. What is said in writing, of course, can never be taken back as what we declare in the heat of discussion sometimes can be. And of course, what is printed on the page risks not carrying the expression of feelings that our voices do. Still I must tell you tonight, and this is the only way I can. So if these words seem dispassionate simply because they are written rather than spoken, do not mistake me for lacking feeling. I love you, Fenton. I love our sons and the men they have become. I love the time we spend together, and I miss you when we are apart. How ironic that the lives we chose have kept us apart so often, and that has taken a toll, I believe, on our marriage and on our family. Our boys feuding, Gertrude at loose ends, and between you and me do I mistake a growing distance? Finally, after being apart so much, we are now accustomed to it, and when we are together, we no longer give the attention to each other that we once did, we simply take each other for granted. We are associates where once we were partners. Nor have I missed the worry in your face. That you remain our sole support when every day living grows dearer. Who could have expected gasoline at eighty cents a gallon? So you are reduced to hushing up scandals for addled old men while I go vagabonding. You are not yet old, I know, but you are weary. When I am truly old, I do not want to look back and see that my neglect had helped to sever the bonds that have been the strength of our family. So, I have decided this will be my last project. When I return, it will be for good. We have some money set by, and I lack nothing in my life but you. Why don't you come in from the world, too? Keep me company, and we will decide what to do.

You see, of course, that is not the end of the letter, so far it has been preamble. Because first, I must tell you something. It might bear on your feelings for me, and thus on your decision. I must tell you a secret, Fenton.

Before I begin, I want you to know that I understand what I reveal may shock you beyond your tolerance. You have always been equitable. It is my faith in that trait where I have chosen to let my hope reside, but that is not my attempt to sway you. You know I have a backbone. I will accept the consequences. If it is so, if you feel you no longer want to have me, I will take any role you would like me to have in your life, even none at all if you choose. I am utterly sincere. You have the right to choose the life that makes you happy. I have faith, though, in your tolerance, and if my hope is true, we will have many more happy days together.

My mother kept a secret from my father to preserve peace in her marriage. I used to see sense in that, but I have realized that a secret is also a burden, and precisely because the secret is held to shield the person it is kept from, the one for whom it only makes sense that he should know, the burden cannot be relieved without telling and violating the secret. You are the only one I can tell, who I should tell, the only one I can share this burden with. I have wanted to tell you more times than I can count, but it was so hard, the effects of its telling could have devastated us. It is easier now, more accepted, and maybe this is the best time to tell it, for you to hear it. So, before you decide if you want to start down a new road with me, I must say this: Eve Halliday and I were lovers. Oh, how can I tell you about the true love and desire I felt for her, my fingers still trembling as I think of it? At the same time I felt that I could not believe it had happened and to never question that it did. I would have given her my life. But she died. She said she would always live in my heart, and she was right, of course, but that is a meager kind of life, compared to her being right there next to me in the fullness of herself, to talk to and to work beside, to take comfort and share burdens with. Remember when you suggested a partner to smooth out the bumps in the road of life? She was that for me, a partner, someone to face life with. After she died, I was dead myself, to anyone else. I couldn't face life alone, and I wanted nobody but her. But time passed, and I couldn't exist anymore with just that meager life. I needed a real partner to smooth out the bumps. And so the time came to give her up and find someone else. And I found you.

I knew very little about sex. My mother had sat me down once and talked vaguely. She gave me a book that explained menstruation and explained love in only the most conventional terms. I accepted what it said and expected, whenever I gave it any thought, to fall in love with a man. I had hints that love could follow another path. My great-aunt shared with her lady friend a Dublin apartment that contained only one bed. There were rumors at school, quickly hushed by the nuns, one of them sent away, and every term, a few mad crushes among the girls on roommates or novice English teachers. They were separated and given penance, their feelings dismissed. I took the nuns' word that it was sin. When I fell in love with Eve, I expected to be in love with her all my life. I didn't have to ask myself if I was a person who fell in love with women. Then I lost her and didn't want to be in love with anyone. Then I fell in love with you and accepted that I could fall in love with anyone. I did wonder if there was a name for someone like me. I tried to look myself up, to find out what I was, but there was nothing there. I even presented myself, hypothetically, of course, to a psychology professor. I asked him what he would call a person like that and he said sick. So I was sick and a sinner. Funny, I felt neither. I had a pretty wonderful life. Perhaps I might have been depressed but for you, and Frank and Joe. And my work, it has been the strong cord that pulls me along. It is the source of whatever strength I have. And you gave that to me, you let me be that person, and for giving me that freedom, whatever happens between us, my heart will always belong to you.

I know I have not explained myself, how it could have happened that I fell in love with a woman. It did steal upon me, that feeling, I thought I was simply diverted by the novelty of my new life, but she went away on a trip once, and I could not concentrate on anything save her return, and the feeling when she did return, I knew, I thought I had been in love, but so pallid were those feelings against this one, it was like water compared to whiskey. When I held her that night, when it was like whiskey, warm and drowsy, I could not have imagined a more complete feeling, a more natural feeling than the one I felt for her. But I think now that biology does not determine destiny, it does not determine love. Love determines biology. That statement cannot stand logical analysis, but I mean, first you fall in love, and only then do you begin to see sex. At least I did, and then I was already in love and sex did not matter, only that I was in love, so I felt as whole, as complete, with you as I did with her, you both had, have, the qualities, the character I can love. The rest is mostly mechanics. And I thoroughly enjoyed those with both of you. When she would touch her lips or the tips of her fingers to my tender places, I felt, aside from the physical senses, which were exquisite, a vibration, a hum, like I was connected to the conduit, whatever it is, that carries the power of the universe. I have never believed in God (I believed in nuns), but her touch brought me as close as ever I would.

With you it was down to earth, straightforward, stronger, in a way, rougher, once you'd overcome your reticence (which vanished quickly!), but rough nicely, it was nice to be handled. Oh, I know some would pillory me for enjoying being handled by a man, but it meant I didn't have to think, I could just relax and feel you, and that was the best part. You have always been a kind and generous lover, and I have never wanted in pleasure. I want you, in fact, here right now, in our big bed upstairs, holding me tight to you. But you are delayed, yet again, and I must leave, yet again. We must put off that night, perhaps to consummate our new life together.

Except, I have told you my secret, because I want to be free of it. I hope that wasn't horribly selfish. So you must decide now what you want to do. If my hope is true, we will have many more happy days together. If it is not, I will still love you and the years we have had together. Until I see you again, all my love,

Laura.

CHAPTER 28
REUNIONS, 1938

Fenton put down his binoculars and sipped from the cup of cold coffee beside him. He'd been watching for twelve uneventful hours and had begun to nod off. He was positioned on the rooftop of the building across the street from his target, an apparently vacant house. Only laborious effort had gotten him this far. He'd started with the blade of grass. He'd been right, handing his badge to O'Malley. He had been cut from the force, a tough blow, but once he got past the shock, he realized he was free, and he had time, to think and wonder, to ask questions, and, finally, to rouse himself and go out looking for answers. And he could think of only one clue which he might still obtain, the blade of grass.

Gertrude had been skeptical. She'd accepted the official explanation that Laura and Halliday had died in the explosion.

"Gert, they weren't there, there was no sign of them. We found you without a scratch, and that Skolimowski walked out of the hospital under his own power. To assume they were immolated, with not even bone fragments left, is ludicrous. No, they got away somehow, and I'm going to find them."

"But why, Fen? Even if they're alive, Halliday didn't kill anyone after all and she probably wasn't even a crook, whatever she was planning. Laura was right about her, and it's not likely Halliday coerced her into going with her. What was it you told me Laura said – that she thought Halliday was her rescuer? Well, there you go, it isn't likely she needs rescuing anymore. You're so fired up, a person would think she'd turned your head."

"Gert, I'm not carrying a torch for Laura van Duyn. I barely knew her. It's just there's something out there, something going on, more than Halliday, she was just one part of it. I want to know what the whole thing is. I am a detective after all, remember?"

"And you would give up your career, your work?"

"This will be my work, Gert. Look, Dad left me a little money, if you're worried about expenses."

"Nonsense, I only want your happiness. If you feel you must do this, then do it. We'll get by. I just want you to be sure."

He had dipped into the inheritance anyway, for the binoculars and a sidearm to replace the one reclaimed by the Department when he'd been let go. He almost never got home anyway, eating on the run, so he'd needed cash. The morning he got up ready to begin, he paid a visit to the landlady at the Royal Arms. When he asked if he might see the room or was anyone staying there, she said, "No, I haven't let it since that woman went away."

A week after Halliday had left, the landlady said, she had received a parcel by mail with no return address. It contained some cash and a letter requesting that the room be left empty. The letter explained that on the first day of every month she would get a cash delivery, money for the rent and even for the room's share of her tax. If she let the room, the payments would, of course, stop. She had gone up to see the room and found it fine. And she thought now she wouldn't have to let it, clean it, manage its tenants, so she locked it behind her and let it be. "And nobody has been in it since, at least nobody has asked for the key."

The blade of grass he found in the room was fresh. "Why," he thought, "am I not surprised?" He carefully levered out the tack with a pocket knife and with a tweezers set the blade of grass into a rigid box lined with cotton balls. He called the switchboard at the Museum of Natural History and inquired of the kind operator whether they had a scientist on staff who could identify a species of grass from its blade. The operator referred him to the resident agrostologist.

When Fenton brought it to him, the agrostologist asked where the blade of grass had come from. "It was tacked to a wall in an apartment in Brooklyn."

"It's crabgrass, probably came out of the alley next to the apartment building." Fenton thanked him and went back to the alley.

He walked it several times, recognizing numerous clumps of crabgrass. He went painstakingly along the alley beside the apartment building, often on his knee with a magnifying glass. He found nothing. He stood back and looked up at the building. Apartments towards the alley each had a window onto it. There were two columns of windows, for the apartments facing the street and for the ones facing the backyard. Running upwards between the two columns was a drainpipe going all the way to the roof. It wasn't in the center of the building, but shifted over towards the apartments at the back. Halliday's had been at the back, on the fourth floor. He went up to the roof and squinted down the drainpipe, wondering if it just looked functional. He returned to the alley and looked up the pipe. The brackets which attached it to the wall seemed numerous and exceedingly stout. He grabbed one and pulled himself up. The brackets fell naturally into place, forming a ladder to the top floor whence a climber could lean over, slide the double hung window up, and swing into the apartment. Fenton let himself down, retrieved his fingerprint kit, and spent the afternoon dusting the pipe all the way to the top. By the end of the day, as near as his practiced eye could tell, he had seven unique prints. He congratulated himself on a good day's work, even though he admitted he hadn't yet really learned anything. He'd have to send them up to Albany, to the Bureau of Identification, to see if they could match his fingerprints with any in their files. They had a new machine from IBM that could sort four hundred and twenty records a minute. If any of the prints had been registered in the state, he'd have an ID in a couple of days.

His request came back negative, no matches, square one. He thought about sending the prints to Washington, to have the FBI look at them, but that could take months. He did not want to wait. So he staked out the place and watched it for a week, but nobody came and he figured they were probably watching him as closely as he watched for them. Frustrated, he made a trip out to Atlantic Avenue, to try to cajole some information from the tobacco shop owner, who stayed mum other than to tell Fenton he would never admit to anything. As Fenton was no longer on the force and had no recourse to coercion, beyond violence, he left empty-handed. He stopped by the Royal Arms to tell the landlady he was done there, he was giving up, and she mentioned, as she had to Laura, the people who didn't call attention to themselves. His faith in the methods of detection led him to believe there must be some way to track them, find out about them. He asked if she had any of the money she'd been sent or parcels she received it in? She gave him samples of both and he took them home.

He had a microscope and a few reagents left over from school. The reagents were useless, their potency long evaporated. He didn't figure knowing the pH was going to tell him much anyway. Under the microscope, he compared her bills with his own and, as far as he could tell, hers were standard issue American currency. Unless his were counterfeit, he thought, sardonically. The parcel was brown Kraft paper, stapled together into a pouch big enough to hold the cash. The paper was clean, no greasy fingerprints, no discernible odor, no other marks except the address, penciled block letters, and the post mark, which showed it had been mailed from a post office in Harlem, probably dropped into a neighborhood box. He went back to the landlady, returning her money, and she said, "You keep looking at things and not getting anywhere. You should talk to people instead."

"Who?"

"The poor, you must talk to them. They know these people the best." She sized him up, jacket and tie and nice shoes. "But if they see you coming, they will think you are the police. You need someone with you they trust."

At home, when he proposed to Gertrude that he go around with her on her visits to clients and interview them about Halliday and her gang, she looked him over, saw him thinning and consumed, sparking again the skeptical part of her.

"Fen, don't you think it's time you gave this up? They're either dead or gone so far away you're not likely ever to find them, and what would you have even if you did?"

He didn't brush her off, because he knew she loved him and spoke only out of concern for his well-being. But nor did he consider even for a moment giving up, and so she relented, and he went to work with her for the first time in their lives. Much as he loved his sister, he'd nursed the half-hearted notion she was a do-gooder, not that she was ineffectual, just that despite her labors, most of the poor remained poor. But when he saw her at her level, alone with a frightened child or a desperate wife, or even, sometimes, a man, washed out and floundering, he saw her for the first time as the very embodiment of a life saver. He saw the hope she rekindled in them and realized this was how you changed the world. It wasn't grand or sweeping, it worked slowly and without precision, but it was dogged, and with enough faith and luck it would make the world better. "Gertrude," he said one afternoon, "you've restored a piece of me, and I appreciate it. Thank you."

She smiled and took his arm. "You're welcome, Fen."

Besides that benefit, the renewed bond between them, Fenton also gained sympathy and respect for the people he met. Despite his proximity to Gertrude and her work, the lives of the poor and dispossessed had remained largely invisible to him. Indeed, he had encountered them only during the few times they had become official police business. Now he saw them in their places, their homes and work, and on street corners, saw the difficulties, the pain, and hardship to which they had to become inured just to live their lives. And still they went out of their way to show courtesy and hospitality, whatever they could afford, even just a glass of hot water, which, truth to tell, was a dear luxury for many of them. He sat in their kitchens and ate their food, food his patrician father had dismissed as "Eye-tie" or "Hebe" or "Pollack" and he couldn't believe how good it was. So even though the winter was a long hard slog for Fenton, his newfound appreciation for the much harder lives that others led held off discouragement.

Earning her clients' trust, even with Gertrude there beside him, required weeks of coaxing and reassurance. And what he got was rumors anyway. He found nobody who could claim direct experience of Halliday's people, at least nobody who would admit to it. As March ground into April, he could still put together only the vaguest picture or pattern, and he began to wonder if Gertrude maybe was right, he could end at nothing but a dead end. About the middle of May he caught a break. Gertrude came home one evening and told him he should have come out with her that day, people were asking for him. She'd asked them why, but they only shook their heads, said he was the one they needed. He went with her next day and listened to half a dozen reports. They were wild, whispers of caches disappearing, of what they couldn't say, a skyship wreaking havoc, two men and a baby carriage with a monster inside, doors broken open in the middle of the night and people roused from their beds, a giant fist looming out of the darkness. He nearly dismissed them as more rumors, but when she, too, had heard generally the same story from everyone, even Gertrude admitted there was something afoot. Her skepticism ebbed; she encouraged him for the first time not to give up.

Then June came, and suddenly the rumors stopped, not that the people stopped talking to him, but because they stopped hearing anything to tell him, as if the agents who had sparked the rumors had disappeared. Fenton made his rounds all summer, keeping his frustration tamped down, and finally, early in September, the whispers began again, although not, this time, stories of violence and destruction, but instead, hints at a possible motherload, a cache of arms with which someone not particularly scrupulous could make a lot of money. Eventually the stories' focus coalesced around a house buried deep in Queens. He sidled out one day to look at it, hoping he was inconspicuous, just walking past. There was a room to let on the second floor across the street, so he took it and set up his surveillance. That was a week ago.

He took another sip of coffee. He tried to watch from the room, but it stifled in the Indian summer heat, so he risked being seen sometimes and, like today, went up on the roof. He put down the coffee cup and rolled over onto his back to stare up into the deepening sky, with evening coming on. In spite of the coffee, he fell asleep. When he awoke, it was dark and he was chilly. He patted himself down, felt the gun still under his arm, so he stood up, stooped to grab the binoculars and went back to his room. His stomach rumbled, reminding him of the diner down the street, and that he'd missed dinner.

Out on the street again, he lit a cigarette and looked over at the house. He crossed and tried the doorknob. The door was locked. He shaded his eyes and peered into a window. He heard a noise, a scuff behind him and when he turned, an arm came out of the darkness, caught him hard across the throat, and pushed him back against the building. A woman spoke. "Don't fight me, just answer some questions."

He tried fighting her anyway, brought his arms up to grab her shoulders, and she turned into him, drove her elbow with all her weight behind it in under his ribcage, stepped nimbly away as he doubled over, jammed her palm between his shoulder blades and pushed him facedown onto the concrete.

"I warned you." She was on him now, her knee hard into the small of his back, and whispering at his ear. She grabbed his right arm and jerked it into a half nelson. "Now stand up and let's start over." He got up, and she kept his arm against his back and her left hand against his shoulder. She pushed him forward under a streetlamp and spun him around.

For the rest of his life, whenever he told the story, he never could describe to his satisfaction the effect of her, in that first second when he saw and then knew her -- couldn't make his listener understand what shook him when her eyes caught his. Never a literary man, he foundered on the shoals of analogy. In truth, he never could have known in a conscious way, it went so fast, was so ephemeral, it didn't register with even the tiniest quantum of memory. It stuck far deeper than that, in a place where only instinct still lived, a place incapable of communion with his higher faculties. Had there existed some mechanism to capture what he saw and to assemble from it something so ordinary as a list, it would have contained strength, tempered by the pure ache of sorrow, and, this was the ineffable part, not maturity, not mere acceptance, and here it would break down, and he'd smile and apologize for the half-assed attempt at expressing himself. "It was just, she understood, I guess that's as close as I can say, she'd unraveled how the world was put together and she'd picked her spot in it, and no one ever would sway her off that." Sometimes the listener would complement him, saying that was actually a pretty good description and ask was that when he loved her? He'd laugh and deny it, "All I could think was I'd just gotten beat up by a woman."

Under the streetlamp, he stood and gawped. Her stance was open-legged, her shoulders up and her arms half-cocked. She was dressed for speed and stealth, a black bandanna around her forehead, black canvas sneakers, loose, lightweight black slacks, a dark work shirt with the sleeves hacked off at the shoulders, and hair short as a bob, a homemade cut, but it suited her, even with it sort of sticking out of the bandanna in all directions. The muscles of her arms seemed etched beneath her skin, that explained how she'd gotten him down, where her power came from. She was as lean as anyone he'd ever set eyes on, but not tough lean, it was a lean that favored her cheekbones, with shocks of that blonde hair driven almost like spikes down beside them, and those eyes, those green and golden eyes, she'd either let you fall right into them, or drill a hole direct to your cerebral cortex and know right away what you were made of. He jerked back, afraid of falling.

She pushed him out of the light. "How long have you been watching this place?"

"About a week."

"Have you seen anyone go in or out?"

He shook his head.

"Good." She smiled at him. "Was that you watching the Royal Arms last fall?"

He nodded.

"I heard about that. You figured out the drainpipe, that was good work."

"Did you put it up?"

"No." Her smile faded. "I was far away from here."

"Why wasn't I spotted this time?"

"Maybe you were, but it doesn't matter, because it wasn't a trap for you."

"Two men and a baby carriage?"

The smile came back, not a smile of pleasure. It might have been a smile that conferred respect.

He waved up at the house. "What's going on?"

She glanced around. "We can't stand out here too long. Come with me." She started down the sidewalk.

"Wait," he called, and when she turned, "what if they show up?"

"They won't until tomorrow night. Come with me please, I will tell you everything." They headed west towards Manhattan, sticking to the dark places, back alleys and the lulls between streetlamp pools. They skirted a commercial district, small shops starting to close up for the evening. Fenton said he was hungry and while she waited in the shadows, bought some hot dogs and two bottles of Coca-Cola at a takeout window and they ate and sipped as they walked. A couple of bums lounged against the corner of a building where an alleyway gaped. They nodded at her as she passed them going down the alley and gave Fenton the eye as he followed. He ignored them. Halfway along the alley another one bisected it, and she turned. Trash cans and some stray cats ranged along the buildings. The cats meowed at Laura and fell in behind her. The alley dead-ended at a brick wall and where it formed an L with the building beside it, in that corner, a little hut was built out of lengths of old board and sheet metal. It had a roof that sloped down and to the left and overhung the walls so any rainwater would be directed into the gutter along the sidewalk. The whole structure leaned over, looking as if it was about to collapse, as if nobody had lived there for a long time.

"I learned to make these in the woods, but they work just as well in the city." She pulled aside a heavy blanket to reveal a door and waved him inside. She followed and began fussing with the roof. "The air's a little close, hang on," and she shoved so the roof came up, rattling and scraping along the bricks, spooking the cats. She put a pole under it to hold it, then drew a chromed Zippo lighter from her pants pocket, struck it, and lit a candle sitting on an apple crate next to her bed, a cast-off piece of sponge rubber that covered about half the floor. She pulled off her shoes and sat on it cross-legged. There was another apple crate along the wall opposite and he sat on that. She watched him as he settled himself. She'd lost all memory of his aspect, his height and the way he took up space. If he wanted to, he could intimidate just by moving up on you. She watched his eyes take in the room's details. A shelf bolted into the bricks held a few articles of clothing. Beside the candle stood a box of Wix, a few apples, a tin of sardines and some crackers, a little metal box, and a half loaf of dark bread. On the wall above where her head would lie as she slept, she'd pinned a fresh blade of grass.

"You chose this? To live here?"

"It's all I need. It's all I want to manage right now."

"Feels damp."

"I live with it."

He looked back at her and waited.

Finally she asked him, "What do you know?"

"Two men have been strong-arming people and stealing, I don't know what or for whom. I assume one of them is Bruno. There's something in the baby carriage. At least seven people have used that apartment Halliday stayed in, but none of their prints is registered with the state. The blade of grass is crabgrass." He shrugged. "That's about it."

There was that smile again. "Horace is in the baby carriage." She explained about him. "Detective…"

"Just call me Fenton, I'm not on the force anymore."

His tone, curt, almost abrasive, left her feeling defensive. "As you wish. If I tell you this…"

"Oh please, what, am I going to run to the cops? Look, I'm not working for anybody but myself, I've got no ax to grind, I just want to know, what was that all about, everything, what was going on with that ship, why you left? If you don't want to tell me that's fine, you don't owe me anything. I'll just keep looking and I'll figure it out myself."

His irritation rankled her, made her obstinate, but it was also a challenge. She couldn't just leave him hanging, stonewalled, so she started in clench-jawed, told him about Horace and Bruno and Gus. She told how they'd been exploiting their knowledge of the network, finding safe houses and their stores. They were looting and selling for profit to whoever would pay the most, and meanwhile, always probing, searching for the arms cache.

"And that woman, Halliday? What's she doing while all this is happening?"

"Nothing, she's dead."

That bald statement, without artifice, shook him, even more than if she'd fallen into hysteria. She saw that it shook him and that he understood, he felt the weight of it on her and so he could let it lie, not worry at it; she wouldn't have to say any more. She saw him, truly maybe for the first time, confused and rattled and deflated. She regretted having beaten him up, and she softened a little towards him.

"She was my friend. My best friend. I was lost without her for a while." She turned profile and her eyes glistened in the candlelight. She patted her heart, "But I have her here, and that must suffice, because she has passed into my history now. And I have much to do." She faced him, and her eyes were already dry. "This is what is happening. Horace must be stopped. He thinks those arms are coming to that house tomorrow night. There is a warrant for his arrest in France. I plan to catch him and put him on a ship. I sent some boys looking for where those arms really are. I think they have found them. If they are right, those arms will go on the same ship."

"Can I help you?"

That was out of left field to her, and she stammered, "No, I don't think, I mean, what would you do?"

He shrugged. "It's a big job. Wouldn't hurt to have some help. I'm available. Besides, I don't know if you can take Bruno alone. I can."

She smiled, with genuine warmth this time. "Are you offering to ease out the bumps?"

He shrugged. "Something like that."

She considered. "I'm used to working alone. I need to think about it."

"That's a start. Why don't you come think at my place and, uh, I hope you don't take offense, but," and he wrinkled his nose. "I have a bathtub! And a couch to sleep on, and Gertrude would like to see you, I'm sure. It's as good a place to think as this is. You can always come back."

She mulled that offer a long time. It meant compromise, surrendering freedom and all of its vexations to the seductions of comfort. Could she give it up, once seduced?

"Have you got subway fare?"

"Heck, I'll spring for a cab."

She wrinkled her nose. "And hope the cabbie doesn't mind." She left the food, opened the sardines for the cats, and the clothes, someone would "...find and use them," she said. She shoved the metal box into her pocket and let the roof down. "Let's go."

***

The cabbie had balked until presented ahead of time with a better-than-average tip. He kept his window down and the heat turned up. Fenton sat up front beside him. Laura perched on the back seat, leaning against the door and watching out the window as the towers of commerce loomed, lit up like Christmas. Fenton sneaked a glance in the rear view mirror, just shifted his eyes, but she caught it. The tiny tic at the corner of her eyebrow gave her away.

"Still sowing your wild oats, Detective?"

He scratched his jaw and squinched up his left eye. "Not lately." He was thinking how good she'd be in a fight. His back still felt her knee, as his stomach felt her elbow. "Where'd you learn to hit like that?"

"A man named Hoyong taught me."

"You been to Tibet or someplace?"

"No, I've been..." she glanced at the cabbie, "...south. I met Hoyong there, but he was from Korea."

The cabbie broke in. "I got a cousin in the Navy, went to Korea. He likes to eat, he said what he ate there was a lot of rice and

184

cabbage, every town's got its own kind of cake made out of rice. He said the cabbage was almost like sauerkraut, only spicy."

"Kimchee."

Fenton turned and looked at her blankly.

"The cabbage is called kimchee. Hoyong's wife, Myoung-Jou, made it."

Fenton nodded and cranked his window down an inch. He took a pack of cigarettes and a lighter out of his shirt pocket, and lit up. He asked the driver, "So what's your cousin do now?"

"Still in the Navy, over at Pearl."

"Yeah? You ever going for a visit?" he kidded, "See some of those hula girls?"

The cabbie laughed. "Naw, me and the missus prefer Rockaway. Don't have to leave land to get there."

"I'll say. Got any kids?"

"Yeah, I got a son, he just made journeyman pipefitter and my daughter's going to business school downtown here."

Fenton continued to draw the man out, absolutely sincere, Laura realized. That he could be truly interested in this working man was something she hadn't expected of him. She couldn't know that a year spent among working people in Gertrude's company had done him good.

***

They found Gertrude washing up some dishes. She could not, of course, immediately place Laura and wondered why her brother would have brought this exotic creature into her staid Murray Hill apartment. She said, "She needs a bath," just milliseconds before recognizing her, so she went on and apologized for her rude behavior. Laura took no offense. She even thanked her for speaking plainly and asked where the bathroom was.

"We have two," Gertrude said, and smiled. "I wouldn't share one with him, and you may use mine." She led the way. "If your clothes need washing, you can leave them outside the door. I'll get something to put you in."

Laura went into the bathroom and began running water. Gertrude tapped on the door and handed in a terry robe.

"Help yourself to a good long soak, you need it. I don't want to see you in less than half an hour."

Laura undressed. She rinsed her clothes in the tub, wrung them out, and hung them over the side. After draining the tub and letting it fill, she lowered herself into the water and allowed herself to feel luxury for the first time in many months. She ranged backwards in her mind along the path that had brought her here. How strange it seemed from her present point of view. She stared idly down through the water at her taut belly and briefly felt Eve's hand like a spider across it, then put that thought away into a far corner of her heart.

A washcloth hung from a rail along the tub next to a recess that held a bar of Ivory soap and a bottle of Breck's shampoo. She lathered up the cloth and scrubbed at her face and her fingernails and toes, along the soles of her feet, and behind her knees. The water was several shades darker by then, and she let it out and refilled the tub. She would do that once more, and then lie to soak until her fingertips were good and wrinkled. She took down the shampoo and washed her hair. It had only had rain and river water for months, that's what had made it spiky, and the soap relaxed it. Later, when it had dried, she would feel it brush against her neck and remind her she hadn't felt that since North Carolina. She let the water out at last and stood, found a towel and dried herself, and slipped into the robe. She found her way to the kitchen, where Fenton and Gertrude sat at a table with two empty chairs.

"Thank you," she said, "I feel much better." Fenton pulled out a chair. Laura went and sat.

"Gertrude," she said, "how have you been?"

"I've been fine, thank you for asking. I have a job, and that's better off than a lot of people."

"And what else, Sis?"

"What?"

"Joe, tell her about Joe, your boyfriend."

Until that moment, Laura could never have imagined forthright Gertrude blushing. Or grinning. "Well, yes," she admitted, "I am still seeing him."

"Seeing him!? Why you two are inseparable. In fact, where is he?"

"He had to visit his mother tonight."

Fenton nudged Laura. "His mother adores her and she bakes. I never had so many cookies. So Gertrude, think he's going to ask his mother's permission to get hitched?"

"Fen, that's simply inappropriate, just random speculation."

He just laughed.

"What happened to you that night, after the explosion?" Laura asked.

"Oh, some silly doctors wanted to keep me in the hospital, for "observation", but I told them nonsense, soon as I came around. I went right back to work. Best cure I could ask for."

Laura smiled. "You're a remarkable woman, Gertrude."

"Just doing what needs doing is all. No excuse not to. How are you? Fen says you were down south?"

Laura's head shook no, reflexively, and her hair brushed her neck, and she stalled. Gertrude, fearing she'd caused Laura distress, apologized. "I didn't mean to ask the wrong question," she said, when she hadn't, because it was the feel of her hair to which Laura responded, and that, of course, Gertrude could not see. It brought on a tug, a memory of that spring evening outside the cave when her hair brushed her neck and Eve, off toward the river, rummaged in the wagon for a coffee can. Her feelings threatened to well out of her and she struggled to put them away, but she struggled with less pain and for not as long as she had the last time. She remembered how it was, when she had failed to put her struggles away and they overwhelmed her. But little by little the pain got less, and, now here were these people, kind and comfortable and offering a hand, and her sorrow, if not yet overthrown, was at least breached. She would go on and after a while the memory would be enough. She smiled at Gertrude. "I'm fine, thank you. I need to tell you a story." And she related to them the events that had befallen her these past fourteen months. Her version was mostly events; she dared not, even to Fenton and Gertrude, reveal her full devotion and attachment. In her relating, Eve was ever and only her friend.

With each new revelation -- the blade of grass, Tony's disappearance, her absence in the wreckage, Halliday revealed, what it was that she, and now Laura, were part of -- Fenton nodded, as if checking off a list in his mind.

Gertrude's reactions wavered between disbelief and admiration. At the end, she stood and said, "Well, Laura, I can't imagine all of that happening to one person, you almost seem to have lived a whole life already." She bent and hugged her. "I am glad you're back." She gave Fenton a hug, too, and advised him to get some sleep, and she left for bed herself. Laura left with her and returned in her street clothes. "I have to go see some people. Would you mind loaning me a key? I don't want to keep you up."

"Of course not." He reached into his pocket and handed her a door key.

"Thank you. I'll be back."

He took that positively.

***

She'd been tracking the man she sought for some weeks, and was finally sure of his routine. She was now occupying the dark corner from which she meant to address him. A shadow cast by a far streetlamp signaled his approach. As he came abreast of her, she called, "Mr. Hirsch."

He stopped and swiveled his head, then the rest of him and started towards her.

"No, please don't come closer. I wish, as much as possible, for my identity to remain a secret. You may know my name."

"Which is?"

"Laura van Duyn."

He sat back on his heels a second. "We thought you were dead."

"That was probably the logical conclusion to have drawn."

"What can I do for you?"

"I have come to apologize and make recompense, if you are willing."

"For what?"

"I abandoned you, Mr. Hirsch, at the very moment you trusted me and without ever a word of explanation."

"Since I thought you were dead, it didn't matter, but now I see your quandary." He retrieved a cigar stump from his breast pocket and began to chew. "How many stories did you deny me, Miss van Duyn?" he asked around it. "I hope whatever you did was worth abandoning your career for."

"It was, Mr. Hirsch. But I still owe you."

"I'll say. So I agree to the apology, what's the recompense?"

"I'm going to get you stories. I'm going to help you sell newspapers."

She'd piqued his reporter's interest. "You want to help me sell papers, Miss van Duyn?"

"That is my intention. And you will owe me no compensation, no attribution."

"You'd be an anonymous source. I'd need corroboration."

"Of course. I'll simply supply the leads. Your own reporters will investigate and write the stories."

"And it will be obvious to me in some way that this is from you, and I shouldn't ask too many questions about how I will know?"

"Yes. Do you agree?"

"Yes."

"Thank you." She'd planned her dark corner as much for its convenient exit as for its darkness, so she was already gone.

***

Her parents' habits she also knew. They'd still be up, even after 10. She had stopped at a spot she knew, where there would be clothes, and now wore a sport shirt, a tweed blazer, tan slacks, and some modest flats, well maintained but several years out of fashion. At the back of her parents' building, she changed her flats for ballet slippers and pulled on a pair of thin, supple leather gloves. She leaped for the fire escape, caught it and chinned herself, then switched to overhand and lifted herself onto the platform. She eschewed the ladders, instead pulling herself by hand up the balconies' cast iron balusters with her legs swinging out over the street, to crouch on the handrail, then to stand and reach for the next floor. She finally came even with an unoccupied apartment and an unlocked window and let herself in. She stopped in the kitchen, changed her shoes, took off the gloves, and went up, in the elevator, to her parents' floor.

Colleen van Duyn answered the door. She stood, gravely taking in the sight of her daughter, then smiled and extended her hands in welcome.

"My how you've grown." She drew Laura inside and gave her a big hug.

Laura pulled back, starting to speak, but Colleen put a finger to her lips.

"Apologies aren't necessary, dear. We never doubted that you were safe. The notice came, a most extraordinary incident." She took Laura's hand and led her down a hallway towards her study. "We were sitting on a bench in the park the day after that dock was destroyed, worrying about you, when a child -- a little, half-grown urchin -- came and sat beside us and said, "Excuse me, I am to tell you your daughter is safe and unless you hear that she is not, she will still be safe." He turned to Charles and said, "I am also to tell you, Sir, that if my saying so isn't sufficient, I may offer you proof for it." Charles was already halfway towards believing the child, but he asked for the proof anyway, and the child produced a sketch of you asleep on a pile of straw. It was drawn on a corner of your newspaper from the day before, the date was there. Whoever drew it had captured you with such care and precision that we both knew we would not have to worry. I admit my faith was beginning just to fray a little, but this message restored it. I prayed every night, and every night He assured us that you were safe and that He would send you back to us when He judged the time was right. And now He has."

Colleen's study bore the essence of comfort. Colleen sat Laura on a high-backed Queen Anne sofa beneath a crucifix hung on the wall and turned to a delicate Chippendale writing desk, where, from amid the clutter of correspondence, ledger books, receipts, and other paperwork that occupied her time she took the scrap of paper and handed it to Laura.

"I'll just fix us some tea," she said, and left the room.

Laura knew hesitation would be no help, and so it was only momentarily that she waited before spreading the drawing out before her, catching it full on. Her thoughts bloomed, of Eve's own hand drawing it, her very hand, and Eve, as she drew, already wanting her perhaps, as likely as Laura had already wanted Eve. This would be as close as she could ever come to touching Eve again. She expected tears, and there were some. She sat, waiting to be engulfed and for the old, grinding ache to take hold. Lightly, lightly did the thought come, how would tomorrow go? She cried some more then, not out of loss or regret, but out of knowing she was letting Eve go. She would never truly be gone, she would always live in Laura's heart, but finally her heart would not belong to Eve. She could begin to say farewell.

Colleen returned with a tea service and poured Laura a cup. Laura gave Eve's drawing back to her.

"I won't have a safe place to keep it for a long time. Except here. You keep it for me until I do. It will remind you of me."

"Then I'll give you something in its place." From around her neck, Colleen drew a fine silver chain that held a pendant of Saint Patrick, carved minutely, as if by insects, into a piece of dark and polished wood. Around its rim in tiny letters were the words "*Mrs. van Daon, go mbeannaí Dia thú.*" Colleen quickly cast it over Laura's head. "May it keep a safe place for you."

"Thank you, Mother."

"Laura, I have to tell you, I followed the reports in the newspapers. I know that you and Miss Halliday disappeared together. It seemed preposterous that you both were dead, killed in the explosion. I can see in your face what you've been through. I know what grief looks like. I know that you would grieve only for someone you loved, and I can see it was sincere, it was true love. Dear, though it is beyond my comprehension to understand, and though my religion stands against you, I cannot find it in my heart to reproach you. I am happy that you found love, and I am devastated that you lost it. I know that I said growth sometimes meant pain, but I had no idea, I would never have wished for you to have been so sad. I am so sorry." She took Laura in her arms and patted her back. "You must have had some very wise help to get you through it. I'd like to meet that person some day. I would shake his hand."

Laura spoke from her place on her mother's shoulder. "There were three mother, one to save me, one to nurse me, and one to put me back on my feet."

"I will hope to shake all of their hands, then. Tell me," she continued, "have you been to see Mr. Hardy? We tried to reach him after the accident, but he's left the police force, and we couldn't find an address."

A tiny smile blossomed, a daffodil in the snow. "Yes, I've seen him just tonight."

"Perhaps you two should go together on some new adventure."

A sound came from the foyer, a key in the bolt, the door opening, and a firm step across the marble.

"Why here's your father, back from his club." She stood and placed a hand on Laura's shoulder. "You wait right here."

Her father insisted on hearing the skinny again, marveling at her daughter's adventures. Laura only hinted at her future plans, not sure herself how they would actually go, but wanting to warn them and to forestall as well as she could their concern. It was after midnight when they let her go, to wend her way back to the Hardy's apartment

***

Fenton sat up, wide awake, to find Laura standing beside his bed. "As a matter of fact, I can take Bruno alone, but I did think, and I decided, it would be good to have you along."

"OK. Thanks."

"Don't mention it. Go back to sleep."

CHAPTER 29
BAYPORT

Gertrude awoke from a delicious dream to the smells of breakfast. She slipped out of bed and into her robe and went to the kitchen. There was Laura busy at the stove frying bacon and scrambling eggs. The toaster hummed and the coffeepot burbled. Three places were set keeping company with butter, a jam jar, the creamer, and the sugar bowl.

"I see you learned to cook."

Laura smiled. "Have a seat. I hope you're hungry."

"I am, and thank you!"

"It was the least I could do. Does your brother use an alarm or does he need to be gotten up?"

"I'll go get him." She came back with Fenton, in pajamas and robe, yawning and scratching his scalp. They both sat and Laura began filling plates. Gertrude said grace and Laura remarked that the Lord still took an interest in her figure. Gertrude thanked her and, noting the portion Laura gave herself, remarked that she seemed to have found her appetite and with no detriment to her own figure. Fenton grumbled amiably about girl talk. Gertrude began to clear the table, but Laura insisted on cleaning up, so Gertrude excused herself to bathe and dress for work and Fenton likewise. Laura did the dishes.

Later, as he and Laura stood on the street outside the apartment, Fenton stepped to the curb and started to hail a cab, but Laura said, "No, let's walk." Laura had procured yet another outfit. She now wore a navy blue, calf-length skirt and matching blazer over a white blouse, and stout, sensible shoes. Fenton paused to light a cigarette, and let out the first drag with a cough.

"I think I warned you about those once."

"You surely did, and you were surely right. I ought to quit before my bellows are shot."

She held out her hand. "Would there ever be a better time?"

He smiled at her righteousness, reached into his pocket, pulled out a pack of Chesterfield Regulars and handed them over. Laura stooped to toss them down a storm drain, and he said, "That's that?"

"We'll see." She led him off down the street. He asked about the boys they were going after, and she realized he still did not know that part of the story, so she told him. "They're my crew now. When I determined to find the arms, and didn't know whom I could trust to ask, I gave the task to them. They know the streets and nobody pays them any mind. They can find out whatever I need to know without arousing suspicions. They started the rumors that set you onto that house in Queens."

"And they have found where these guns are hidden?"

"I think so."

Forty-five minutes' walk left them in front of Bruno's last known address. Laura approached three charged-up boys gathered on the stoop. Laura introduced them to Fenton as Andrjez, Franz, and Rasheed. Rasheed invited them up to his family's apartment to hear what the crew had found out.

Laura, Fenton, and the boys stood a moment in the small, dim space, letting their eyes adjust; the room's single window let onto a narrow alley. Five mattresses stacked on end sagged against the wall ahead of them, next to a door that led to the only other room. Beneath the window to their right stood a stove and small counter with sink and two rough cabinets nailed to the wall on either side of the window. A table and four chairs sat on the floor before the counter.

"Do you live alone, Rasheed?" Fenton asked.

"No. My mother is at work, she cleans houses uptown. My dad's gone down to Maryland to help his cousins with their farm and my brothers and sisters are at school." They all gathered at the table.

Andrjez spoke up. "Miss van Duyn asked us if we could find any of the men who had driven a truck down to the dock that night, then we could find out where he picked up his freight, and that might be where the depot is. We was gonna ask at the Union Hall, but Miss van Duyn said these guys probably didn't belong to no union. She said try the shantytowns over by the river, wave a piece of grass around, and ask after any out-of-work drivers. We finally found a guy, and he said it all came from some place called Bayport."

"Bayport!" Fenton perked up, intrigued. "I know Bayport, I went to high school there, at the Woodson Academy. Quiet town, hard to think of it as a smuggling den, but then it just might fit. Not the first place someone would look."

"Yes," Laura mused. "Let's go to Bayport."

***

Neither one of them had a car, so they caught a bus. They had a brilliant and warm Indian summer day. After they left the city, Laura opened the window to let the breeze into her hair. Fenton tried to doze with his hat over his face, but soon began to fidget for a cigarette. Laura laid her arm over his on the armrest.

"Untie your shoes."

He glanced at his brown brogues and raised his eyes, quizzically, to hers.

"Let your feet breathe a little, they're too hot."

He shrugged and bent to loosen his shoes. "Glad I used foot powder this morning." He leaned back and sighed. "Say, that does feel better. You got any more strange ideas?"

"Be serious," she scolded.

"I am, I am. I'm all jumpy, I hate that, and you made me a little relaxed. Make me more relaxed."

Laura smiled and turned toward him. "All right, lean back and close your eyes."

"You're not going to try and put me to sleep!"

"I said be serious! Close your eyes."

He grumbled, but closed them.

"Don't go to sleep, just think of only one thing."

Fenton blindly grinned. "A foot long hot dog with chili and mustard!" His knees bounced and swayed.

Laura squeezed, hard, and got his attention. "Breathe. With me." Her breath came like a slow wave on the beach. When he had the drift, she let go his hand, and began a contralto hum as she exhaled, soft, then strong, then soft again before the inhale.

The bus driver glanced into his wide mirror and back to the road, sipping from a bottle of buttermilk. They were his only passengers.

After five minutes, Fenton's knees slowed, then stopped. Laura turned back to the window. After fifteen minutes, Fenton opened his eyes and watched the fields go by. "What do you know? That worked."

***

The driver dropped them on the street outside Bayport's bus station just before noon. As they stood gathering their bearings, a police car stopped at the curb beside them. The young man at the wheel leaned across to the open passenger window.

"Good afternoon, folks. I'm Patrolman Collig. Do you need any help?"

Fenton started towards the car, but Laura caught him up and spoke. "Can you tell us, please, where the library is?"

"Why, sure." He pointed straight ahead. "You go down to the next street, that'll be Pleasant Street, take a right, and it's a block down, on the right. Can't miss it. Would you like a lift?"

"No thank you. I think we'd like some lunch first. Can you recommend a place?"

"Morton's, just across the street there. Nice lunch counter, good hamburgs, coffee, and great apple pie."

Laura thanked him, and he pulled away.

After hamburgers, pie, and coffee at Morton's, they walked to the library, a tidy, square, single-story, yellow brick building set back from the street among laurel hedges and azalea bushes, and shaded by four or five tall elm trees. Inside, the smell of beeswax emanated from the walnut wainscot and mingled with the slightly musty odor of books and, from the tweed-clad woman behind the counter, the hint of Fleurs de Rocaille.

Laura breathed. "My mother's perfume," she said.

The librarian beamed, her dark eyes twinkling behind wire-rimmed glasses, and graciously asked how she could help.

Laura glanced at her nameplate. "Mrs. Braithwaite, my name is Laura van Duyn and this is Detective Hardy." She waved towards

Fenton. "I'm looking for a house. I wonder if you might know where it is. It would have been used on the Underground Railroad."

"Why, yes, there is one, over on Elm Street, I did the research myself, you see, my grandfather passed the night there once, on his way to Boston. Why do you ask?"

"Personal interest. A kind of investigation. Might you know if its owners are at home?"

"Well, that's the shame, really, it's just a derelict. I'm not sure even who owns it. Nobody in town, certainly."

"Is it far? Could you please give us directions?"

"No, it isn't far. Look there behind you." She pointed to a large map of the town mounted on the opposite wall. "You can find Elm Street by the key. The house is at number 23."

"Thank-you, you've been very kind."

"My pleasure."

***

23 Elm Street looked familiar enough to make Laura smile. It loomed behind a crumbling stockade fence, standing in a yard gone weedy and coarse, clad in narrow strips of silvered wood, some fallen. With its hanging gutters and shattered windows, it looked as if the merest nudge would bring it down. She turned the corner onto Elm Street to walk past the front of the house. Someone had built on a short, sagging porch that stretched the width of the house. She strolled past it trailing Fenton and, at the next corner, turned onto the cross street. Halfway along, she went down the alley, shadowed and dimmed by overhanging trees, and came up at the rear of No. 23, where a large, rustling oak tree stood over the remains of the fence. She parted the grape vines and brambles that overgrew the fence to reveal a wide gap in the pickets, through which they stepped into the yard. An extension, perpendicular to the house, ran out towards them. It had no door, and windows were placed up towards the eaves, too high to see in without a ladder.

"Funny," Fenton remarked, "it's done so it looks normal from out on the street."

Laura stood gazing for a moment, nodding in agreement, then started down the right side of the house along a brush-choked gap between the extension and the neighboring house. Halfway along, the vines and brambles grew thick enough to stop their progress. Laura turned to face the wall. Starting as high as she could comfortably reach her arm, she scanned back and forth and downward until just at waist height she stopped and gave a little cry. To Fenton, she pointed out the tiny likeness of a blade of grass carved into the wood. She pushed upward on the length of siding, and it slid smoothly beneath its overlapping neighbor in the course above. A small door, raggedly edged with wood ends, swung outward, centered on the hidden mechanism. Fenton gave a low whistle. "Good work," he breathed. They stooped to walk through and down some stairs a good six feet to stand on a packed dirt floor. The sunlight streaming through the door revealed the room's dimensions, twenty by thirty feet and the ceiling sixteen feet above them. As near as Laura could tell, all of the crates that she and Eve had worked so hard to deliver were there, stacked floor-to-ceiling and wall-to-wall with just a few narrow aisles between them for walking space. Fenton whistled again. "Jackpot," he said.

They reconnoitered the room, each by a different path, and returned to stand by the door, framed in sunlight. Fenton appraised the stacks of crates.

"Now we head back to New York? Pick up a couple of trucks and your boys?"

"That was my plan."

They set off for the bus station. Laura wanted to see more of Bayport, so they went by a different route, which brought them into an industrial part of town. The street led them past the back lot of a construction company, full of stacked lumber, tufts of grass, spools of cable, and assorted trucks. Beside the fence that separated the lot from the sidewalk stood a semi-truck trailer. On its side, in red plain block letters were the words "Evelyn Frances Cosmetics."

Laura said, "I need to see these people." She led Fenton around to the front of the yard, where a sign above the gate read "Prito Construction. Land and Sea." Inside the gate was a small office building. Laura went up its steps and entered. Behind a counter stood a stout, balding man in denim jeans and a blue work shirt. He was bent over a desk, examining a blueprint. He looked up as the door squealed open.

"Can I help you?" His voice was rough, but not unkind. As he waited for Laura to answer, he picked a pack of cigarettes off the desk with his right hand, shook it, and drew one out between his lips. He put the pack down.

"I'd like to know about that trailer out in your yard. The cosmetics trailer."

In the man's left hand, hanging limp at his side, was a lighter. He flipped it open with his thumb and flicked the igniter wheel a couple of times. When the lighter flared, he grabbed his left arm with his right hand and lifted the flame to the cigarette's tip, pulled, got it going, then dropped his arm and flipped the lighter shut. He drew deep and exhaled, squinting against the smoke. Fenton fidgeted, but Laura stilled him with a hand across his shoulder.

The man held out his right hand. "Anthony Prito," he said, "Pleased to meet you."

Laura shook the offered hand. His eyebrows rose at her grip.

"What happened to your arm?"

He grinned. "Took a bullet for Joe Hill in '05. Didn't ever hurt. I figure because of the privilege."

"I don't remember anyone taking a bullet for him."

"Well, I don't talk about it much."

"Why did you tell me?"

"You must've known Evelyn," he replied.

"I'm Laura van Duyn."

"I figured."

Now Laura's eyebrows rose, and settled, and then the corners of her lips slowly lifted. She pulled Fenton up beside her. "Mr. Prito, my associate, Fenton Hardy."

Prito held out his hand, and they shook. Laura said, "I'd like to talk with Mr. Hardy privately outside. I don't mean any offense."

He grinned again. "I don't generally take offense at people I like."

Out on the porch, with the door closed behind them, Fenton asked, "What's up?"

"Marine construction. He must have access to boats, docks, trucks. We're already on the coast, why should we haul those crates all the way back to New York? I want to ask him if he would help us load the ship."

Fenton considered. "What about Horace, Gus, and Bruno? Can we get them down here? And if we do, can we hold them?"

Laura shouldered open the office door. "Mr. Prito, do you have a ship to shore radio?"

"Of course."

She turned back to Fenton. "I can arrange a truck and getting the boys ready. Mr. Prito," she called, "could you keep three men shut up overnight?"

"Sure could."

Laura nodded at Fenton. "Then it's set. You and I will capture them tomorrow night, put them on the truck, and bring them down here with the boys to stand guard during the trip."

Back inside, Laura laid out her plan. Anthony signed on enthusiastically.

"There's a cove north of town, company has a dock there and a motor launch, some construction equipment." He gave Laura coordinates to pass onto the ship's captain, so he'd know where to meet them. "You get your crew, your ship, and those three bad men down here. I'll take care of all the rest. What time?"

"Eight o'clock?"

"That's not a problem," he said. "See you then."

CHAPTER 30
AN EVENING OFF

Back at the Hardy's apartment that evening, Gertrude met them at the door and held out her right hand. "Joe's asked me to marry him," she gushed. "Look, his mother's ring." The platinum band sparkled in the light, as did the quarter-carat stone that topped it. Fenton, with a grin, swept her up and spun her around, set her back on her feet.

"Gert, that's wonderful! Is there a date?"

"No, I told him I'd want to discuss it with his mother."

"Well I think we ought to celebrate. Shall I run out for champagne?"

"Don't be foolish, Fen. I have all I need right here. You've heard my news. Now you must tell me about your day."

They gathered in the kitchen and, between them, Laura and Fenton filled Gertrude in on the afternoon's discoveries and the next day's plans.

"That's a lot on your plates. And you intend still to apprehend those three criminals tonight, too?"

Fenton looked to Laura, who nodded.

Gertrude slapped the tabletop. "You'll need some fortification. Fen, peel some potatoes, please, and slice them up." She went to the refrigerator, retrieved eggs, milk, and a block of cheddar cheese. She pulled down two mixing bowls from a cupboard overhead, and began separating eggs for a soufflé. Laura, anticipating Gertrude's intention, lit the gas on the stovetop, rummaged under the oven for a saucepan, and began the sauce, melting butter, stirring in flour, adding milk, salt, ground pepper, Worcestershire sauce, and finally, when the sauce had thickened, a handful of grated cheese. While Gertrude whisked the egg whites into stiff peaks, Laura stirred some of the sauce into the separated yolks, poured in the rest, and handed the bowl to Gertrude who folded the mixture into the egg whites. She spooned the batter into a soufflé mold and set it to bake in the oven.

As they were working, Laura asked, "What will your wedding be like?"

"Oh, I don't know, I hardly thought about it. I'm no spring chicken, probably no need to get all in a fuss about it. Maybe he and I'll just go down to the courthouse."

"Oh, my goodness, Gertrude, no! How could you think that? You must have a proper wedding."

"Well." Gertrude blushed, "I-I did some window shopping last week. I saw some lovely gowns. You don't think it's just vanity?"

"It's not, Gertrude. It should be in a church, with all of your friends. It needs a best man and a maid of honor. And afterwards there should be dancing and champagne. It's what you deserve. Don't you think so, Fenton?"

"These spuds are ready," he announced, "and Gert, she's right, it's your special day. You deserve all you can get from it."

"Well, goodness, I wouldn't know where to begin."

Laura reassured her. "I'll help you Gertrude. Don't you worry."

Laura rinsed the potatoes, put them in a panful of water on the stove to boil, and when they were tender, fried them up crisp and golden. She lifted them onto a platter with her spatula and set them onto the table next to the soufflé, just out of the oven and already beginning to sink in the cooler air. Gertrude plopped ladlesful onto plates, and they all sat to eat, silently for a time, concentrating on their food. After a second helping, Fenton pushed his plate back.

"I thank you, ladies. Didn't realize how hungry I was."

"Words are fine, Fen, but deeds are even better. How about you do the dishes?"

Fenton sighed, but guessed that was fair and started clearing the table. Laura volunteered to dry if he wanted to wash, and they made an efficient pair, getting the job done in a jiffy. With the table cleared, Gertrude brought out a cribbage board and a deck of cards, and they traded off playing, two at a time, sipping lemonade, while Red Barber called the Yankees against the Cubs on the radio, and a light breeze brought the sounds and smells of the slowly darkening city through the window open beside them. The time came when Gertrude yawned, stretched, wished them luck, said goodnight, and padded off to bed. Fenton gathered up the cards and slid them into their case and switched off the radio.

"Look, I don't want to intrude or impose. I'm happy to help you, but if I get to be a pain the neck, you let me know, OK? I mean it."

"OK."

"Glad that's out of the way. How do you want to split up on those three?"

"Either of us can take Bruno, and Gus shouldn't be a problem."

"Do you have any kind of backup? In case there's trouble?"

"I can always call the police. There's a call box down the street."

Fenton had walked that street and didn't remember a call box.

"You wouldn't have seen it."

He grinned.

"What?" she asked.

"Like you're a secret agent or something."

She turned away and smiled to herself.

***

They were on the roof across the street at 9:00. Laura was in her street clothes again, and they both reclined with their backs against the parapet and their legs stretched out in front of them. Fenton said, "I'd like to ask you about something."

"What is it?"

"Where'd you go, what did you do after the attack? You kind of just skipped over that part."

It was true, she had, and consciously. She had feared betraying her true feelings for Eve. It had been a black time, and if that was a cliché, nobody ever said clichés weren't apt. She had kept that blackness bound up tight in her, afraid of it coming loose, but now she took a deep breath and ventured to tell him, a version of it anyway, the part where Smith rescued her and Amos cured her.

The version she told Fenton was abbreviated, bowdlerized -- a word she dredged up from an old English class. She left out the song, afraid he'd ask her to sing it. It pained her not being utterly honest with him, but he took it as she told it. He wasn't a devious man,

Laura thought, he wasn't given to teasing out bias or motive. She told it steady and straight out, and her fears went unrealized.

"You don't seem very angry."

She slipped fingers into her pants pocket and withdrew the little metal box and Zippo lighter. "How do you mean?"

"Just seems like someone that brutal, caused me all that pain, I'd be thinking about putting the gun to his head myself. I mean, I wouldn't pull the trigger, but I'd be raging some. You don't."

She opened the box, took out a tiny brass pipe and a block of material wrapped in tinfoil. "Anger is a wasted emotion. It would only distract me from what I need to do." She began to unwrap the block -- some dark material, Fenton saw, that gave off a spicy odor, not quite pine. He watched Laura pick bits of it off with her fingernail and put it in the pipe. His eyebrows rose when she put the pipe to her lips, set fire to its contents, and inhaled the vapor.

"What is that?"

She exhaled. "Hashish."

"Are you kidding!? That'll make you crazy!"

"It hasn't yet."

"Then you'll get addicted. The government says so. Besides, isn't that a double standard? You told me not to smoke."

Laura took another hit at the pipe, then knocked out the ashes, and put away her rig. "Yes, I suppose it is, although I use it very little. I saw you get jittery on that bus ride today, because you didn't have a cigarette. I don't ever feel that compulsion, and because I do not feel compelled to use it, I believe if I ever came to see it as a crutch, I would give it up. To its benefit, I find it improves my concentration. I'm able to see choices more clearly and to take the correct one. We may end up in a fight, and I want that clarity for it." She smiled, remembering. "And it improves sensation. If it disturbs you, though, I won't use it around you."

"Each to his own poison, I guess, and you're an adult, you can do what you want, I just..."

"Sh." Laura put a finger to her lips and spun to crouch behind the barricade. Fenton heard feet scuffling and a faint squeak. Laura raised herself to peer over at the street. Fenton joined her. They saw six men approaching, among them Bruno, unmistakably large, and a smaller man beside him that must have been Gus pushing the carriage. The four others went ahead of them, and when they drew abreast of the house, Bruno gestured, and they came across the street to stand apparently directly under Laura and Fenton. Moments later, they heard the building's door open and shut. Laura turned and sat.

"What do you want to do?" Fenton asked.

"We have no choice, we have to take them."

"That will scare off Horace."

"We can hope it won't. That's better than just sitting here."

"I'm ready when you are."

The four men loomed in the foyer. They saw Laura and Fenton coming down the stairs, and their hands headed toward their jackets. Laura went in first, executing a move Fenton had heard of only as myth. When her opponent's fist got to where he'd aimed it, she wasn't there anymore, she was way over on her other foot, kissing the side of the goon's neck with her heel. He dropped, out cold. She'd had dancing lessons, too, Fenton noticed. He preferred a direct approach, parrying with his forearm, knocking the pistol out of his opponent's hand, and swinging his other fist up, into a roundhouse at first, but the guy was slow, so he switched mid-punch and got in a solid uppercut instead. The dope's head snapped back and his eyes rolled up, so he was down. When Fenton went after one of the other two, he saw Laura had taken on the both of them. They couldn't move fast enough, never got a hand on her, and she split between them almost flickering to the eye, sliding in and throwing body blows, her fingers stiffened at the second knuckle, blunt as broomsticks and too quick to see, while she gave out a sort of yelp at each hit that Fenton found somehow amusing. Left long enough, she'd wear them down all by herself until they slowly collapsed, bruised and exhausted, begging for the cops to come and make it stop, but Fenton was there, too, contributing his own, less subtle, form of justice until they were laid out beside their brothers in short order.

Laura and Fenton rushed the door, but the street was empty. In frustration, Laura stalked stiff legged in circles, burning off energy and thinking. Fenton stood by, helpless.

"What do you want to do?"

"Bayport, we'll get them in Bayport."

CHAPTER 31
ARRANGING THE RENDEZVOUS

The next morning, they all three stood together on the sidewalk outside the apartment. Gertrude said good-bye and gave them each a kiss on the cheek. "I love you both. Come back safe. You have to dance at my wedding."

Laura and Fenton walked to Grand Central and took the subway to Union Square. Laura headed west on 14th Street and soon turned south into the meatpacking district, a warren of dead end streets, and back alleys suffused with a rancid odor. They threaded their way through legions of husky men in blood-soaked shirts hauling sides of beef from the backs of trucks into dusky buildings sounding with the whine of electric saws and the whacking of large knives. Laura turned west down a dingy alley. Beneath a popping and buzzing neon sign promising "C--cktails", Laura pulled open a heavy steel door and ushered Fenton into the murky interior. Laura reassured him. "I know the owner." He shrugged and went in.

The room was longer than it was wide, and as high as it was long. Four dim light bulbs suspended from the murk up towards the ceiling on long conduits and surmounted by tin shades provided the only illumination. A mahogany bar down the left side dominated the room, leaving an aisle only wide enough for a line of men standing at the bar and another to pass sideways behind them. Behind the bar, his backside reflected in the mirror running the bar's length, stood the room's only other occupant, the bartender, a skinny old gentleman with a bald and wrinkled head, dressed in a white shirt and a regimental tie in navy and maroon patiently wiping spots off the beer glasses. The light streaming through the slowly closing door momentarily dazzled him.

"What can I get you lads?" he called without looking up, knowing from experience not to even try to make out his customers.

"It's just me, Reggie," Laura replied, "Is Jake in?"

"Oh hello, dearie. I expect he's catching a nap in the back room. We were busy last night, a couple of knife fights, and some nasty business with one of those wenches hangs about, he had to run her over to St. Vincent's for some medical attention."

"Will she be all right?"

"Oh yes, a broken arm and some stitches. She'll be back on the street soon enough. The blokes who worked her over got rather the worse end of the deal once Jake was done with them."

"Jake and you, too, I don't doubt. Don't be modest."

He smiled. "Well, yes, still good with a cricket bat, I suppose." He lifted a delicate china cup. "Would you like some tea? Just brewed."

"I'll take a slug of that, Reggie. None of your dainty teacups, though, milk and sugar, too." Jake stood in a doorway at the back of the room, a fit, heavyweight-sized black man in a white dress shirt with the sleeves rolled up and crisply-pressed black slacks. While Reggie mixed his tea, he strode across the room barefoot, belying any formality, and took Laura in a big hug. "How's my favorite singing girl?" He let her go and said to Fenton, "She stands right up on that table back there and sings to a roomful of men. Sad songs mostly, I've seen men cry." He extended his right hand. "Name's Jake. You a friend of hers?"

Fenton nodded towards Laura. "If she says so."

"Of course you are, Fenton."

Fenton took Jake's hand, but couldn't shake it, the man was immovable. "Fenton Hardy."

"Hardy! You were on the force a while back. About the time that building blew up over in Brooklyn?"

"Yes, I had something to do with that."

"Pleased to meet you. Hope you had something to do with cheering her up, I don't know if I've ever seen her happy before. If that was you, you'll be a friend of mine."

He took them down to the end of the bar to sit at the table. Reggie set mugs, a sugar bowl and a pitcher of milk in front of the three of them. Jake emptied half his mug in one swallow and let out a bellow of satisfaction. "That's good stuff. Hey, Reggie," he yelled towards his bartender, "I am glad I hired you."

"Have you heard from Smith?" Laura asked.

"Oh, that cousin of mine, he gets all over the place. Last I heard he was out in Uzbekistan, mixed up with a bunch of Gypsies were taking a beating from some local warlord." He called to Reggie, "Hey, how about some grub for my friends, sausages and tomatoes, and some of that black pudding. Join us." He turned to Fenton. "You going to go back into police work?" He took another gulp from his mug.

Fenton was a little startled at Jake's directness. After a minute of consideration, Laura's eyes searching his face, too, he said, "No, I don't think so. I'd like to strike out on my own with something. I'm a good detective, but I don't like a lot of rules and regulations. I work better alone."

"You ought to open a shop, private investigation. Sounds like it might suit you. I've been reading this guy, Dashiell Hammett, he writes about that line of work, sounds like a good one."

"I don't know how much life is like books."

"He was a Pinkerton man, knows what he's talking about. You should look into it."

Fenton shrugged. "Maybe I will. Thanks for the tip."

Reggie arrived with a platterful of food. "That was fast," Jake said.

"I knew you'd be hungry. It was already done, just had it warming in the oven."

Jake, taking in Laura and Fenton, jerked his thumb at Reggie. "Is this guy a jewel or what?" He pulled out a chair for Reggie, who sat and passed around forks, and they all dug in communally. When they had finished, Reggie took the platter and went back to his beer glasses. Jake turned to Laura.

"What happened last night, you never came for the truck?"

Laura related the previous night's events. "We need to change our plan a little. I need you to plant some information and make sure it gets around. I don't think we need to be mysterious anymore. Make it plain where those arms are. That will get them to Bayport where we'll figure out how to round them up. And I didn't tell you yesterday, it's too sensitive to broadcast, we need to change the rendezvous with the ship."

"Well, all right, let's do it." He pushed back from the table and motioned them to follow. "Going downstairs, Reggie," he called. They went through the doorway into a back room. Jake switched on a bare light bulb dangling from the ceiling to reveal shelves lining the walls, on which were stacked the bar's supplies, and, clear at the back, a comfortable-looking bed surrounded by a crammed set of bookcases. There were more piles of books on the floor and nightstand beside the bed. Shoved into a small crevice between two piles stood an alto saxophone. Jake knelt, flipped aside a small rug, and pulled at a brass ring set into the floor. A trapdoor came up. Jake stood and started down a steep set of stairs, almost a ladder, really. "Watch your heads," he warned, as Laura and Fenton descended after him. By the time they got to the floor below, Jake was already warming up his radio set. There was no microphone, just a telegraph key. Jake sat before it, strapped on a pair of headphones, dialed in a frequency, and began tapping on the key. The flurry lasted about thirty seconds, and then he stopped to listen for a reply, his face screwed up in concentration. He turned to Laura. "He says he knows the cove. He will be there at 10 pm." Laura nodded. Jake tapped some more, listened, nodded, tapped again, listened for the reply, then took off the headphones. "OK, it's all set up. Meet you night after tomorrow night at Bayport."

"Thank-you so much, Jake. You've been a wonderful help."

"Hey, my pleasure. You just watch yourself, OK?"

Laura nodded, then stepped up and gave him a kiss on the cheek.

"Why thank-you darlin'. Now you'd best go on home and catch a nap. Busy day tomorrow."

"Busy day today, but thanks." While Jake shut down his radio, Laura and Fenton climbed the ladder to the storeroom, and walked out through the bar, waving to Reggie and thanking him for breakfast as they passed.

They walked back to Union Square and used their last few coins to take the subway downtown so they could meet the boys and map out a plan to get them to Bayport.

Out on the street, Fenton recognized a branch of his own bank and stopped to withdraw some cash. They strolled towards home through the tenements, a tough neighborhood. Without warning, two men jostled them. One of them shoved a pistol barrel into Fenton's ribs, "Saw you at that bank back there, and me and him, we could use that dough, so why don't you and the dame step into the alley, and we'll be happy to lighten your load a little." The other man put his arm around Laura's shoulders, steering her after them, and they all four disappeared into dimness. A passerby might have a heard a shout of surprise, some grunts, and a noise like a couple of sacks of potatoes hitting the ground. A minute later, Fenton and Laura emerged from the alley, Fenton shaking the pain out of his contused knuckles, and Laura straightening the hat on her head.

"You're pretty good in a fight."

"Likewise."

"Might be I could show you how to take a man down without you getting your knuckles dusted."

"If that's an offer, might be I'll take you up on it."

CHAPTER 32
NIGHT WORK

The full moon in a clear October night shone upon a dozen or so boys dressed in dark clothes, standing before the office of the Prito Construction Company. Laura and Fenton had a hectic afternoon getting them into town a few at a time. Some of them took the bus, some hitchhiked, several came in an old jalopy that now stood behind the company office. Here they were, finally, facing the office's porch where Anthony Prito, Laura, and Fenton stood. Anthony spoke.

"OK, boys, we're going to take a couple of trucks out to the house, we're going to move around a hundred crates onto them, then take them north of town and unload them. The trucks will make some noise, but other than that we've got to be quiet as possible. Working people like yourselves will be sleeping. And no heroes, OK? I want four to a crate, no less. They're heavy and we can't afford to lose any of you, especially by trying to show what a man you are. Work hard, but work smart. Now, the trucks are around back. Let's go. "

He stepped off the porch and led the way behind the office. There were two stout freight trucks, snub-nosed, and with canvas tents over the beds. The boys climbed into the back of one. Anthony turned to Laura and Fenton, held up a pair of keys.

"Which one's driving?"

Laura insisted Fenton drive. They arrived at 23 Elm Street in just a few minutes, down the alley behind the house. Anthony looked the stockade fence over skeptically. "It'll be a chore getting those crates through that fence. Would you mind, Miss van Duyn, if we disassembled it a little?" When Laura said no, he took a couple of crowbars out of the back of one of the trucks and handed them to two boys. "Know how to use those?" The boys nodded. "OK, take out about a three-foot section of that fence, just take off the pickets." The boys went to work, prying out nails. Some of the nails squealed. Fenton asked if the noise and activity wouldn't raise some suspicions.

"The way I've heard it told," Anthony explained, "is that the neighbors are pretty well used to the activity and, in large part, sympathize with it. Doubt they'll give us any trouble."

When the boys had finished their work, Laura led the company through the gap the boys had made, then along the house to the secret entrance. She raised the activator panel and opened the door. She told the boys to wait and felt her way down the steps, then turned to take lanterns the boys passed down the line to her. She got the lanterns lit and placed where they would shine the most light on the work, and then the boys began to file in. Anthony handed out work gloves, and organized them into teams of four, himself, Laura and Fenton included, leaving several in reserve, so they could spell each other when they got tired. Anthony warned them again not to overdo it, to ask for help or a rest if they needed it. Then they got to work.

Each truck took twenty-five crates. They would make two trips that night. The first load up took two hours. Before they left for the dock, Anthony fed them thick beef sandwiches, brisket he'd probably braised himself that morning, moist and spicy with horseradish and mustard that made their eyes water. When they were done, he let them flop on their backs and digest for a half an hour, then roused them up and shepherded them onto the trucks, telling them not to hang off the back of the truck, on pain of...well, he didn't want to say.

North of town they pulled off the highway onto a sturdy gravel road. A half mile in, they stopped so Anthony could unlock the gate in a chain link fence. Inside the fence sat a few small buildings and some stacks of materials covered with tied-down sheets of canvas. The road extended across the beach to a dock running broadside of the shore. A small shed perched on the inland edge; to seaward, a barge and Anthony's motor launch were docked. Anthony trusted his dock but still allowed only one truck at a time to drive onto it. He reassembled the teams and they got to work. Laura toted her share. The boys could not believe her strength.

Mid-way through unloading the second group of crates, Fenton found himself working alongside Anthony.

"How did a Wobblie come to own the means of production?"

Anthony threw back and laughed, almost dropping his end of the crate. "That's how it's supposed to end up for us workers. Yeah, I make a profit, but most of it goes back into the business, better equipment for my guys and paying their families' doctor bills. Don't get me wrong, they work hard for it, but I keep them longer if I take care of 'em, and the more experience, the better they work. Something those robber barons never considered, I'll bet. Who knows what shape this country'd be in today if they'd only paid better attention to their men. Lot better than it is, I think."

Fenton considered a minute, huffing a little under his load. "You know, a year ago I wouldn't have bought that, but it starts to make sense the way you explain it. I'll bet your men get weekends off, too."

Anthony grinned. "If that's what they want. Usually their wives push them for overtime, though, always saving up for something better."

The night's work ended. They pulled heavy beige tarps over the crates to protect them from all but the most determined eyes, which, in any case, were unlikely to appear along this lonely stretch of beach. Everyone collapsed wearily in the trucks going back to the construction yard. Anthony had fitted out the cosmetics trailer with mattresses and blankets, old and musty, but the boys were too tired to care. They were asleep before they could take in the smell. For Laura there were a sleeping bag and mattress in the office ("Wished it was a feather bed," Anthony declared. "Nonsense," Laura replied, "this will do fine."). With everyone else settled, Anthony turned to Fenton.

"Got a little fire set in the pit out back. Mind sleeping under the stars tonight? Might be I could offer you a nip of something to warm your belly."

Fenton grinned. "Why that sounds just fine." He held out his hand. "Thanks."

***

They each nursed a second whiskey, poured straight into coffee mugs. Fenton lay stretched out by the fire on a couple of blankets, up on a hip and a forearm, staring into the flames, and shadows flickering across his face. Anthony reclined in a wooden beach chair he'd dragged up.

"She's quite a woman."

"Who, Laura? Yeah, she's got a lot of sides to her."

"And they're curvy, too. You have a girlfriend?"

Fenton searched Anthony's face, trying to judge the intent of his inquiry and decided it was a suggestion. "Aw, well, she doesn't see eye to eye with me, all I ever do is rile her up."

"I ain't seen her riled up yet."

"Give her time."

"No, that's what you ought to do."

"What?"

"Give her some time. She'll come around."

Fenton had to laugh. "How do you know that?"

"I guess I don't for sure. But a lot of people get riled at someone they like, someone gets under their skin a little and that spooks them, they don't know what to make of it, so they react, they try to push it back. It takes courage to let someone under your skin."

"You can't say she isn't courageous. She fought down two men big as me all by herself just yesterday."

"There's different kinds of courage. But listen, I ain't trying to run your life. Maybe she ain't your type. I'm just saying, I ain't seen her close to being riled in two days now. You give her some time, give yourself some time, and who knows?" He raised his mug. "Here's to giving things time." They both drank off their whiskey. Anthony stood. "Busy day tomorrow. Better get some sleep."

"Going home?"

"Heck no, this is an adventure! I'm staying right here."

CHAPTER 33
UNDER ASSAULT

They let the boys sleep late the next morning. Anthony brought donuts and coffee while they roused. One by one, he directed them to the privy. It was a nice privy, they all said, with its shaped, honed, and varnished wooden seat. They stood together beside the trailer drinking cups of steamy coffee, dunking their donuts, a few of them smoking. Fenton leaned over as Laura came up and said, "Let 'em be, just let 'em be."

Anthony figured the boys ought not to stand around all day, so he set them to work, hauling and stacking. Around mid-afternoon, the heat began to tell on the boys. Anthony told them to knock off and passed around sandwiches and sodas. The boys dug in with gusto, and settled down for a quick snooze. It would be another late night.

***

Anthony fired up one of his pickups at 9:00. He, Laura, and Fenton took the cab, and the boys piled in back. When they got to the dock, the boys went down the beach into the darkness, stripped to skivvies, dove into the water to wash off the day's sweat, and stayed to cavort a while. Laura tilted her head. "Sounds like somebody's coming." Against the horizon, the ridge at the top of the dune, a light played across the sky. A low rumble began off in the distance. A single headlight broke the crest of the ridge and the rumble swelled.

"That'll be our librarian, Mrs. Braithwaite." She roared onto the dock and climbed off her 1930 Indian 101 Scout, rocking it forward onto its stand. She wore blue jeans and a leather jacket. She wore no helmet, but the wind hadn't even ruffled her closely cropped and curled hair, black and shot through with gray the color of steel.

Anthony nodded. "Evening, Eleanor."

"Evening, Anthony. Miss van Duyn, how nice to see you again, and you, too, Detective."

Laura and Fenton returned her compliment.

Anthony kicked at the bike's rear tire. "How's she running?"

"Very well, thank you. I tuned her just last week."

"What's up?"

"A Packard sedan and a large truck drove into town this evening, filled with large, unpleasant-looking men. I saw them parked in front of Morton's after work. I followed them long enough to see them headed this way. I passed them six miles back. They are keeping the speed limit. I didn't. They should be here in ten minutes. Miss van Duyn, may I assume that you intended for these men to find you?"

"Yes. How did you know?"

"I am a librarian. It is my job to know. You also intend to keep these boys out of harm's way."

"Yes, of course. Anthony will supervise them loading the crates."

"That leaves the three of us to fend them off. There are seven men. Several of them moved slowly, stiffly, like they'd been injured. They should be easily disposed of. They've got little fight in them."

"Did they have a baby carriage?"

"I didn't see one. They could have hid it in the truck."

Laura glanced at Fenton. "We'll just have to trust he's with them. He wouldn't be part of the fight anyway."

The Librarian broke in. "What is your objective, Miss van Duyn?"

"I need to capture three men. One is crippled, one is small, and one is large, and he won't be injured."

"Very well. What are your tactics?"

"I don't understand, Mrs. Braithwaite."

"This is a military exercise, Miss van Duyn. Surely, you have a plan for deploying yourselves! Has nobody read you Sun Tzu?"

"I. . .No, they haven't."

Fenton felt it would be impolite of him if he snickered.

"Very well, I will take command. You still have much to learn,

Miss van Duyn."

The errant boys, attracted, like moths to light, by the sound of the motorcycle had joined them on the dock. Anthony gathered them around. "Got your gloves?" They all raised them in their hands. "Good. Let's get to work. We'll haul I figure about ten crates each trip, that makes ten trips or so to get them all out there. Since there are twelve of you, I want three teams of four. You'll go with me out to the ship to help unload, and you'll just rotate turns, so you all pick someone to remember when you last went, and he'd better keep track." He selected a team of four boys. "I want you in life jackets right now, we don't want to be fussing with them getting onto the boat, and you never take them off until you're back onshore, do you hear me?"

They all nodded. Levi asked excitedly if they could go aboard the ship. Anthony shook his head. The boys started to protest; they wanted to see the ship, but Anthony held up his hand, settled them down. "Too much extra work getting you on and off, rounding you up when it's time to leave, not to mention, one of you might fall overboard. We haven't got time for any of that. Listen, there's ships aplenty, and if you boys want to be sailors, let me know, because I can get you on to one." Several faces brightened at the prospect.

"The ship is here," Fenton cried. Outside the cove, two hundred yards away, a light blinked three times and once more.

Anthony and the boys swarmed over the stack of crates, pulling them down and passing them, bucket brigade-style, to the launch.

Eleanor marshaled her troops. "Do we have any weapons?" Fenton reached under his jacket and pulled out his pistol. Laura stood shaking her head, and Fenton, astonished, called her out. "Laura, your whole body's a weapon."

Eleanor squinted at her. "Is this true?"

Laura nodded.

"What style?"

"Korean."

Eleanor dared to crack a grin. "That's nice." She reached over her shoulder. Laura noticed for the first time a long, narrow leather tube at her back from which Eleanor drew forth a stick, not much thicker than a pool cue, but stout, and spun it about her wrist. "So. We have your pistol, my asaya," she held up her stick, "a pair of hands, and a pair of feet. I like these odds. May I assume, Mr. Hardy, that you know how to use your pistol well?"

"Yes, I do." He brandished it.

"Fine. It may be necessary for you to disable the truck. Can you do it?"

"Why, of course he can," Laura said.

Fenton grinned. "I guess I've got no choice."

"Good! If you're lucky, the car will be in front. We'll do this right outside the gate. The front vehicle will be disabled, and the one following will not be able to get around. The men will exit the cars, and you and I, Miss van Duyn, will disable them. We must assume they will have guns. I trust you understand the importance of silence and speed."

Laura nodded.

"Excellent!" Eleanor cocked an ear sideways. "They are coming. Keep alert. This plan could go awry any number of ways. You may have to improvise. Let's go."

She led them down off the dock and out to the gate. They found a packing case big enough for Fenton to crouch behind and moved it to the middle of the drive just inside the gate. Eleanor and Laura went beyond the fence and the circle of light cast by the streetlamp over the gate. Headlights swept the horizon, and the two vehicles came grinding slowly over the ridge of the dune. Fenton had been lucky, the car was in front. He knew he didn't have a lot of range with any force strong enough to puncture a tire. He'd have to let them get close.

The vehicles continued down the slope towards him, still slow, and Fenton was glad for that, it gave him more time. He cocked the pistol and suddenly it felt awfully small.

When he judged they were fifty feet off, he squeezed the trigger and lofted two slugs of lead in high and gentle arcs that took out one headlight and then the other one. The truck's headlights, coming up behind, gave him a perfect silhouette by which to place the car's tires, and he popped the two in front, and, after it slewed around a little, got a bead on one of the rear tires, took it out for good measure. With one bullet left!

As Eleanor had predicted, both vehicles came to a stop. The car's doors fell open, and its passengers crouched behind them. Bullets spattered against the packing crate as they returned fire. Fenton hunkered down to weather the barrage. It stopped suddenly amid a different barrage, a collection of cracks, yelps, grunts, and sighs. Silence fell, and then filled with the whine of the truck, as it labored in reverse back up the hill. Fenton stood and sprinted up the drive to the car. Behind him, the launch roared into full-throated, rumbling life and sprang from the dock, trailing a foamy wake that glittered in the moonlight.

Laura and Eleanor were, between them, hauling one of their unconscious chumps down under the streetlamp. Fenton knew the face, one of the guys they'd beat up last night.

"Any sign of them?"

Laura shook her head.

"These will come round soon," Eleanor announced. "Can we do something about that?"

"Well, I can put them out for longer." Fenton pulled a small brown bottle out of his shirt pocket and a handkerchief. "Ether."

Laura broke into a huge grin. "Why Fenton Hardy, you've been holding out on me."

He shrugged. In the dark you couldn't tell if he'd blushed or not, but it sounded like he had when he said, "Just a tool of the trade."

He dabbled a few drops of ether onto the handkerchief and held it over the man's nose. The only sign that the ether had caused an effect was his deepened breathing. Fenton put the other three men under.

"You want to try and get to that truck, Laura? See if they're there?"

"No. Loading is more important."

"What about Horace?"

"Give up on him for now. As long as he's out there, he can be captured. There will be other chances, and we have the guns. We will make do with what we've got."

They returned to the dock. Eleanor said goodnight, and Laura offered heartfelt thanks. Eleanor climbed onto her Scout and wended her way into the night. Laura and Fenton helped to move crates over to the edge of the dock to be loaded when the launch returned. When it did, Anthony yelled, "Hey Hardy, think you can drive this thing? My arm's getting tired."

Fenton said he could figure it out and climbed aboard. Anthony showed him where the throttle was, and how to put it into reverse, and that was about all he needed to know.

The work ground on, hauling crates to the boat, helping to swing them over the gunwales, dragging themselves back for more crates. A faint glow just lit the rim of the eastern sky as the launch docked for the last time. While the band were wearily slinging the last crate aboard, rifle fire crackled behind them. Bullets splintered the dock. Anthony made sure all of the boys were safe, sheltered behind the little shed, and lifted Laura bodily into the boat. He clapped a hand on her shoulder, said into her ear, "Take him with you. Drop the drag anchor, we'll pick the boat up later."

Laura looked into Anthony's eyes and nodded. "Watch my boys?" He grinned back at her. "You bet. Go on then." He cupped his hands, and roared, "Hardy, get out of here." Fenton pushed forward the throttle, and the launch surged, soon outpacing the rifle fire, with the bullets falling harmlessly astern.

The trip took only a few minutes. They pulled up to the ship and sailors jumped down with ropes to secure the two craft. They helped Fenton and Laura pass the crates into the hands of their brethren waiting aboard. When the loading was done, Fenton stepped back to the wheel. A sailor on the ship extended his arm towards Laura. She said, "Wait a minute, please." She found the launch's drag anchor and dropped it overboard.

"Anthony said he could pick the boat up later. Come with me, Fenton."

"What?"

"There's nothing for you in New York. You need a change, an adventure. Come with me."

"Wait, no, I didn't bring anything, no clothes, no plans. I can't just up and leave."

She pulled at his arm and smiled. "Yes, Fenton, you can, none of that matters, we'll make our way. Just come with me."

He fidgeted a few seconds. "Can I get a message to Gertrude?"

"Of course, the captain will radio Jake."

"Well all right. I guess I will." What else could he say?

***

On deck, the ship's captain, a tall African man, held out his hand. "Simon Katanga," he said. "Welcome to the *Bantu Wind*." Laura and

Fenton introduced themselves. Simon addressed Laura.

"There are cabins below deck. And clothes, you are not the first woman to travel with us. Come, I will show you." He led the way aft to the bridge and down a steep flight of steps, along a narrow corridor and showed them their rooms and the bathroom, a head, he called it.

"There is no shower, I am afraid, but you may wash up as best you can at the sink. Salt water, from the sea, you know. If you will excuse me, I must get us underway."

When he had gone, Laura turned to Fenton. "Think you'll get seasick?"

He grinned. "Hope not."

"Are you tired?"

"Bushed."

"Let's see each other tomorrow, then."

CHAPTER 34
DECKHANDED

Fenton awoke, restless, after about five hours. He got up and dressed, looked in on Laura, still sleeping, then trailed after some crewmen on their way to breakfast. One of the hands had landed a tuna the night before and put it on ice until the cook, Aloisio, could cut it into steaks. He fried them in butter, onions, garlic, bay leaves, and a little white wine, and served them up with fried potatoes, crusty bread, and tiny cups of strong, bitter coffee. When he had finished, Fenton pushed himself back from the table and patted his full belly.

"My compliments to the chef," he said, to nobody in particular, "Now I need a turn on deck to walk that off."

The First Mate sitting at his right hand said, "No walking around the deck without you pick up a mop and swab it as you go. Hey Izzy, grab him a pair of dungarees, some boots, and a shirt out of the locker. He don't want to get them nice slacks and those wingtips dirty." He turned back to Fenton. "Sorry, but everybody's gotta work, otherwise the ship falls apart, see? No hard feelings?"

Fenton grinned. "Nope, no hard feelings."

"Thanks, buddy. Some of our passengers ain't always so cooperative, puttin' on airs, see? You do a good day's work, you're welcome to all the chow you can hold. Long as you don't mind fish and potatoes."

Fenton collected his "uniform" from Izzy, changed clothes in his room, and went topside. He found a mop and a bucket in the bow, dropped the bucket over the side by the rope tied to its bail, pulled it up, and set it on the deck. He stood a moment leaning against the gunwale, facing east into the sun, up straight ahead twenty degrees off the horizon in a cloudless sky. A light headwind stirred his hair as he gazed across the open sea. He heard a splash and turned to see a dolphin breach, fall back into the water to race alongside, and leap again. He bent to his work, dunking the mop in the bucket and spreading the water across the deck. The day warmed, and he began to sweat, and to glance overboard at the cool water beckoning. A blister formed on his right hand where the mop handle rubbed the tender skin between thumb and forefinger. He switched hands, trying to place the handle so the weight fell more against his palms. He kept at it, head down, and began to anticipate the short breaks afforded by an empty bucket, when he could go to the side and drop it overboard for more water. A gull settled onto the anchor windlass, turning to fix Fenton first with his left eye, then his right. Fenton leaned on his mop handle and stared back.

"What do you think," he asked the bird, "would she go for a guy like me?" He bent and scrubbed at a stubborn scuff on the wooden deck. He glared at the gull. "You're not much help." The bird just watched. "Oh, go on, then." He swung the mop, scattering water in the gull's direction. It briefly lifted off the windlass while the droplets passed beneath it, and settled back. "Well, you're just a bird."

The First Mate appeared at his elbow. He flopped a pair of work gloves into Fenton's hands. "I need to apologize for forgetting these. How're your hands?"

"Fine. Thanks."

He handed Fenton a packet done up in a dish towel. "Brought you some lunch." Unwrapped, it turned out to be a thick chunk of leftover tuna between slices of bread soaked in olive oil and sprinkled with minced garlic. The mate produced his own sandwich and motioned for Fenton to sit beside him in the sun, their backs up against the gunwales. He glanced at the gull. "Talkin' to the birds, eh?" Fenton blushed. "Yeah, well, you ain't the first. I wouldn't worry about it." He offered his hand. "Name's Bernstein. Albert." Fenton shook, felt the thick calluses formed by a lifetime of hard work. "Pleased to meet you Albert."

"Word going around is you used to be a cop? That right?"

Fenton nodded. "I was a detective, on the New York force."

"But you don't do that no more?"

"No. I sort of quit."

"Sorry to hear that." He bit off a hunk of bread and tuna.

"No need to be. It was the right thing to do."

Albert nodded towards the mop and bucket. "How'd you like to be a sailor? Could use a guy isn't afraid of hard work."

Fenton smiled. "Thanks, but I'm considering something else."

"Yeah, you'll probably settle down some day, this kind of work sure don't do nothing for a marriage, gone all the time, temptation in every port."

"You're not married then?"

"Yeah, I am, one of the few, long time even, got a couple of grandchildren. It ain't been easy on either of us. It helped that her dad was a sea captain, she knew what she was signing on for."

Fenton nodded, pondering as he ate, tasting the bite of the garlic against the mild fish and the richness of the oiled bread. Albert broke his reverie.

"That lady that come aboard with you, is you two a couple?"

"No, we're not. Just friends."

"She sure is pretty. Works hard, too, she's been scrubbing pots for Lois all morning. Maybe you ought to be more than just friends."

"You're not the first person to suggest that. She's been through a wringer, though, I don't want to push her too hard."

"That's one way to look at it. Another is she's waiting for you to say something."

Katanga yelled from the bridge, "Albert, come, take the wheel. I must pray."

Albert and Fenton stood. "Thanks for the advice, Albert."

"Don't mention it. See you at dinner."

He didn't see much of Laura all day, only once when she came up to empty a bucket of kitchen scraps overboard. With most of the ship's length separating them, she turned to smile and wave before disappearing below. By dinnertime, he'd mopped down most of the deck. He could feel the day's work in his shoulders and hips.

Laura wasn't in the dining room; Albert said she'd already eaten. After he was done, polishing off a big bowl of fish and tomato stew and more bread, he went up on deck, wanting a cigarette. Forward, in the bow, in the lee of the windlass he found her barefoot in a fluttering white dress that must have been in her cabin, sitting with her feet behind her knees beside a few guttering candles, eyes closed, chanting low and soft. With the sky darkening against her back, the golden candleglow seemed to him, for a moment, to shine out from within her, and she, utterly at peace. He turned to leave, but she spoke.

"Come, sit beside me, breathe with me," and when he had, she took his arm and smiled. "I missed you today. Was the work awful?"

"No, well I mean it was hot and all, but the fresh air was good, and the work was simple, left me alone with my thoughts."

"What did you think about?"

"Oh, a lot of stuff. What I'm going to do. I thought about you."

"Oh?" Her brows peaked and she smiled. "What did you think about me?"

"People seem to want to make us a couple."

"Well, and do you think they're right?"

"Gosh, I don't know."

"You still have oats to sow."

"No, it's not that." He hesitated, half-smiling. "Honestly, that doesn't seem so important anymore. It's, well, do you want us to be a couple?" He waved his hand around the ship. "With all this that you do, this life of yours, is there room in it for another person?"

"There is, for the right person."

"Is the right person me?" Suddenly shy, he stared down at the palms of his hands facing upward in his lap.

"Kiss me."

"What?"

"Kiss me. Then we'll see."

"You mean it?" She nodded, smiling. "Well, all right." He swiveled to face her, put his arm across her to steady himself on the deck, and leaned in. As their lips touched, she trembled, and he hesitated. "No," she murmured, "don't stop. It's all right." Her arms went around his neck and she leaned back against the gunwale slanted outwards above the sea. The ship pitched up and over a hard swell and sent them tumbling full length along the deck with Laura beneath him, and then their lips did meet. As their kiss continued, they settled into each other, Laura taking his full weight upon her. She moved her hands down his body to loosen his shirt, to slide them beneath and up along the smooth skin of his back. At that, Fenton got his hands back down flat against the deck, pushed himself up and, sitting, scrambled away crabwise with a very red face. Laura raised herself on her elbows to watch.

"S-sorry," he said, "never did anything like that before."

She gave him a lazy grin, her hair mussed. "That's okay, I think we settled the issue." She drew the rucked up dress back down to her ankles and stood, smoothing her tousled hair. When he'd come up beside her, she was already gazing over the water at the big orange moon, just risen. She took his hand. "You're a good man, Fenton Hardy." She turned and softly kissed his lips. "There's a proper kiss." She faced the water again, pulling his arm across her shoulder, and they stood together in silent communion, watching the moon, the stars, and the sea.

CHAPTER 35
HIJACKED

Next morning after breakfast, Albert set Laura and Fenton to shifting crates in a half-empty hold. Fenton cast a skeptical eye. "Doesn't look like a whole day's work here." Albert winked. "I'm sure you two'll think of something," and he left them to it. They finished in little more than an hour, heavy work, so they both took a breather, sitting side by side on a crate. Fenton asked her, "You think you can throw me?" Laura smiled at him sideways, then stood and assumed her stance. He took a run at her and she flipped him, flat on his back. He nicked her elbow on the way down, though, with just the right touch to ruin her balance, and she landed on top of him. "You didn't let me win, did you?" he asked. "I don't agree that you did," she replied.

From above, against the sky, Katanga shouted down to them. "You two must come up here, quickly." On deck, he turned Laura around while he pointed astern, but she'd already caught the terrible drone she knew so well, knew what he was pointing at before she even turned to confirm that she did. The black dirigible stood off half a mile or so, high up and pacing them.

Katanga spoke. "I have been wondering when we would see him."

"Yes, so have I. I assume you know him."

"Yes, we have encountered each other many times."

"What is he like?"

"He is a despicable man. No conscience. He has no scruples about who he does business with, and he does it with the worst. He indentures and starves his crew."

"He helped to kill some friends of mine."

"Yes, I know."

"What would you do if you had him in your hands?"

"I know an island. It is large enough that, with hard work, a person could survive there. It is far from any shipping. I would make it his home."

"Do you know of three more islands like that?"

Katanga grinned. "I think we would put all four on one island and let them fight it out."

Fenton came up behind them. "Well well."

"Katanga," Laura asked, "can you stall them?"

"Of course I can, ma'am."

"Good. Fenton, we need to take control of that ship."

"I figured that's what you were thinking."

"Did you figure the odds?"

Fenton scratched his head. "I figure it's mostly Bruno and Gus we have to worry about. Crew'll be busy."

"Do you still have your pistol?"

"Yes. And one bullet."

"Don't shoot anyone. But it might help to damage something. As Mrs. Braithwaite taught us, we'll have to improvise."

"I'll keep that in mind."

"Do you know what they're like inside? I've never been in one."

"I have, in this very one," Katanga said. "They will take you up into a room amidships, for cargo storage. From there, a ladder takes you up inside the ship. You will come onto a gangplank, a catwalk, that goes the length of the ship, and a framework of metal hoops going up and down the ship and long ones going from front to back. And all that space that you see within its skin will be taken up by the bags of gas, twenty of them maybe, all filled with hydrogen, two million square feet of it, he bragged to me once."

"I thought they used helium now?"

"This one is old, from World War One, it was designed for hydrogen. Helium does not have sufficient lift."

"Mr. Katanga, this is invaluable information. We are fortunate to have your expertise."

"I have no expertise other than to listen carefully and observe well. Necessary behavior in my line of work. Are you ready to begin immediately?"

"I can't think of any reason to wait."

Katanga called to Albert in the deckhouse, "Signal all stop."

"Aye-aye, Sir." Moments later the propellers spun down, but still the ship's momentum carried them another mile. Crewmen put a drag sail over the side to hold her steady. The dirigible trailed them until they stopped, then moved in slowly, descending as it went until it stood directly over their heads, one hundred feet up. A hatch opened in its belly and a steel pallet began to descend, held by cables at each corner that, like the corners of a pyramid, ascended to a point and were bound into a single cable a dozen feet above. The pallet came to a stop a foot off the deck and from it stepped Bruno, dressed in a silk suit and gray fedora. His cool eyes ran Laura's length, and he started forward to take hold of her, but Fenton intervened.

"You're looking a little soft, Bruno. Too much easy living?"

Bruno grimaced. "I can still take anything you can dish out. Last time you hit me, you was more sore than I was." He guffawed and it sounded like sandpaper on a blackboard.

Fenton grinned, and playing the good-natured kid on the sandlot, he said, "I wasn't going to take you down, Bruno, I wanted Miss van Duyn here to have that satisfaction. You're easy pickings for a gal like her."

"Why you…" Bruno raised a massive fist, but Fenton stood his ground. "I suspect, though, that might displease your boss." He jerked his head up at the airship.

Bruno lowered his arm. "Yeah, well he's got plans for you. Wouldn't want to spoil them." He turned to the Bantu's crew gathered around them. "If you don't want to get sunk, you'll do what I say. I need you to start hauling them crates on deck." Katanga nodded. Albert came down from the deckhouse and began to assemble men at the hold. Bruno crooked a finger at Fenton and Laura. "You two come with me." He stepped back onto the pallet and they followed. Bruno waved at the airship, and the pallet began to rise on the winch motor's whine.

A breeze, cool and brief, stirred Laura's hair, and she glanced towards the horizon. With a nearly imperceptible touch, she drew Fenton's attention to a tall band of dark clouds, twenty miles off, flat-topped and with tendrils already streaming towards them. He nodded, barely, in acknowledgment.

As they drew near the airship, Fenton reconnoitered. The dirigible easily filled the sky above them. Forward, a car hung, suspended from the airship's belly by struts and guy wires. It was shaped like a teardrop, its stem pointing towards them, where it ended in a propeller with eight-foot blades, cutting the air with a whoosh as each blade slowly passed. Another, smaller car hung aft. Four more motors stood out from the sides of the craft in matched pairs, one amidships, the other, a quarter of the way from the aft end. Curious eyes looked them over, mechanics working in the engine nacelles, and crew members stationed in the rear car.

The platform came to a swaying stop inside the airship's bay. The bay's doors whined closed beneath them. Bruno stepped down and off onto the gleaming metal deck. Laura and Fenton followed him. Bruno waved his arm, showing off the expansive hold, the size of a small house, lit up by ranks of giant incandescent bulbs. "We can put a lot of stuff in here, stuff'll make us rich," he bragged. He gestured off toward the far end, where racks of bombs and torpedoes hung from the ceiling. "We could of sunk you five times over." He guffawed again, clapped a heavy hand on each of their shoulders, and steered them forward. Close by in front of them was the bay's forward bulkhead. A ladder bolted onto it led up to the ship's interior. Beside it stood a control booth from which the winch and weapons racks were operated. A man stepped out of it, rubbing his hands together and cackling.

"Got them, I see," he gloated.

"Yep." Bruno took his hands off Fenton and Laura and stepped forward while he opened his jacket and pulled out a big stogie. "Hey, Hans, how about a light?"

The man's smile vanished. "How many times do I tell you, do not call me Hans. My name is Friedrich."

"How many times do I have to tell you, you Krauts all look the same to me, so you're all Hans, get it? Now gimme a light, or I'll punch your face."

The smaller man grumbled, but pulled a lighter out of his jacket pocket, waiting while Bruno leisurely carved off the cigar's tip with a pocket knife. He held it up to his ear and rolled it between his fingers, then ran its length under his nose sniffing noisily, and finally champed down on the tip while he lowered his head toward Friedrich's lighter. As Bruno sucked the flame into the cigar, Laura barely nodded at Fenton, and together they crashed into Bruno's backside, pinning Friedrich between him and the bulkhead, and the burning cigar and lighter against Friedrich's cheek. Laura leaped onto Bruno's back, hooked her forearm around his neck and kicked him hard behind the knees. They buckled, and as he tilted backwards, Laura's feet touched the deck, and she jerked him towards her, then got out of his way as he crashed to the floor, dazed. Fenton kicked the still-lit cigar far across the floor and then he was on Bruno slapping a cloth over his nose and dripping ether. Bruno relaxed unconscious. They turned their attention to Friedrich, collapsed against the wall, holding his face, and screeching in pain. He cringed when they stood over him, but Laura knelt, her hand on his shoulder.

"Relax, Friedrich, we're only going to put you to sleep. The pain will stop." She took Fenton's hand and pulled him down, then turned back to Friedrich. "Ready?" He nodded, still apprehensive. Fenton dripped ether onto the cloth and held it to Friedrich's nose. "Breathe," he said. Friedrich did and was soon slumbering.

"So far, so good," Fenton said. "What now?"

"I think the captain, Gus, and Horace are probably in that forward car. Let's see if we can sneak up on them." She climbed the ladder, pushed open the hatch at the top, and hauled herself up. As Fenton followed, Laura looked around. Light from the cargo bay beamed upward through the hatch like a spotlight, but it illuminated only a small part of the vast interior, making it seem as if Laura were in a huge, echoing cave. She felt the wind's constant beat against its skin; it whistled through girders and wires. She stood on a catwalk that ran along the keel of the craft from bow to stern. A series of girders forming an inverted V marched forward and aft overhead. At their vertex ran a string of bare incandescent light bulbs that illuminated the catwalk. Above the vees, draped on either side of her and parted by them were the silvery bags of gas billowing gently, constantly. Fenton closed the hatch, and the light dimmed. The catwalk remained deserted. Toward the nose of the ship, they saw an opening down into the forward control car. They crept up to it and peered over the edge. Their view was constrained by the width of the shaft, large enough to let one person through. They could see no men. Laura said into Fenton's ear, "I'm going to jump, maybe I can startle them. You get down fast as you can after I'm out of the way." Without waiting for his reply, she placed a hand on either side of the opening, swung her legs out over the free air, and waited a moment, suspended, balanced on her outstretched arms, then flexed them and threw herself upward, pressed her arms against her sides and dropped, straight as an arrow into the room below. Fenton watched her hit and flow like soft wax into her stance. She pivoted on her right foot out of the way, and Fenton scrambled over onto the ladder and, using its uprights to guide himself, slid down to the floor, staring out the front of the control car. Before him stood Gus with a pistol trained on him.

"Mister, I've never been on one of these before." Fenton nodded upward at the hydrogen-filled balloons. "But I ought to know enough not to risk shooting in one. We aren't going anywhere, so why don't you put that pistol away?" Gus scowled, but dropped his aim.

Behind Gus, the ship's controls lay in the forward third of the gondola, open to the sky except for a glass windscreen. A steering wheel, a map table, speaking tubes, a humming and glowing electronic array, levers for adjusting ailerons and rudders, and an engine telegraph were all crammed into a space barely large enough for the captain and his two officers, who stood now, laboring at the controls in their effort to keep the ship steady over the freighter floating below. They paid Gus, Fenton, and Laura no notice, so consumed were they by their tasks. Laura chanced a look over the side and saw Katanga's men slowly working at bringing the crates up from the hold onto the deck. In the half hour they had been gone, only a few crates had made the trip. She continued her turn about the car. To the rear, a polished mahogany door, trimmed in shining brass began to open, and she squeezed Fenton's hand to draw his attention. Though Laura had done her best to prepare him, still, at the sight of Horace's ravaged body, he stepped back. He could not help himself. The move did not escape Horace's attention. He laughed, a raspy kind of whisper.

"I ain't pretty." He laughed again, sounding like the death rattle. "So I decided to be rich. Come on in, I'll tell you about it." He sat upon a small, motorized chair fitted with straps and a metal frame to hold him upright. To his arms were fixed grasping devices with which he had opened the door and now manipulated the controls that moved the chair, gliding backwards to make room for Laura and Fenton to enter. As they stepped toward the door, the captain approached from behind them and barked, "There is a storm coming. We must cut our losses and leave. You have the woman now. Let us go."

"We'll go when I say," Horace snarled. "We got a deal, we're going to deliver."

"An hour I will give you, then I will take us up whatever you say. A few dollars are not worth death." Horace jammed at the chair's controls. It spun, struck the wall, and stuck. Growling in frustration, Horace backed, turned, and steered on into the room.

It was done up like a Victorian saloon car -- tufted green velvet and mohair banquettes, purple brocade curtains and silk shades with tasseled pulls, a red Turkish carpet on the floor, and wainscotings of polished English oak. A window in the ceiling offered a view along the fuselage, the tip of the propeller attached to the rear end of the car, and a strut. A bright poster featuring a couple sipping champagne in evening dress hung on the wall. At the far end of the car, a brazier stood, wafting smoke; the air in the room was heavy with its scent, cedar and cinnamon. Laura sneezed. Horace, his composure restored, swiveled his chair to face her. His awful grimace stretched a bare half-inch, the only evidence that he smiled.

"Didn't catch a cold did you? You ain't much good sick."

"Good for what?"

"Ransom. Figured your daddy would put up a fortune to get you back."

"I'd never let him."

"Whatever. I can always sell you." He looked her over. "Dish like you, worth a lot in some places."

Fenton started forward, fists raised. Gus collared him, stuck the pistol in his back.

Horace regarded Fenton through his good eye, then nodded at Gus. "Shoot him. Throw him in the ocean."

"With pleasure."

"Wait!" Laura batted away Gus's gun hand and drew up to Fenton, her arms around him, lips to his ear, and whispered, "It's OK, Fen. We'll get out of this. Please, don't die." She turned back to Horace. "I'll go over the side right after him, and then where would you be? If money is your interest, you could sell him too, he's got a strong back. But you haven't the right to sell anybody, or to bomb a village, or to kill people."

"Lady, on this balloon, in this room, I got the right to do anything

I want because I got the power."

"You can't truly believe that. There must be some conscience left in you."

"Listen, I'll tell you the story about my conscience. First thing was my ma died of having me. Second thing was, my pa was too drunk to attend the funeral or to mc, so the third thing was when your pampered butt was still in diapers, I was out on the street hustling food. Empty belly stunts your conscience. So after that ship blew up, Gus here fishes me out of that harbor, knocked out and half drowned -- thanks Gus, I guess you got a little conscience...."

"Don't mention it."

"...and hauls me off to some Chinatown doctor who can get me on opium and some herbs, but smart enough to get some germ-killing medicine, too, and I'm laying there for six months all bandaged up with nothing to do but think, and this is how I took stock. Can still smell some, but I can't taste anything, can't hardly hear or see anything. No woman's ever going to look at me again, besides which I got nothing left between my legs anyway. Nobody's ever going to give me a job, except maybe the circus, and I ain't no freak. I must have some kind of head on my shoulders to get this far alive. I got a briefcase full of cash, a little singed maybe, but still legal tender. I got a couple of guys who can help me out, long as I give them their fair share. And ain't nobody, in my whole life, ever looked out for me, except me, so I don't owe nothing to anybody except me. And what do I owe myself? A chance to be happy, and what's going to make me happy is to get back at what done all this to me. And what done all this to me besides Halliday is everybody in the whole world who ever put me down, kept me down, denied me the chance to become somebody." He was in high heat by now, his emotion driving his wasted body beyond its limit to contain or control it, and he slumped writhing in his chair, the stumps of his limbs jerking randomly, breath whistling along scarred passages, spitting bits of saliva and phlegm.

Laura rounded on Gus. "Do something," she demanded, "can't you see he's suffering?" He stood blinking before her onslaught, his jaw working, and finally stammered out, "I don't know, I never seen him like this before." He stepped around them, laid a hand on Horace's shoulder, and bent down. "Hey, buddy, can I get you something?" Horace's flailing arm knocked him away, whether by purpose or by chance they could not tell. The fit began to subside, and within a few minutes, he sat, breathing hard, but still.

Laura knelt at his side, speaking so only he could hear her. "Horace, you aren't a happy man. I don't believe you ever will be unless you stop," she waved her hand around the room, "this path you have chosen. Please, just say you will give it up, and I promise I will help you find a better life. Happiness lies in peace and forgiveness, not revenge and destruction." She laid a hand on his cheek, turning his head to face her. "Please," she begged, "I promise." Laura would always swear that he began to cry then, that blocked ducts prevented the tears, but that she could feel him tremble and a sob build in his chest. "I had him," she would say. "Right then I had him." A fearful pounding sounded on the thick door and a muffled shout, almost a scream, came. "The storm is upon us, you have doomed us all!"

CHAPTER 36
MAËLSTROM

Fenton wrenched open the door to see the captain frantic at his controls and the two crewmen disappearing up the ladder into the ship's interior. Laura glanced out the window and saw only formless gray mist. A blast of wind caught the dirigible amidships, and above them, they saw it buckle and its skin go wrinkled and lax. Overhead, metal groaned and rivets popped, ricocheting off girders. The gust passed, and the airship snapped straight again, almost throwing them over.

Fenton strode into the control cabin, shouting, "Can I help?" The captain, straining at the wheel, freed an arm to motion him forward. "Hold the wheel," he gasped, "We must turn her into the wind." As Fenton stepped up beside him, the captain shouted into a speaking tube, "Steuerbordmaschinen, voran voll. Portmaschinen, voller anschlag." He jabbed at a switch on the console before him, and the engine behind Horace's room sang to life. For what seemed an eternity, Fenton and the captain labored with all their strength against the mighty forces that battered the bucking and swaying ship. Slowly the compass needle before them spun until finally it held steady on a course due south. Once again, the captain shouted through the tube, "Portmaschinen, voran voll." From beyond the cabin, they heard the port-side engines rev to speed. The captain pushed Fenton off the wheel.

"I will manage now. Take them…" He nodded back at Horace's cabin, "…up there. It is safer."

"Where are your officers?"

"There is a second control room aft. From there they will steer if I cannot."

"If you're dead, you mean."

The captain shrugged. "It can happen. Now leave me to my work."

Horace had a sling rigged by which he could be raised from the gondola up inside the ship. It was connected by a winch that could haul him all the way to the top of the ship, if he wanted. Through a trap door up there was a machine gunner's nest, Gus explained. Horace liked to sit out in the air sometimes. This time, Gus was going to raise him only halfway up and strap him onto the ladder that led to the gunner's nest. It was safer than remaining in the car. Fenton and Gus fastened him into the sling, and Gus touched a switch mounted on the ladder. They watched him ascend, and then followed him up. Inside the balloon, Gus switched on his flashlight and climbed monkey-like up the ladder to where Horace hung, midway to the roof. He passed a belt through loops in the back of the sling and secured it to the ladder.

"You ain't going anywhere, buddy," he said, squeezed his shoulder, and climbed down to rejoin Fenton and Laura. "I oughtn't to leave him alone, so I'll stick around until things calm down. You two do what you want, I don't much care anymore. Looks like a situation we might not survive. Revenge don't mean much if you're dead."

Bruno loomed out of the shadows aft. He snatched at Fenton, who backed out of his reach, and Bruno stumbled, still groggy. "Was a lousy trick," he slurred. He sat down on the catwalk, dipping his head.

A lightning bolt's flash came up the tube from the gondola and thunder boomed around them. The airship's nose came up, and they began to slide down the catwalk toward the stern. As they scrambled for handholds, the ship lurched back level, then dipped downward. They scrambled again to keep from pitching forward into the access tube. Laura thought she heard a thump from Horace's cabin, and, as the ship rose level again, remembered the incense brazier. She swung herself over onto the rungs and began to descend. Fenton yelled and grabbed for her, but missed; she moved too quickly. She glanced into the cabin and saw her worst fear realized; coals had spilled across and ignited the carpet. Even now, flames began to lick at the paneling and climb toward the window shades and curtains. She pulled the door closed, hoping to starve the fire of oxygen. When he heard the latch snap to, the captain turned from wrestling with the aileron controls. "What is it?" A hint of panic.

"Fire. Extinguisher?"

He reached beneath the map table, pulled it out, brushed Laura aside, and pushed open the door just as Laura shouted at him to stop. The smoldering coals erupted on the inrushing air, sending the captain reeling back. Laura just managed to step aside as he surged past her. He tripped, cracked his head on a steel beam, and fell senseless to the floor. Laura tried to close the door again, but the fire was too hot. She heard Fenton land on the deck behind her. She pointed to the captain. "Get him out of here," she yelled. Fenton hauled the captain's inert form over his shoulder and started up the ladder, calling for Gus. Laura picked up the fire extinguisher, inverted it, and aimed its feeble stream at the flames, but got only hissing and steam for her trouble. The fire roared on. Fenton was back at her side asking what they could do. Before she could answer, the bolts holding the strut to the rear of the car failed in the heat. The car sagged, and the engine, running at speed, tried to drive it up into the balloon itself. Guy wires snapped, and the access tube, the car's only remaining means of support, began to groan and buckle. Fenton shoved Laura towards it, shouting, "That solves the fire problem."

Moments after they regained the catwalk, the access tube gave way, and the gondola plunged out of sight through the mist. The airship's nose, now lightened, once again pitched upward, knocking Fenton and Laura backwards. They found themselves on a rising slope, feet slipping towards the abyss. They snatched at the girders and hung on. Air rushed through the breach. The gasbags snapped in the wind.

Gus, clinging to a girder, collared the still unconscious captain as he slid past. The jerk when he stopped at the end of Gus's arm woke him up demanding to be set free. When Gus let go, he went aft, lurching, trying to walk. Laura, looking around, called out, "Where's Bruno?", and it was true, he was gone.

A wild howl sounded above. Gus's head jerked up. "That's Horace." He hauled himself to his feet and began to climb the girder beside him.

Beneath them, under the catwalk where Laura and Fenton could not see, the titanic forces beating against the airship's wounded frame began to tell. As the ship's nose fought to come level, girders, weakened by wind and fire, gave way just at the spot where the car had torn loose, their sharp ends plunging through the ship's skin. It promptly began to rip, with the effect that the onrushing wind both forced the nose more sharply upward, and as it rushed into the gap, forced the rest of the ship downward, overloading the remaining girders, which failed, causing a larger rip. The cycle fed on itself. Soon, the gap widened beyond the catwalk. Fenton and Laura, dangling, began to see daylight, and the angle of the forward section of catwalk steepened.

"Laura, she's going to split right there, and this whole front end is going to tilt and float away like an egg standing up. Everything horizontal is going to be vertical and vice versa. We have to climb away from here."

Even as they pulled themselves up, the separation accelerated. Within minutes, the catwalk was vertical. Popped rivets and bolts spun around them like shrapnel, and sparks flew as conduits snapped.

"Hope she doesn't blow," Fenton yelled, "we'd burn up in here." He stared past his feet into the storm swirling directly below. With a final groan, the two sections parted, and the forward, as Fenton had guessed, floated free like an eggshell with them inside it. The rear section hung silently, level at last. As they drifted away, more and more of its open end came into view. The foremost gasbag, pierced, had collapsed and hung ragged, flapping in the wind. At the very center of the opening, occasionally hidden by the bag, Gus clung to a beam, one arm outstretched. He seemed to be calling, but the wind snatched his words. More men began to appear, some almost tipping over the edge only to be hauled back by their fellows. Their perches began to shift as the aft section, now tail heavy, began to tilt and slide backwards into the mist. As it disappeared, a muffled thump reached them. Moment by moment, the mist changed. Its uniform gray took on a reddish tinge, brightening from carmine through scarlet to vivid orange until the whole sky around them glowed, and then slowly went out.

"I hope they jumped for it, poor devils." Fenton peered downward, then up into the interior. "Don't know how long we'll be in here. Might as well climb up. It'll probably be warmer."

"Fenton, we need to get to Horace. He's out there in the storm all alone."

"The footing's difficult."

"Then it's good I wore sensible shoes. Let's meet at the point of the V."

They shuffled sideways up their respective legs of the V and met at its vertex.

When he stood at last, facing her, he asked, "Don't you ever sweat?"

"When it's hot I do. Why?"

"Aw, nothing. What's your plan?"

She patted the girder between them. It had once been at the top of the Vs running horizontally the length of the ship. Skeletons of the burst light bulbs rattled against it. Now vertical, it would serve as a way down to the ladder from which Horace hung. They started to descend, taking care not to trip each other up. Looking down made them giddy, so they looked at each other instead.

"Of all the things I ever thought I'd do with a girl, this surely wasn't one of them."

"What were?"

"Sorry?"

"What were the things you thought you'd do?"

"Oh, marriage. You know, house, kids. A pipe and the Sunday paper. Dog."

"Right now, those don't sound too bad to me." She smiled and reached to pat his hand, stepping down as she did so and nearly falling. She had reached the bottom of the girder, and her foot hung off into space. Ahead of her, the ladder extended across the ship leading to the gunner's post. Laura maneuvered around Fenton and the upright girder, dropped onto the ladder on hands and knees, and inched toward Horace, twenty feet ahead. Snapped off cables, ropes, and conduits dangled, whipped by the wind. The gasbag billowed and snapped a scant few feet above her head. To forestall dizziness, she kept her eye fixed only on the ladder a foot before her. The wind picked at her and the ladder's rungs shifted beneath her hands. She reached Horace, lay flat on the ladder, and patted his shoulder. He started. She twisted down from the waist to catch his eye.

He hung over the void, goggling and petrified, save for his jerky breathing. The wind rippled his skin and the loose tunic he wore. He began to turn towards her, slowly, fearing that a jar could knock him loose. When finally their eyes met, he said, "C-c-cold. Please help me."

Laura sensed Fenton behind her. She drew herself back flat on the ladder, crawled past Horace, and swiveled to face Fenton. She lay down again on the ladder. Beneath her, the mist parted for a moment. She stared three hundred feet straight down a hole in the storm, where the savage winds roiled the cloud, tearing off scraps of mist. She took a deep breath.

"Horace, Mr. Hardy is going to unfasten you from the ladder. You will swing free, but I have the rope, and I promise I won't let you fall. Do you trust me?" He nodded.

The sling that held him to the ladder was also attached to the rope that would, when the ship was level, have taken him all the way to the gunner's nest. Laura grasped it a foot beyond Horace's head, caught Fenton's eye, and nodded. He crawled forward and began to unbuckle the strap. He got his hands through the ladder and took hold of Horace's sling, let the buckle slip, and then lowered him until the rope and Laura took Horace's full weight, not more than sixty pounds. Even so, she had little leverage to pull him up, but Fenton got him by the sling again, and together they maneuvered him out from under the ladder, and then up and on top of it. They freed him from the sling; it swung away, and they laid him flat on his back on the ladder. He thanked them both in a nearly inaudible scratch.

"What'll we do with him?" Fenton asked.

"We need to get up, out of the wind."

"I can take him on my back, I guess. How will he hold on?"

Horace cleared his throat. "Turn me over, I can pull myself." He snapped open and shut the prosthetics at the ends of his arms, three-forked like talons, and as savagely clawed.

Laura sat up, straddling the ladder, riding it like it was a horse. She tilted Horace from the waist and then somersaulted him onto his stomach over towards Fenton, who caught the rungs.

"Laura, I'm going to back up, I don't want to try to turn around on this thing, and I can give him a hand if he needs it." He locked his heels under a rung, slid his arms along the ladder's stringers, got them under his shoulders, unlocked his ankles, and pushed himself, feet leading, back along the ladder. Horace freed an arm, reached to the next rung, and pulled himself forward. The wind battered, twisting the ladder, and he began to slide towards the edge. Fenton reached for him, but he shook his head, grimacing. The gust passed, the ladder came horizontal, and he shifted back. He and Fenton danced twice more, and then Laura lay on her stomach and pulled herself along. They crossed in only five minutes, hours though it seemed to them.

As Fenton's feet hit the upright, Laura caught a flicker, and looked up to see Bruno's arm waving a pistol around.

"Hey, boss," he shouted over the wind, "nice setup here, they screwed us over pretty good, but now we got 'em where we want 'em." He cocked the pistol and aimed at Laura's head.

"God damn it, Bruno, put that piece away," Horace snarled, "she's the only one I trust to get us off of here alive. You kill her, and we'll all die."

Bruno squinted, thinking. "Yeah, all right," and he slid the gun into a side pocket. He pointed at Fenton. "You, get up here."

Fenton wrapped his ankles around the girder. He propped himself on his hands, then reached behind him one at a time, grabbed the girder, and let go with his feet. His legs dropped free. He swung one up on to the ladder, bent it at the knee, and pushed himself standing. Then he turned into the beam and climbed overhead.

Bruno peered down. "Hey, Horace, think you can hold on, around my neck?" Horace nodded. Bruno climbed onto the ladder, turned his back to Horace, then sat down. Horace came clanking down the ladder, got Bruno's jacket, and hoisted himself until he had caught Bruno around his throat. Bruno talked over his shoulder. "I pass out, we both die. Don't go hanging on too tight." He began to climb. Laura came up below him. Bruno continued over his shoulder. "Boss, I found us a way down. I punched a hole out the top and punctured one of them balloons. It'll let the gas out, and we'll land in the ocean, see?"

"Kind of stupid, Bruno," Fenton drawled, "what'll we do when it sinks?"

"Hey, I had enough of your lip. The boss here didn't say nothin' about saving your hide," and he reached a hand into his side pocket and pulled out the pistol, took aim, and fired just as a gust caught his arm. The shot went wild. Laura swarmed up the ladder, grabbed Bruno's belt and jerked, trying to knock the gun out of his hand. Bruno angled a vicious kick into her stomach, broke her hold on the ladder. Horace swung one-handed off Bruno's neck and caught her wrist, and for just a moment it looked to Fenton as if they would come to some balance, but the sudden shock of Laura's weight across Bruno's neck clamped shut his windpipe, his eyes rolled up, his grip failed, and, suddenly, they were gone.

For Fenton, it was as if they vanished. They did not even cry out. Bewildered, he climbed down the ladder, looked around and then down, and found Laura. A length of snapped manila rope dangled twenty feet past the end of the craft, and to its end she clung with both hands. Her face was calm as she focused entirely on that thick thread. Even as he watched, a gust took her and left her hanging by one hand. A whiff of air brushed Fenton's cheek, and a piece of dislodged girder fell past him, not heavy, maybe only a few pounds, trailing a piece of electrical cord that whipped spiraling through the air. Fenton followed its trajectory for the fraction of a second it took to reach Laura, watched as the cord wrapped and then caught around her ankle, saw the jolt as the weight hit her, saw her grimace in pain as her rope-burned hand was jerked inches farther downward.

He took out his pistol.

CHAPTER 37
LOST

He had never done, nor would he ever do, anything so hard in his entire life. He could see her hand loosen, stressed beyond all endurance. He knew he had only seconds, and one bullet. "She never sweats," he told himself. "Neither can I." His target was so slender, but in his favor, it was not a long distance to shoot, and there was light enough to see. He cocked back the pistol's hammer, drew his bead, and squeezed the trigger. He'd heard people who had been in similar situations describe time as slowing down or stopping. Maybe because his hope ran so high it would not endure such a wait and so he saw, almost instantaneously, the wire part, and the girder spin off into the sea. With her burden lightened, Laura managed to swing her loose hand back and pull herself up until she could entwine her legs around the rope. Hand over hand and with knee, ankle, instep, and infinite care, she began to raise herself. The wind did its best to dislodge her with its chilly and prying fingers. She began to tremble -- from cold or fatigue Fenton could not tell -- and she raised her eyes to him. He knew then she wouldn't make it, not by herself. She couldn't hang on, the storm was too strong against her and the rope too slight. He saw no fear in her face, only sadness. "I'm sorry," she mouthed.

"The heck you are!" He crouched, then swung over and down, locked his feet on the rungs and hung there, a daredevil acrobat. She had managed to come more than halfway up, and with his long reach overhead, he spun her so she faced away from him and he got her under the arms, his hands locked across her chest, and lifted so she could free her arms and take a higher purchase.

"Wait," he said, and he let her go, then adjusted himself upwards to hang by his knees, caught her and lifted once more. Then she was close enough, he could kneel on the girder and bring her in his arms the rest of the way up, and they lay there for a while, straddling the ladder, him with his back against the upright girder and she against him. Her blistered and abraded hands lay open on her lap, and she sobbed, with equal parts pain and relief.

"We need to find a safer place to rest," he said. "Think you can climb?"

She nodded, and they slowly disentangled and got themselves stood. They began to ascend. At the gap between gasbags Laura stopped. "Fenton, I think it could hold us." She leaped, twisting, and landed, as if for snow angels, on the billowing cloth, where it rippled and swayed. Fenton went more gingerly, putting a foot forward and promptly sank to his thigh. He pulled back, shrugged, and followed Laura's lead. They lay there with their heads tilted together.

"You saved my life."

"I didn't have a choice."

"Thank you anyway." She curled into him, draped her arm across his chest, and went to sleep. Soon, he did, too.

***

A jar and a hollow thump brought them awake into pitch dark.

"Do you hear water?" She tried to push herself up on her hand, but the balloon only gave way beneath her. She rolled onto her stomach, grasped handfuls of fabric, and hauled herself towards the edge. The catwalk and its overhanging girders split the bag like a slice of cake. Laura got herself over onto a girder and climbed down. At its end, she found, by plunging a foot suddenly into the water, that they were afloat upon the gasbag in the sea. A glimmer of daylight came through the water. She climbed back up. By feel alone, she found Fenton on the upright. The light did not penetrate that far.

"Do you think it's stable?"

"As long as the sea's calm, I don't think it will tip over, but that water's cold, it'll shrink up the hydrogen in the bag, and then we might start to sink."

"We should be on the outside, anyway, if a ship should come. We can climb down and swim out underneath. It's only twenty feet or so."

They climbed back to the water's edge. Fenton took a breath and was about to dive in, when Laura grabbed his arm and pointed to the water. Dark shadows slid below them, sharks in silhouette.

"They must have come around after those other men."

"Yes." She stood, thinking. "We can try through that trap door, where you get to the gunner's nest. Up and across the airbag. Then down to the water. We'd only have to swim down and open the door, and then out the other side. They wouldn't have time to attack."

Back on their stomachs on the airbag, they decided to circumnavigate rather than strike out across it because in the darkness they feared they might lose their way. The work exhausted them. The bag had begun to shrink, as Fenton had foreseen, and enfolded them ever more closely. They could not gain a purchase with their feet and were reduced to dragging themselves along by their arms. At intervals, they passed girders, the ribs of the airship running from bow to stern. After the fourth, they took to climbing down to the water to see if they'd gone far enough, first Laura, then Fenton. At the sixth rib, Fenton yelled up to Laura, "I can see the ladder, it's probably ten feet down. I'm going to dive down there, see if I can open that door." A moment later, as she started down to the water, Laura heard his splash. By the time she got down, he was back at the surface, shivering.

"It's cold down there. I can't open the door. Come give me a hand. Didn't see any sharks."

Laura climbed into the water. They dove together and Laura quickly joined Fenton in shivering. They pulled themselves down along the rib. When they reached the ladder, they turned to the trapdoor, and with the two of them pushing, managed to swing it outwards. Laura glanced backwards, and even though the water blurred her sight she saw a dark shape cruising out of the murk. She took Fenton's shoulder and shoved him towards the opening. They both got through and turned to close the door in the shark's face. They swam up, and with their lungs near to bursting, broke the surface. An ominous fin drifted a hundred feet away.

Along the outside of the airship's skin, a skein of ropes wound around cleats bolted through the fabric to the ship's superstructure.

With their waning strength, they grasped the ropes, hauled themselves up and climbed to the pinnacle. The sun stood low, dipping towards the horizon. A light breeze blew, and they continued to shiver. "We'll freeze to death," Laura said through chattering teeth, "hold me." Fenton put his arms around her, but she drew back. "Not close enough." She threw back his jacket, unbuttoned his shirt, threw it back, too, then opened her blouse, and pulled him close, skin to skin. "That's better." He reddened, shifting his legs. "It's all right, Fen, I don't mind." By entwining their arms and legs through the ropes, they managed a kind of equilibrium against gravity, and so could relax against the vast and silent sea. The sky bled light and the moon and stars appeared, the moon a little smaller than yesterday. The breeze died. The sea rocked them gently. Their island shrank. Fenton began, "We won't last long…," but Laura hushed him.

"We don't have to decide anything until the last. Just be warm with me," and so they were -- as comfortable as they'd been in a while. They even managed a little sleep. The moon was halfway across the sky and the water lapping at their toes when a deep thrum and the sound of water churning awoke them. A spotlight flashed out of the darkness, and there stood the Bantu Wind, one hundred yards off and closing. Even as they raised their arms to wave, its horn blew and they were saved.

CHAPTER 38
THE RESCUE

Albert piloted the launch that brought them in. He told them on the way back that the dirigible had stood its ground against the storm, was nearly overhead of the ship the whole time, and only a few ship's lengths in altitude. They spotted the aft section when it caught fire, and arrived in time to begin pulling the crew from the sea. Most had fallen not more than twenty feet, and some had ridden the ship down to the water. They all got out, banged up and singed, but otherwise healthy.

"It's a ragged bunch, from all over the place, didn't look like they got fed too well. Lois is taking care of that."

After he heard about the craft's break-up, Albert continued, Katanga stayed on patrol to see if the bow section landed. Several of Katanga's crew saw it fall into the ocean thirty knots away over the horizon. Katanga had gotten good azimuth and range readings off it before it disappeared, and trued up his course. By the time darkness fell, they could see it bobbing just at the edge of sight.

Back on board, Laura and Fenton joined the rescued men in the hold and in devouring Lois's rich stew out of any container they could scrounge. The exception was the airship's captain, locked securely and sourly behind a cabin door below. It had a little flap through which he could get his food.

After stilling their hunger, Laura's and Fenton's next priority was a decent night's sleep.

Alone that night in their individual beds in their separate cabins, they each lay awake, surprised that sleep did not come. Laura watched stars wheel across the porthole. At times her eyes filled. At one of these times, so deep in thought she didn't notice, she did sleep and awoke into sunshine with gulls in place of the stars. She dressed and went out on deck. There she found Albert, whittling on an oar. He nodded forward to where a man sat alone on the anchor windlass. It was Gus, hunched over and silent.

"Don't know what's gotten into him," Albert nodded.

"He's just lost his best friend," she said.

"That a fact? Well I know just the thing." He grabbed a couple of mops leaning on a bulkhead and strode forward, clapped Gus on the shoulder, and handed him a mop.

"Best thing I know for the blues is hard work. Come on, help me swab down the deck." Gus looked him in the face and stood. Albert took his measure. "Wiry," he said, "and quick." He spun Gus towards the stern, and gave him a nudge. "You ever thought about sailoring? I'll tell you, the sea's a fine mistress, she'll teach you lessons you'll never learn anywhere else. Say, why don't you tell me all about your friend. When did you two meet?" Gus began to speak, too low for Laura to hear. She glanced into the wheelhouse and saw Katanga's eyes following them, a smile on his lips. She waved to catch his attention, then climbed up beside him to ask if he'd seen any sign of Horace or Bruno.

"No. With the water so cold, and the sharks...". He shrugged. "You must presume them lost I am afraid. God's will."

"Thank-you, Mr. Katanga, for not giving up on us."

"That is not necessary, Miss van Duyn. The privilege was mine."

She climbed down to the deck, and met Fenton coming up from the galley. They leaned side-by-side against the deck rail. She told him there had been no sign of Horace or Bruno, and of their likely fate. The ship churned beneath them. "I did make a difference in his life, if only briefly. I will learn to be satisfied with that, I guess."

"Are you mourning him?"

"His life was wasted. Nobody ever took care of him except himself. If he'd had a mother, who knows how he'd be today? It's that waste I mourn."

"Surely Evelyn's life was wasted because of him."

"No, it wasn't. She lived enough for two lives. She saw places, she met people most of us can't even dream of, and she saved them, she rescued them. Fenton, she rescued me. And for that, nothing she did was a waste. Even the loss of her -- she said once sorrow was like heat to her steel. I understand now what she meant, and it's because she died that I do. I wish she hadn't died, but she did, and I can't do anything about that. But I didn't succumb to sadness, and so, having come through it, the sadness made me stronger."

***

Days passed and they fell into an easy camaraderie, between themselves and with the crew. The weather stayed fair and warm. The food was plentiful. Laura's hands healed, and she was able to work again. The work was hard but simple, the kind where you could carry on a conversation with the fellow beside you to make the time go.

In the evenings sometimes Katanga came down to eat with them, conjuring hair-raising stories of smuggling and piracy, swashbuckling archaeologists, beautiful women and Nazi submarines. One night they were all down in the hold, swapping stories and passing around a couple of bottles of cognac to warm themselves against the chilly air. A crewman brought out a concertina and another one a fiddle, and a third, a guitar, and they started singing and playing. After a while, Laura got up and called out a song and a key, the first of many, and she roused and bewitched them all. She sang worker's songs and fighting songs and patriotic songs, love songs and ballads and songs about the old country. Many a tear rolled down many a cheek that night, and all of them at one time or another raised a bottle high to her. Fenton advised her maybe if this other thing didn't work out, she ought to think about show business. "Pshaw," was all she said.

Gus, nudged by Albert, came out of his shell. He took to whistling as he bustled around the deck, coiling rope, scrubbing on hands and knees, or hanging over the side scraping rust and painting. Life on the sea suited him it seemed, for now anyway, and Albert couldn't have been prouder.

Before they knew it, the voyage was over.

CHAPTER 39
PARTINGS AND PROMISES

They anchored off Dieppe one midnight, under a clear and moonless sky. A hint of autumn's chill graced the air.

Swarms of men in rowboats came to meet them, preserving silence. Out of the first one climbed Dominique, the former French nun, dressed in black beret, wool trousers, and a leather jacket. She called for Laura.

"We are glad you made it." She glanced into the hold beside her, at the crates stacked under gleaming lights. "Those are the last of them. All of the other shipments arrived safely. Evelyn planned well. She will be missed."

"Yes."

"I am sorry for your loss. But our work must go on. We have not the luxury to mourn the past." She caught Laura's eye. "I have a job that needs doing. You are the best person for it. Are you willing?"

"Yes."

"Good. I want you to take one of these boats ashore. There is a farmhouse at the top of the cliffs. Wait for me there. I will see you after the ship is unloaded."

She climbed onto the winch hook dangling over the hold and called up to the wheelhouse, "Katanga, let me down please." The winch whined, and she descended.

Laura found Fenton and told him about Dominique's instructions, and they both caught the first rowboat that left. On shore, they helped unload boats, hauling crates to the top of the beach, to be hidden in a cave at the foot of the coastal cliffs.

A man came to speak to them, said they could leave, Dominique was coming. They climbed a ravine alongside a creek that chattered among the stones to emerge into the farmlands verging on the cliffs' edge. They were now close by the house, and finding its doors unlocked, went into the kitchen and sat at a table to wait. An hour passed. Laura dozed, her head on her folded arms. Fenton occasionally stood to walk around the room, watching from the windows. A barn door slammed. A moment later came the sounds of jingling tack and horses' hooves on gravel. They walked out to meet Dominique with her party of three or four others, shadowy in the dawn, horses trailing behind them.

"There is a village south of here," Dominique said. "The orphanage there is poor and full of sick children. There is money, but the mayor is, how do you say it? A greedy son of a bitch, yes? And he will not let it be spent for the medicine. You must come and be an American woman, you will tell him you have been denied your inheritance of 1,000,000 francs and you wish it to be transferred to his bank account to hide its trail. For his trouble, he can keep twenty percent, but you need 10,000 of his francs to bribe the banker in Paris to transfer the money to his account."

"Why ever would he think I would come to him in his little town to ask him this favor?"

Dominique looked her over. "Let us say also the mayor thinks he is a man for the ladies. We will dress you up and then you will convince him, yes? I do not think you will find it hard."

Laura took Fenton's hand. "Ready for another adventure?" She started forward with him.

"No, he cannot come," Dominique objected. "There are only these many horses, and you may not ride double, we must go fast. So you will say your good-byes now. We will go on and wait, you must want your privacy." She and the others mounted and rode off.

Laura turned to Fenton. "I'm sorry, I didn't mean for that to happen. I wanted you to stay."

"It's okay, Laura. I made a promise."

"But you're not a pain in the neck." Her eyes glistened.

He nodded after Dominique. "I am to her. My promise didn't refer to anyone specific. But look, it's okay. One thing I've learned, you don't need anybody's help, Laura, and you're on to something grand, one big adventure. I want you to go out and live it. But it's more than that. I need to go back. I need to build something that's my own. I thought about what Jake said, and I think he's on to a good idea. Being a detective, why that uses everything I know, and I could use it any way I felt like, any way *I* felt like. So if you'll release me from my promise, I think now that we're done, that's what I'll do." He watched his shoe, scuffing dirt. "Only thing is, I don't know what that means about us being a couple." He searched her eyes now. "Should I wait for you?"

She came into his arms then, kissing him, and it was a proper kiss, true and long and sweet, and then, "Yes, please wait for me. If you love me you will. It will be wanting you that brings me back, I promise."

With his thumb, he wiped the tear off her cheek, and held her out to his arms' length. "Don't forget to write." He smiled, turned her towards the horse, and tipped his hat. "Now, let's see you ride."

She swung into the saddle and rode up close to him, leaned, took his lapels and with blazing eyes kissed him fiercely as an angel -- God's own soldier -- might, to draw out his very essence and keep it strong within her. She wheeled and galloped up a long gentle slope, easy in the saddle and the brightening sky ahead of her.

She rose into the light and was gone.

POSTSCRIPT

Danny Hirsch removed the unlit stub of a cigar from between his teeth as he finished reading a piece of paper, a letter he'd just received special delivery.

"Mr. Grant," he yelled, "get in here. Got an assignment for you."

ABOUT THE AUTHOR

Jeffrey Pike works as a librarian in Massachusetts. *Laura* is his first novel.

32455553R00150

Made in the USA
San Bernardino, CA
06 April 2016